Anna Bell is a full-time writer and writes the weekly column 'The Secret Dreamworld of An Aspiring Author' on the website Novelicious. She loves nothing more than going for walks with her husband and Labrador.

don't tell the groom

ANNA BELL

Quercus

First published in Great Britain in 2013 by

Quercus Editions Ltd
55 Baker Street
7th Floor, South Block
London W1U 8EW

A CIP catalogue record for this book is available
from the British Library

ISBN 978 1 84866 361 9 (PB)
ISBN 978 1 84866 362 6 (EBOOK)

10 9 8 7 6 5 4 3 2

Printed and bound in Great Britain by Clays Ltd, St Ives plc

Typeset by Ellipsis Digital Limited, Glasgow

For Steve:

Without your encouragement
the words would never have been written.

chapter one

Every woman should feel like a princess on her wedding day; it's practically the law. As I gaze down at myself in my sparkling dress, a dress that would make Mary Berry's meringues weep with jealousy at how light and fluffy it is, that is exactly how I feel: like a princess.

My dad's just about holding it together as we glide into the room to the wedding march. He's choked up and I think there might even be a tiny glint of a tear in his eye. Walking down the aisle I see all of my friends and close family beaming at me. I know what they're thinking: that I'm wearing the most beautiful dress they've ever seen. All except my aunt Dorian. Her face is full of thunder as I've quite possibly upstaged my precious cousin Dawn's wedding.

And then I notice my handsome groom, my most favourite

person in the whole wide world. He's standing there in his bespoke suit looking sexy as hell. To think in mere minutes I'm going to be Mrs Mark Robinson. The Lemonheads' song 'Mrs Robinson' is playing loudly in my head, drowning out the wedding march.

There's my mum sitting in the front row looking like the cat that got the cream. I can almost imagine what she'll be writing in this year's Christmas-card round robin. All her friends' kids will be made to feel inferior when they're shown the photos of me and Mark looking absolutely stunning, at the most wonderful wedding in the world.

The room in the castle looks even more beautiful than I ever could have imagined. The candles flickering in the alcoves give off a dusky glow, and the simple vases of long-stemmed white roses adorning the ends of the rows are like the icing on the cake.

Approaching the end of the aisle, I come to a halt alongside Mark. He leans over to me and whispers that I look beautiful, just like Prince William did to Kate. I smile back and gaze into his eyes, which are easier to see than usual because my to-die-for Jimmy Choos make me only an inch or two shorter than him.

I hand my bouquet back to my friend Lou, my maid of honour, who's dressed in a simple purple empire-line dress, which I love almost as much as my own gown. My sister is standing next to her with my little niece clinging on to her leg and looking angelic and lovely.

This is the happiest day of my life. I. Am. A. Princess.

It is at that blissfully perfect moment that the computer makes the worst sound imaginable. The synthetic crowd-cheering noise snaps me out of my daydream and back to my poky little bedroom. The strategic lighting of the candles is replaced by the dim light of an energy-saving lamp, and instead of Jimmy Choos and a Vera Wang wedding dress, I'm in my baggy boyfriend jeans, an oversized woolly jumper, and a pair of cartoon-character slippers.

The words on the screen are there in Day-Glo pink and yellow: Bingo. I was just about to call it. I only had one number to go. This was *the* game. The game I was going to win. The one which would have allowed me to actually buy the Jimmy Choos. The one that would have got me one step closer to the wedding of my dreams. The wedding in the castle where I'm the most beautiful bride that anyone has ever seen.

And now 'LuckyLes11' has won my £500. Goodbye, Jimmy Choos.

There's a feeling of nausea that creeps over my body when I lose a game of bingo. But the feeling is so much worse when I'm so close to winning that I'm practically spending the money.

Not that I do this often, you understand. Just every now and then. It just happens to be now as while I was waiting for Mark to come home from work, I was flicking through the latest copy of *Bridal Dreams* and they had these top ten must-have wedding shoes. I fell in love with pair number two and at £550 I thought a cheeky little go of 90-ball bingo might just get me them; you know, if it was meant to be.

Turns out it wasn't. I bet LuckyLes11 has fat ankles and wouldn't look good in the Choos anyway. Not that I'm bitter.

'Shit.' That's the sound of the front door slamming. Mark is home.

I log out of Fizzle Bingo quicker than you can say 'goodbye, Jimmy Choos' and switch off my private browsing. By the time Mark makes it over the threshold and I hear him kicking his shoes off, I'm idly surfing for books on Amazon. God, I'm quick, or well practised. Either way, I still feel like I've just cheated on my boyfriend.

Oh yes, that's right, *my boyfriend.* You were expecting me to say my fiancé, right? Seeing as I've planned the most wonderful wedding in the world and that I was trying to win myself the money for *the* perfect shoes.

The truth is we aren't engaged. But that's not to say we're not getting married, as we are. We just haven't got engaged *yet*, but we will. We have a wedding fund and everything.

Mark, my hopefully soon-to-be-fiancé, is very sensible like that. He has our life planned out in stages and everything.

'Penny?'

'Up here.'

'Are you ready to go?' he says as he opens the door.

He's staring at me with a look of horror.

'Yes,' I say, peeling back the covers of the bed to reveal I am fully clothed and not half in pyjamas. 'What?'

Mark sent me a text at work earlier to tell me he's taking me out for dinner. Which can only mean one thing on a Monday: the all-you-can-eat buffet at our local Indian. For some reason they always have the air-con on, even in winter, and so I'm dressed appropriately, in layers that would give the Michelin man a run for his money.

'That's what you pick to wear when I'm taking you out for dinner?'

'Yes, but I was thinking why don't we just get a takeaway and watch a movie in instead? We could eat in bed?'

I should probably stress at this point that I detest eating in bed. But there are some things you should know: a) it's January, b) our little Victorian terrace does not have good central heating, and c) our bed is the comfiest bed on the planet. Pretty much nothing could drag me from my bed at this point. Not even the thought of unlimited poppadoms.

'In bed? Are you feeling all right? No, come on, I fancy

going out. We haven't been out in ages. And now I'm not revising for my exams I fancy being spontaneous. You know going out on a work night feels slightly naughty.'

'I could think of other things to do to you if you want to feel naughty.' I'll do anything he wants at this point if I can stay in bed. Well, almost anything – I'm no fan of *Fifty Shades of Grey*.

'Penelope, get out of bed and put on a dress. We're going out.'

Uh-oh. He's played the Penelope card. I must be in trouble. Before I know it Mark is pulling me off the bed.

'So if I need to put a dress on, where are we going?' I say, sighing. If we're not having curry, I quite fancy pizza, maybe Pizza Express or Ask.

'I've made us reservations at Chez Vivant.'

'Chez Vivant? How on earth did you get us reservations there?'

My voice has gone up an octave. Chez Vivant, for those not in the know, is *the* restaurant around the area where I live. It's the kind of place that the fancy people, who fly in and out of Farnborough in their private jets, eat at before they jet off to their exotic destinations. It has a waiting list as long as your arm and it's got a number of Michelin stars. Mark and I have never graced it with our presence before.

It is the place I'd always imagined that Mark would take

me to pop the question. Suddenly The Lemonheads' song is playing up-tempo in my head. I've started to have palpitations and I'm sure that I'm breaking out in a cold sweat. This is what I've been waiting for.

'I've just been assigned their account and in return for sorting out their rather bungled tax return from their previous accountants they've offered us a complimentary meal there.'

The Lemonheads on loop comes to a dramatic halt. Suddenly it makes sense. Mark wasn't about to shell out part of the mortgage on our house to pop the question. He was clearly treating me to a freebie from work.

'Great,' I say. I need to keep the disappointment out of my voice. I am still getting to go to Chez Vivant. I can still make my friends weep with jealousy. And a few months ago Posh and Becks were spotted there, so at the very least I can hope to see a Z-list celebrity like someone from TOWIE.

'Come on. Table's booked for seven thirty, so we should get a wriggle on.'

'OK,' I say. *Seven-thirty?* I've got less than an hour. An hour before we have to leave! Clearly Mark doesn't understand that you book to have your hair done before you go to a place like Chez Vivant. Less than an hour to get ready is an impossibility.

* * *

Exactly one hour later and we're walking through the doors of Chez Vivant. It just shows that my teachers at school were right: I would be able to succeed in life if I actually put my mind to it.

For once my frizzy hair allowed itself to be blow-dried straight to within an inch of its life, and so far, thanks to a whole can of hairspray, it is staying up in a chignon.

I'm also dressed in a hideously expensive, I'll wear it one day, I really will, Mark, dress. And look, here I am wearing it! It has only taken three years, and I don't know if you'd call that value for money, but it looks amazing. And I'm even wearing a proper cheese-wire thong and a sexy lace strapless bra. Of course both are killing me, but the overall effect is worth it.

It's just a shame that the shoes I've got on are from Next and not the Jimmy Choos that I could have owned if it weren't for LuckyLes11. I close my eyes. I'm not allowing myself to think about that now. Besides, even if I had won, it wasn't like there is a Jimmy Choo shop in Farnborough I could have raced to tonight to get them.

'You look so good,' says Mark as we deposit our coats in the cloakroom, 'I almost thought about throwing you on the bed and changing my mind about going out.'

Now he tells me! If I'd known all it would have taken was for me to put this dress on to get him to stay in bed, then I would have put it on two hours ago. What am I saying? I'm standing in Chez Vivant!

Inside it is exactly like I'd imagined it would be. Huge glass chandeliers dangling from the ceiling. There are thick red heavy velvet curtains hanging around the outside of the room. There is even a black-and-white movie being projected onto the ceiling. It just screams expensive.

'We've got a reservation, under Robinson,' Mark says to the maître d'.

I can't believe how grown-up and confident he sounds in this place. There's something about walking in here that has made me suddenly feel like I'm a child at an adults' party. I'm hit with narcissistic thoughts that everyone in the whole restaurant is going to be looking at me as if they know we're getting our food for free and that we can't normally afford to eat here.

So much for my celebrity spotting. I'm terrified to even look at anyone for fear they'll be pricing up my outfit and thinking that my dress is far too many seasons ago to wear.

The maitre d' nods at us in that discreet posh way, and he leads us across the restaurant. It's at this moment that I notice the floor. It's super-shiny black tiling with diamantes buried in it. The lights keep catching the sparkles and they're twinkling like stars in the night sky. I'd usually be dead impressed, but as well as being super shiny it's also super slippy, and it seems that I might as well be wearing heels with soles made of ice, as I appear to have absolutely no resistance.

Gone is the panic that people are going to be judging me on my looks. They're now going to be judging me on the fact that I'm waddling like a duck and doing windmill arms like I'm walking a tightrope. I manage to grab hold of Mark's arm just as I'm about to do the splits. Not only would I have ripped my amazing dress on its first outing, but with the cheese-wire thong I'm wearing, I'm sure I would have put a lot of diners off their dinner.

'Here you are,' says the maître d', unaware of the Bambi-on-ice impression I've being doing behind his back. He points towards some curtains in the corner and I'm wondering just where he's taking us. He pulls them open to reveal a velvet-covered booth. Maybe they keep the curtains closed when it's not in use to make the restaurant seem fuller. I shimmy into the booth. It is almost as comfortable as my bed; maybe it was worth getting out of it after all. As Mark slides in opposite me, the maître d' shuts the curtains around the booth.

Oh, my God, they really are embarrassed to have us here.

'Are we like the poor relations?' I ask. I think it best to make a joke out of it before Mark gets embarrassed.

'What do you mean?'

'Well, he shut the curtains.'

'Pen, that's to give us privacy. These booths are for their guests who want their dining to be a bit more discreet.'

'Oh. Right,' I say, nodding. 'I knew that.'

I did *not* know that. Now we're going to spend the entire night starving as we'll never get the attention of the waiter.

Mark presses what looks like a doorbell and seconds later a waiter appears from behind our curtains.

'Yes, sir?'

'We'll have a bottle of the Châteauneuf-du-Pape to start with,' says Mark.

Having the wine list in front of me at that particular moment makes me gawp at the price. Thank God this is a freebie.

'An excellent choice, sir. I'll bring it straightaway.'

Minutes later the waiter is as good as his word and he's poured me the best wine I've ever tasted. Oh, how the other half live! I could get used to this.

'Here's to the start of an excellent night,' says Mark, as he raises his glass.

I chink his glass with mine, making sure we have strong eye contact. The more intense the eye contact the more intense the sex, or so my friend Lou always says.

* * *

By the time my trio of desserts arrives I am full, but there's no way I am going to leave here without three courses. Especially when someone other than me or Mark is paying. Why is it that food always tastes better when someone else picks up the bill?

Mark presses the little buzzer.

'I can't eat another thing, Mark,' I say, groaning under the weight of my belly.

'We'll have a bottle of the Möet,' says Mark to the waiter.

Möet? There is no way that they are going to give us Möet on a free meal. They're not that bloody stupid, are they? Or else my boyfriend Mark is the best accountant in the whole world.

'What did you do that for?' I hiss over the table.

'Because, Penny, we are celebrating.'

'We are?' I ask. 'What are we celebrating?'

Maybe we're celebrating the fact that he has been crowned world's best accountant. Maybe this will be the start of more amazing free dinners.

'This,' says Mark.

Oh. My. God. There it is, in his hands. Stage four of the life plan Mark's mapped out for us. Aka an engagement ring. A small, perfectly formed, princess-cut diamond that seems to tick all the four Cs, (colour, cut, clarity and carat,) and is by far the most amazing thing I've ever seen.

'So will you marry me, Penelope?'

Thank God for the curtains, is all I can say. As the next thing I know I've thrown myself at Mark like a desperate woman who thought this day would never come.

'Of course I bloody will!'

'Ahem.'

I stop snogging the face off Mark and wipe my mouth, embarrassed, as the waiter is standing next to us, popping open our champagne.

'Here's to you, the future Mrs Robinson,' says Mark, as he raises his glass.

We chink glasses, and this time there is no Lemonheads, only the wedding march ringing in my ears.

I glance down at the ring on my finger. It's perfectly weighted so that I know I have something ever so special and precious on my left hand. It's like my whole life my left ring finger has been lacking something, and finally it's lost its virginity and it feels complete.

I'm just starting to drift into a wedding fantasy where I'm shopping for the perfect dress to match my ring, when I realise Mark is talking to me.

'We'll have to get out the bank statements for the wedding fund to see just how spectacular our wedding can be.'

Uh-oh. My cheeks suddenly feel heavy as I push every muscle I can to hold my fake smile in place. Mark can't see the bank statements, as that's linked to my bingo account. He'd be able to see all my bingo win payments going in. Even though I've probably topped up the account with thousands of pounds of winnings by now, he would never approve of me playing bingo.

'How about I plan the wedding, honey? I can make it my present to you? Then all you have to do is turn up. It will be like that TV programme, *Don't Tell the Bride*, only I won't tell the groom.'

'Sounds even better. To us,' he says, taking a sip of champagne.

'To us,' I echo. Oh, bloody hell. There suddenly seems a lot already that I can't tell the groom.

chapter two

'Are you sure you wouldn't rather just go straight to bed?' I ask. 'I mean, aren't we supposed to consummate our engagement? Won't it not be binding if we haven't done it?'

I look up at Mark in the hope that the lure of getting me naked will be stronger than the urges of the accountant inside him.

'Come on, we didn't open them yet so that we could have the big surprise when we got engaged. I want to know just how big this wedding you're going to plan will be.'

I fail to correct Mark, that we didn't open the statements because I didn't want him to see my bingo winnings going in.

'OK,' I say reluctantly.

This is not how I imagined the night of our engagement ending up. I imagined we'd spend the time after the proposal screaming down the phone at our nearest and dearest, but as it was after ten o'clock on a Monday night we thought we'd save that pleasure until the next day. Then after shouting from the rooftops, I'd envisaged that we'd probably be so amorous when we got over the threshold that we'd end up having sex on the stairs. Not that I imagine it would be a) very comfortable on our wooden staircase or b) very warm in our poorly heated house. But surely when you get engaged you're supposed to have acts of passion like that. Checking bank statements did not appear in any of my fantasies. I guess that's what happens when you're going to marry an accountant.

I sit on the bed in the spare room in my sexy dress, hold-ups and Mark's dressing gown, as he hands me the envelopes for our bank statements.

I take a deep breath. You see, with weddings the difference of five hundred pounds is mammoth. It's the difference between having, or not having, luxuries like a magician to entertain the guests, or a candyfloss machine and sweetshop stand at the evening reception.

I find the most recent statement from the franked date on the envelope, and I almost wince at it through closed eyes. Does that say fifteen thousand three hundred and fifty-five pounds? A smile breaks out over my face. Fifteen thousand is OK, although I was expecting it to be around twenty thousand. But fifteen thousand will still get me my Vera Wang dress, right?

'So how much are we talking?' asks Mark.

I'd almost forgotten he was in the room. I'd been imagining how I was going to eat candyfloss without getting it on my Vera Wang gown.

'I'm not telling you, Mark. We said we were going to do this "Don't Tell the Groom" thing, and I think we should take it seriously. Besides, you'd probably do a spreadsheet, and it would be like the whole household expenses fiasco.'

Mark makes an all-singing, all-dancing spreadsheet for our household budget every year. It was depressing enough to discover that we spent £3.50 on toilet rolls every two weeks, but then he manipulated the data into a graph that showed me that it cost £91 a year, and that it literally went down the toilet. That's a pair of boots!

'OK,' says Mark sulkily.

I look down at the statement again and I'm about to drift off into a wedding fantasy once more when I look at the total. I'm sure it said £15, 436.50 the last time I looked, only now it seems to be missing ten thousand pounds. That can't be right.

'What's wrong, Pen?'

In the horror of realising that I'd read the total wrong, a look of panic has replaced my smile.

'Oh, nothing, I was just feeling a little sad as I realised

that my gran wouldn't be able to see the wedding,' I lie. I'm definitely going to hell after that. Dragging my poor dead gran into things.

Mark supportively rubs my feet in comfort and I try to force a fake smile on to my face again. It's the kind of face you pull when you're opening a present that you can just tell you're going to hate in front of the person who gave it to you. A smile on the face that grows wider and faker, and gets an accompanying head-bob as you pull out the microwavable slippers that smell like your great-aunt.

£5,345.50. How can that be? Our combined bonuses last year came to eight thousand pounds. Why is there only just over half of that amount in there?

Surely Mark hasn't been helping himself to the wedding fund? What would he have spent the money on? My eyes fall on my beautiful, perfect, sparkly ring. No. Surely not? He wouldn't have used the wedding fund to pay for the engagement ring, would he? He must know that that was not what the fund was for and that he was supposed to pay for it out of his own account.

Of course he would know that, and besides, I've got the debit card for the account. We just thought that when the time came to it I'd be the one spending the money. Which means there has to be some other explanation for where the money has gone to.

I start trying to focus on the payments going out and going in, but there are just so many of them.

Inside I'm freaking out, wondering where the hell my money is, but outwardly I've got this painted smile on my face which seems to be making Mark look deliriously happy.

I slowly open some of the other statements, and read them over, doing a head-nod and a smile as I do. I can clearly see the payments made in from both Mark and my bank accounts, but there are all these other debits made to Carnivore Services. That doesn't ring any bells with me in the slightest. It sounds like some weird male-blooded dating agency or an upmarket butchers. It does not, however, sound like something that should appear on my wedding bank account.

And where are all my payments in from my winnings from Fizzle Bingo?

These are not my transactions. Someone has clearly been stealing from my account and paying this Carnivore company for whatever they do.

What I need to do is march to the bank and demand they sort out the problem for me, only I've got nine hours to wait before it opens, and then there's the small matter that I have to go to work tomorrow. Somehow, showing up late with an engagement ring on my finger, I'm not going to be able to convince anyone I had an emergency doctor's appointment, or at least without the rumour mill starting that it's going to be a shotgun wedding.

'Well, now that we know we're going to have one great big party, I think we should go and consummate this engagement after all,' Mark says.

I look up at him, careful to keep up the fake smile. Sex is now the last thing on my mind. Why couldn't he have just been like any normal, red-blooded male and we could have had the sex in the first place instead of looking at bank statements?

I stuff the statements back into their folder just as Mark begins to run his hands up my thighs. While on the one hand I want to go all Nancy Drew and solve the mystery of the meat-eater and the missing money from our account, another part of my brain is telling me that the bank is going to sort the little mix-up out in no time, and that really I should concentrate on the fact that my fiancé is taking my hold-ups off with his teeth. Yes, I really shouldn't be worrying. Who knows, the bank might even give us extra money – you know, to compensate for the trauma of what went on. Maybe it will be enough so that I can even have doves released at the wedding.

It's depressing enough going to the bank at lunchtime, but it's even more so when you've had to turn down the offer of going to the pub with your work colleagues. They wanted to help celebrate my engagement. Instead I'm having to celebrate it by standing in a queue, along with the whole town of Farnborough, at the bank. I glance at my watch. I'm going to be lucky if I make it to the counter this century, let alone before the end of my lunch break.

I haven't really given the bank statements much thought since last night. I went to sleep pretty quickly, thanks to the naughty things that Mark did to me and the amount of alcohol we'd consumed. Then today, I've barely had time to think of anything other than how lucky I am to have the best engagement ring in the world. Colleagues from all over my office have been coming to admire the diamond dance I've now perfected with my hand. But shuffling forward in the queue, I'm growing ever more nervous about the statements. By the time I've shuffled all the way to the counter, I'm feeling quite sick. Now I know this could have everything to do with the amount of alcohol Mark and I had last night, but somehow this feels different.

'Can I help you?' asks the woman behind the counter in a way that makes me think that she'd rather stab her own eyes out with a fork.

'I've noticed some unusual activity on my account and I think someone's been spending my money.'

'Right. Can I have your account details?'

I hand over one of the crumpled bank statements and she taps the number in.

She scrolls down her screen for what seems like hours.

'Which bit of it is unusual activity?'

'There are some transactions to Carnivore Services on there and I don't know who they are, and they've taken out an awful lot of money from my account and it's our wedding fund. I've just got engaged, you see.'

'Ah, that's sweet.'

'Thanks,' I say, flashing my left hand so that my engagement ring catches the light. It seems to have become a default spasm that I do when I announce my engagement to anyone.

'It appears to be a regular payment,' the cashier says. 'And it has been happening since last August. Have you not noticed before now?'

'No, I don't usually open the statements,' I say quietly.

The woman rolls her eyes at me.

'You know that you're legally obliged to open them,' she says sternly. 'Right. I don't think I can sort this out. I think I'll have to make you an appointment with the bank manager. Are you free next week?'

'No,' I practically scream. 'I've got to get it sorted today. I mean, it's imperative. If someone's been stealing my money, how do I know they're not going to steal more? You'd think you as a bank would take this seriously.'

I look round to make sure that the other customers are looking, which they are.

Clearly embarrassed at the potential for bad PR, the cashier mutters that she'll go and see if the manager is free.

A few minutes and a lot of tuts from customers behind me later, the cashier returns. 'Miss Holmes, would you step this way, please?' says the bank manager, emerging from the back office.

I give him the biggest smile I can muster. I want to give him the best possible impression of myself to counteract the fact that I probably still stink like a brewery from last night.

'Now, I've had a very quick look at this bank statement and it all seems very standard. It doesn't really count as unusual activity,' he says as we sit down in his office. I needn't have worried about the smell of alcohol coming from me – this office smells of nothing but egg and cress sandwiches, the stinky kind that is not helping with my sick feeling.

'But I don't know who Carnivore Services are,' I say in frustration.

If a company like Carnivore Services doesn't sound unusual then I don't know what does.

He sighs so loudly that he causes the papers on his desk to lift and fall. He taps away at his computer. That's what always disconcerts me with banks. I'm always terrified that they have secret information on there. Or that they're analysing your account to see whether you buy your knickers from Ann Summers or M&S. Whatever they do on their computers, I always feel like I've been violated.

'Oh,' says the bank manager.

'Oh' is never a good sign. He gives me a look up and down and then he gives me a look of pity. Is it just me, or is he now avoiding eye contact too?

'What is it?' I ask.

I put my arms on the chair rest and grab hold of the handles as if I am in an aeroplane during take-off. My knuckles have started to turn white and I start to feel sick again, and this time it isn't due to my hangover, or the egg smell.

I know exactly what he is going to say. My fiancé Mark has been using a vampire-impersonating escort agency, Carnivore Services; it is the only logical explanation. It had come to me on the drive into town.

The bank manager now knows that I have a cheating fiancé and he is feeling sorry for me. Will I break down in tears right here in this office?

'It looks like Carnivore Services is . . .'

Why's he pausing? This isn't like the bloody *X Factor*. There's no audience here to hold their breath in anticipation. There aren't going to be any ticker-tape-fuelled explosions and there will be no Dermot O'Leary to wrap his arms around me in consolation. He just needs to spit out the ugly truth.

'Let me put it another way, Ms Holmes. Have you been using the site Fizzle Bingo?'

'Well, yes I have, but I don't see what that has to do with anything. Although that reminds me, their payments are missing from my account. That is one of the reasons why I think that your records are wrong and that my account has got linked to someone else's by mistake. I think that–'

'Ms Holmes.'

He's stopped me mid-flow without letting me explain.

'Ms Holmes, Carnivore Services is the company that runs Fizzle Bingo. I've done a Google search and on their site's FAQs it tells you that Carnivore Services is how it appears on your bank statement.'

This is all too much to take in. If that was Fizzle Bingo then why was all the money being taken out? Where were my winnings going in? Don't tell me that they've cocked it up their end and I've got to try and sort it out.

'But this can't be. I mean, I win. I win all the time.'

The bank manager sighed again. 'Do you also lose?'

'Sometimes.' I mean, I do lose. I lose most of the evenings I play, you know, the odd game – but then I win. I'm sure I must win more than I lose. But it is so hard to keep track of exactly what is going on as there are all the people to talk to. Like Bride2BKay who I love chatting weddings with, and then there's bitchySue and we always slag off the other people who win, privately of course. And then added to that I do fantasise a lot about my wedding and sometimes I realise that I've been playing multiple games without realising. That's the problem when you use auto-dab. It just tells you when you win.

Oh. God. How have I done this?

'So you're telling me that I really do only have five thousand three hundred and forty-five pounds left in the account?'

The words are starting to stick in the back of my throat; my throat that has suddenly gone remarkably dry.

'And fifty pence,' says the bank manager.

I swallow. Fifty pence? That wouldn't even get me a packet of confetti.

'But I don't understand. I really don't.'

I look up at the bank manager for words of wisdom. They must have to deal with this stuff all the time, mustn't they? They are probably like counsellors. The next step will be for him to make me a strong cup of coffee and we'll work out my options. Maybe I could invest my remaining five grand in a high-interest bond. Mark and I haven't even set a date yet; I'm sure we'll have plenty of time before the big day. And between now and then I could be super-good and not buy anything for myself and the money would be topped up in a jiffy. Or I could try and win the money back by playing bingo . . .

'Right, Ms Holmes. I'm actually at lunch, so if you wouldn't mind.'

He's pointing at the door. I think he actually wants me to leave.

'But aren't you going to talk me through what happened? Go through my account with me and tell me what options I have? You know, savings account, high-interest bonds?'

'High interest? You're having a laugh. There isn't anything high interest in this economy. Look, if you're looking for advice you've come to the wrong place. I'm not an agony aunt.'

'But what am I supposed to do? I'm supposed to be planning a wedding.'

'Look, love, I'm afraid I can't help you. If I were you I'd buy a lottery ticket. Or, thinking about it, with your gambling habit that is probably not a good idea.'

Hey, I scream in my head. I'm not some addict. That makes me sound all seedy and dirty. All I did was play a bit of bingo online while watching TV. That is hardly in the same league as men who spend all day in the bookies'.

He reaches into his drawer and hands me a business card.

'Citizens Advice?' I say, reading it out loud.

'Yep, go and see them. They'll make you feel better.'

He is actually standing up now and I really can't stay in the bank any longer. Walking back out I don't know what I am going to do. How am I going to tell Mark that I have lost over ten thousand pounds on online bingo?

Mark always laughs when those adverts for bingo come on TV and he says 'Who would be sad enough to play that?' I always laugh along, thinking, *Just wait until we have the most amazing wedding and then I'll tell you about the bingo.*

Only there's not going to be a wedding as we've only got five grand. Not unless we elope, but then both our sets of parents would disown us.

What am I going to do? Then it hits me. We'll just get married next year. Who says we have to get married soon anyway? We'll put it off a bit and I'll save my arse off.

Yes, that will be it. A wedding next year. What's the rush? We've got plenty of time until we need to start thinking about stage five of our life plan (get married) and stage six (have babies). Plenty of time indeed.

chapter three

'This summer?' I splutter. A cold sweat starts appearing over my forehead, which has nothing to do with my hangover from our impromptu engagement celebrations with our friends last night, and every bit to do with the bank statements. 'The summer, later on this year?' I ask again, just to make sure that I've heard her right.

'That's right, Penny,' says Nanny Violet.

'But surely that won't give us enough time to plan?' I say in horror. Or save up to replace the money I've lost playing internet bingo.

'Of course it will. In my day people got married a few weeks after announcing their engagement. Of course, in my day people saved themselves for when they got married.'

My cheeks start to burn in shame, as they do every time

Nanny Violet mentions us living in sin. She's not been our biggest supporter in that field. She rarely sets foot in our terraced house. I think she's worried she'll be struck down by the evil that clearly resides inside.

'Things are a bit different now,' says Mark, reaching over for his second mini Battenberg. 'You have to book your venue quite far ahead.'

I smile at Mark and my heartbeat starts to return to more of a normal resting pulse, rather than racing like in a spinning class.

'We were thinking it's going to be sometime next year,' I say. I've gone through it in my head, and if I save really hard, like over five hundred pounds a month, then I'll have replenished the wedding fund. I haven't really given a lot of thought to how I'm going to save five hundred pounds a month but I'm sure I can make some cutbacks somewhere. I probably don't need to have my hair dyed – isn't the odd hint of grey fashionable these days? And I'm sure I could stop buying shoes. No, really, I *could* stop buying shoes.

'Oh no, Penny, that just won't do. I don't think I've got that much time left.'

Mark's nan is always a bit of a doom-and-gloom merchant when it comes to talking about the future. I think it's her way of making everyone go and visit her more. Just in case it is the last visit. I hope I'm not that morbid when I'm eighty-eight.

'But next year would give us time to plan and give us our choice of venue.'

'No, next year won't do at all. I couldn't bear to die knowing that I wasn't going to see my youngest grandson get married, and you wouldn't want to get married without me, would you, Mark?'

I wasn't aware that I had to plan my wedding date around Nanny Violet. I look over at Mark. Surely he's going to step in and put his manly foot down? But upon looking at him I realise which woman in the room he's going to listen to.

'Don't worry, Nan, we can bring it forward. Can't we, Pen?'

I'm about to argue how we couldn't possibly, but it seems like Mark's question was rhetorical.

'I'm sure we could get somewhere for September or October, a nice autumnal wedding.'

I try not to get too caught up in an autumnal-themed wedding fantasy with me in a dark ivory dress and my bridesmaids in brown or burnt orange dresses, with dried flowers in our hair. Before I mentally plan the flowers, I stop myself. We can't possibly get married in September or October, no matter how great the autumnal theme could be. Unless we take it to extremes and have the wedding in a forest, and we do a variation on harvest festival from our school days where you bring cans of food with you, only this time we cook and eat them rather then giving them to the needy.

But before I can protest that that is far too soon, Nanny Violet is back to her head-shaking.

'No, no, no, Mark. That's far too far away. You really are going to have to do it sooner, like May.'

May? What is Nanny Violet trying to do to me? At this rate I'll be the one in danger of not making it to our wedding, if my racing heart is anything to go by. May is only three and a half months away. There is absolutely no way we can get married in three and a half months.

'Is there something you're not telling us, Nan?' asks Mark. I can see the look of concern written all over his face.

'I just think you'd be better off having a wedding in May.'

'Well, that will be fine, won't it, Pen? We all know you've got the wedding planned out on your mood boards and Pinterest, anyway.'

I shoot a look at Mark and wonder what else he knows about my secret wedding planning. If he knows about Pinterest, maybe he knows about my online memberships to Confetti and Hitched. And if he knows about them, what if he knows about the bingo? But I shake my head. If he knew about that there wouldn't be a wedding to plan at all.

'That is a relief then,' says Violet, staring directly at me.

There's something in the way she's looking at me that makes me think she knows what I've done. It's like she knows that I am a bad egg her grandson shouldn't marry. Maybe this is a test.

'Yes, May is it then,' I say, holding Violet's gaze to show her I'm not scared. 'I can plan a wedding in that time. It will be no problem at all.'

'Splendid,' says Violet, as I try to come to terms with what I've just agreed to.

If only I could share her enthusiasm.

To be honest I don't quite know why I agreed to take Nanny Violet to the library. I should have just run as far away as possible from her. I guess I naively assumed that I'd be able to use the time in the car to try and push the date of the wedding back. Even if we went for Mark's autumnal suggestion I might be able to save some of the money.

'Right, Penny. It will take me about half an hour to choose my books. Is that OK?'

I glance at my watch. I'll never make it back in time for the Saturday afternoon *Midsomer Murders* repeat now. 'Yes, Violet, take your time.'

Violet walks off with a spring in her step that makes me doubt that she's an eighty-eight-year-old who won't be with us next year.

It's been years since I last set foot in a library, and I look around to see if it's changed. It still gives me that I'm-scared-to-breathe-too-loudly feeling, but somehow there's something comforting about the space. I walk around seeing if anything takes my fancy – and then I see a sign on the door 'Citizens Advice'. I remember the card the bank manager gave me and what he said about them being able to help me.

I walk across to the door, looking over my shoulder to check that Nanny Violet isn't watching, and when I see the sight of her blue rinse over in the large print section, I hurry through it.

I wait outside on an uncomfortable plastic chair, and it isn't long until a woman pokes her head out of an office door.

'Do you want to come through?'

I follow her into the little office and sit down opposite her. This time the chairs are more comfortable; it's like I'm progressing to the headmaster's office.

'So what can we do for you?'

I had expected the woman to be older, but she is probably only in her mid-thirties. I'd pictured a little old lady dispensing the wisdom.

'Well, I sort of need financial advice.'

'OK. Are you in debt?'

'Not really.'

'You either are or you're not.'

'Not, then,' I say for clarification. Blimey, this woman isn't taking any prisoners.

'Well, what financial problems are you in then, if not debt?'

'I've lost ten thousand pounds.'

'Ten thousand of your pounds?'

'Yes. Well, I had joint access to it.'

'Hmm, yours and . . . ?'

'My fiancé,' I say, doing my obligatory diamond-waving dance, then instantly regretting it.

'Right,' says the woman as if I'm completely nuts. 'So you said you lost ten thousand pounds. How did you lose it?'

'Bingo.'

'You lost ten thousand pounds playing *bingo*?'

It really does sound bad when you say it out loud like that. I can't bring myself to say anything, that's how embarrassed I am right now. My eyes are firmly fixed on the old brown carpet and I just nod my head.

'I see. Well, that isn't very good, is it? Right, so you have a gambling addiction.'

'I'm not an addict.'

I'd like everyone to know I'm not an addict. It isn't like I couldn't give up the bingo. I'm sure I'd be able to give it up just fine.

'You lost ten thousand pounds at bingo. I take it not in one go?'

I shake my head.

'I'm afraid to tell you this, but I do think you are probably addicted to it. When was the last time you gambled?'

'A couple of nights ago.'

Don't hate me, I just needed to play once more before I quit. Just in case I could somehow win back all my money and then there wouldn't be a problem.

'So what was the ten thousand pounds? You said you weren't in debt, so was it ten thousand pounds of savings or from your current account?'

'Savings.'

'OK, so what do you need advice about?'

All those questions and she still can't tell me what I need to know.

'I want to know how I can recover the money. My fiancé and his nan want us to get married in May, and I want to know how I can make five thousand pounds suddenly pay for a twenty-thousand-pound wedding.'

'I'm afraid I can't help you with that. Would you like to know about support groups and Gamblers Anonymous?'

'I'm not a gambler.'

'Look, you seem like a nice girl.'

I sit up a bit straighter at that compliment.

'But you have to realise that you have obviously got a problem. Whether you've got it under control or not, it is a pretty big deal. Now, I suggest that you go to a counsellor or Gamblers Anonymous. Or at the very least a support group.'

I wince at the fact that she keeps calling me a gambler. Gamblers are people with actual problems. Like last year when a guy in our office gambled so much that he had his house repossessed. It was awful. I had to help him arrange temporary accommodation and help with the paperwork as he filed for bankruptcy.

The advisor reaches down into a drawer and gives me an A5 flyer for a local gamblers' support group. I take it to be polite – I can always throw it away as soon as I get out of the office.

'Can't you help me?' I ask, pleading. The bank manager sent me here and now she's going all slopey shoulders on me, too. What is it with these people?

'I'm afraid I'm not a counsellor. I'm just here to give you advice. Like seek help.'

'Great,' I say sarcastically. I hadn't meant it to come out that way.

'I'm sorry, but I'm doing the best I can for you.'

Now she is making me feel guilty.

'No, I get that, I do. I'm sorry, it's just all coming as a bit of a shock to me. You see, this isn't very me. I don't usually do things like this.'

The woman is nodding her head as if she's heard it a million times before.

'No, I mean it. It isn't like me at all. We were saving for our wedding and we were being sensible. It all started when Mark was studying for his accountancy exams in the evenings and I would think of the wedding and how Mark could contribute more for it than I could. One night I just thought I'd try another way to help out.'

I wish she would stop nodding her head; she is reminding me of one of those nodding dogs you put in your car – the ones that freak me out.

'Well, why don't you postpone the wedding until you can save up? I take it your husband-to-be knows about your gambling.'

I can't meet her eyes as I don't want to see her look of disapproval.

'Don't you think it might be best if you started by confiding in him?'

'Look, I just need some advice about the money,' I say, ignoring her. There's no way I can tell Mark. No way at all.

'OK,' says the woman, sighing. 'While I usually talk to people about managing debts, maybe we could talk about how you're going to budget your money, if you're not going to postpone your wedding. Have you given budgeting any thought?'

'Not really. I did try to look into investments and interest rates in the week, but I'm never going to be able to scale my money up four hundred per cent in three months.'

'OK,' says the woman after a long pause. She starts to talk to me like she is talking to a simpleton. 'How about you budget your wedding for five thousand pounds?'

I laugh out loud. I laugh like it is the funniest thing anyone has ever said. A wedding for five thousand pounds. Is she kidding? I look up at her face. Evidently she is not kidding.

'How do I do that?'

My palpitations have started again. I'm beginning to panic and my breathing is getting shallower. I am starting to feel like I'm slowly suffocating.

'I think it would help you if you made two lists. At first, why don't you write out exactly what you would like – a dream budget – if you will.'

That would be easy. I could practically give that to her off the top of my head, I know it so well.

'OK, that's easy.'

'Yes, that one always is. Then in the next budget why don't you try to forecast using the funds that you *actually* have.'

'But I've got to shave off sixteen thousand pounds. How am I supposed to do that?'

'Start with making a list and put things under columns of essential, nice extras and luxuries. Then you can go through the essentials and find if there are ways to make them cheaper.'

'Like how? Get married in a sack?'

'No, like buy a cheaper wedding dress. Marriage is not all about the wedding, you know.'

Tell that to the magazines I've been subscribing to for the last two years. I don't want to come across as a bridezilla as I am totally in touch with reality. It is just that I do want to have a princess wedding. I don't want to scrape by with only the essentials.

'Here,' she says. She reaches down into her desk of ever-helpful leaflets and she hands me one marked *Budget yourself out of debt.*

'Catchy title,' I say.

'Unfortunately, it's our most popular leaflet. It's slightly different for you as you're not in debt but the principles are the same. It is all about making a budget and sticking to it. Now, is there anything else I can help you with? Perhaps you want to do some volunteering work to fill your time to stop you gambling?'

Has this woman not heard me? I'm trying to make money, not give myself away.

'I don't think so,' I say attempting to be polite.

'Well, if there's nothing else?'

'No,' I say. She's already ruined my dreams of a castle wedding and made me feel like I ought to be appearing on *The Jeremy Kyle Show*.

'Great. Well, good luck with the wedding,' she says.

'Thanks,' I mutter, pushing the leaflets into my pocket.

What on earth am I going to do now? Thoughts of Mark flash through my mind. You see, it's his wedding that I'm messing up too. I've told him that I'll plan him this utterly spectacular wedding and I've totally fucked up. I've wasted our hard-earned money on empty dreams. And now we're going to be eating something like baked beans on toast for our wedding breakfast.

I go back into the main library and sit, trance-like, at one of the research tables. I cast my eyes over the budgeting leaflet the woman gave me. I don't usually do budget forecasting, working in HR, but this leaflet seems to suggest that it isn't that difficult. I take a pen out of my bag and start writing down the essentials.

I've already blown my budget by the time I've written wedding dress (£3,000), suits and bridesmaid dresses (£1,500) and reception entertainment (£2,000). I continue writing my list, incorporating venue hire, catering costs, alcohol, cars, and before I know it I'm looking at my dream budget of £21,000.

I take a deep breath and try desperately to channel some inner calm from my yoga classes. My pen hovers over the wedding dress total. I can't take any money off that now, can I? I mean, that's the only wedding dress I'm ever going to wear.

But amazingly I do manage to shave something off each of the other totals. I mean, Mark doesn't need a bespoke suit made in Savile Row, does he? Surely we could hire his suit? And I'm sure the bridesmaids wouldn't mind a dress from Coast rather than made-to-measure ones. And maybe we don't need a hundred guests. If we had, say, eighty, we'd save on both the catering and the alcohol costs. See? I'm a savvy saver after all.

But after doing the calculations, the figures still don't add up to anything manageable. I know what I have to do. My pen hovers over the wedding dress total and I have to use both hands to put a cross through it. There goes any hope of a designer dress.

I look down at my budget on the page and I wince in horror.

Wedding dress – ~~Vera Wang~~	~~£3,000~~	*£1,000*
Suits/bridesmaid dresses	~~£1,500~~	*£700*
Venue		*£4,000*
Catering – ~~100~~ 80 guests @ £80 per head	~~£8,000~~	*£6,400.*
Alcohol	~~£1,000~~	*£800*
Entertainment: band, and DJ	~~£2,500~~	*£1,500*
Misc. (favours/cars/presents/etc)	~~£1,000~~	*£700*
Total:	~~£21,000~~	*£15,100*

I'm practically weeping. If I had never played any bingo, then that would have been the budget for my wedding. And that looks totally doable. But now, thanks to my flirtations with Fizzle Bingo, that's £10,000 over budget. Damn my attempts to get over twenty thousand pounds! If I hadn't been so obsessed with having a Vera Wang wedding dress, we could have had a lovely wedding.

The more I look at the numbers, the more I can't see how I am going to skim anything else off this wedding. Really, I can't. The figures look as squeezed down as I can make them.

Which leaves me with only one other option. I somehow have to find £10,000 without Mark knowing about it. Great. Another secret to add to my 'don't tell the groom'. I do the maths on the calculator on my phone. I just have to save £3,300 every month until the wedding. Which would never happen, as for starters I don't get paid anywhere near that. Unless I got a second job, but how could I do that without Mark finding out? I work fulltime as it is.

Too bad that Carnivore Services didn't turn out to be a real escort agency or else I could have gone to them for a job. I am just going to have to find another way to come up with the cash.

'Are you all right, Penny?' says Nanny Violet, coming up behind me. She is giving me a curious look.

'Fine, thanks,' I reply through gritted teeth. I know it's not her fault that I'm not going to have the wedding of my dreams, but I can't help feeling a little bit resentful towards her and her suggestion of a May wedding.

'I picked up a book for you,' says Violet, handing it to me. It's a WI wedding planning book circa 1970.

'Thanks.'

'You're welcome, dear. Should be a doddle planning the wedding with that.'

I look at Nanny Violet and I wish that were true, but somehow I feel that my wedding planning is going to be anything but a doddle.

chapter four

'So when's the big day then?' asks Jane.

I'm about to throttle her, but then I realise that she's brandishing a bottle of Veuve Clicquot. I imagine in a struggle that she'd drop it and that would clearly be a waste. Instead, I restrain myself and take the bottle and give her and her husband Phil air kisses.

'Give the woman a chance – they've only just got engaged,' says Phil.

Thanks, Phil. At least someone is talking some sense.

'Whatever, honey. After all our years of marriage you still don't understand women, and you obviously don't know Penny that well either. She's been planning the wedding secretly for years.'

I clearly only have myself to blame for the fact that

this is the only topic on people's minds when they see me now. I used to talk weddings a lot before we got engaged, so people just assume that I'm steamrolling ahead with the planning, and they think it's perfectly acceptable to press me for the details like when, where, and what I'll be wearing.

'Now, let me see that ring,' says Jane, grabbing my hand before I can do the obligatory wave. I don't need to worry about trying to make the diamond sparkle in the light – she's pulling my hand this way and that to inspect my ring.

'Excellent choice,' Jane says to Mark as she walks into our hallway.

'Thanks,' says Mark, beaming with pride. 'Do you want to come on through?'

We gravitate to the lounge while Mark opens up a bottle of Prosecco that's been chilling in the fridge. I perch on the arm of the sofa and try to tell myself that Jane is not judging me. Just because she and Phil live in a fancy-pants five-bedroom house that's practically a mansion does not mean to say she's judging my living room or what I'm wearing. She's the only woman that would warrant me changing my outfit three times before I settled on something, aka, ran out of time. I'm now wearing a pair of Karen Millen jeans I bought in a sale once and a chunky Warehouse knit. It's about a million miles away from my usual

Saturday slobbing of bleach-stained tracksuit bottoms and a hoodie.

'So are we waiting for Louise and Russell?' asks Jane, as she looks curiously at the vases by the fireplace. I bet she just instinctively knows they're from Asda.

Yes, thank goodness, I almost say.

'Yes, they should be here any minute,' I say, glancing at my watch. I told them to come half an hour ago, so by their late meter they should be arriving any second now.

Please don't think I hate Jane, as I don't. Mark is Phil's best mate, and therefore I've got to know his wife Jane pretty well over the last few years. It's just that she's always impeccably dressed, she never has a hair out of place and her roots never need touching up. She just always makes me feel so ordinary and like the poor relation, which means it takes me a while to relax around her when we're the only females in the room. Lou, on the other hand, is my best friend and she's like the anti-Jane: as down to earth as you can get.

I'm never entirely sure whether it's a good idea to have them in the same room together, but as Phil is best-man-to-be and Lou is maid-of-honour-to-be, we thought it might make for a nice lunch. Or at least Mark did when he invited them when we were out drinking to celebrate our engagement. Personally I'm still trying to avoid all things wedding until

I work out how to beg, borrow, or grow a money tree to the value of ten thousand pounds.

'I want to hear all the details about your proposal then, Phil tells me it was at Chez Vivant. Such a lovely restaurant. I always go for the venison, what did you have, Penny?' asks Jane.

I'm about to reply when I hear the doorbell ring. I'm saved from having to declare that I boringly went for the steak with pepper sauce. In my defence it's one of my favourite foods, and to be fair to Chez Vivant and its mammoth price tag, it was worth every penny.

'Be back in a minute,' I say, dashing off to let Lou and Russell in. I take a moment in the hallway just to revel in the silence and the lack of wedding-related conversation. Unfortunately for me we've got a big frosted glass pane and I know that they can see me lurking out here.

'Hey, hey, hey, lovely,' says Lou as I open the door.

She hands me another bottle of fizz and I take them through to the lounge, where there's more kissing and drink-pouring. Since leaving the room, much to my relief, the topic has changed to Phil and Jane's annual pilgrimage to an exotic destination that the rest of us can only dream of. This year, they've apparently booked to go to the Turks and Caicos islands. Cue lots of 'if only' looks between me and Lou.

* * *

The lunch has passed in a haze of too much food, or in my case, too much wine. The boys are like naughty schoolboys when they are together and today they're on fine form with banter flying around everywhere.

'So, we haven't talked about your wedding yet,' says Jane.

I nearly spit out my dessert, but then I remember the fight I had to secure the last box of profiteroles from Marks and Spencer's and I try to keep them in my mouth as a sign of respect.

'We can't talk about the wedding. Well, not in front of me,' laughs Mark.

Yes! Thank you, Mark. This 'don't tell the groom' thing might not be so bad after all.

'What are you talking about?' asks Jane. Her gaze flicks from me to Mark like she is watching Olympics table tennis.

'Penny thought it would be fun if she organised the wedding herself. You know, like the TV programme *Don't Tell the Bride*, but we're doing "don't tell the *groom*".'

'That is a legend idea,' says Phil. 'I wish I hadn't known anything about our wedding. The run-up to it, with Bridezilla over there, was a nightmare.'

Oh no, you didn't, Phil. Jane's face is like thunder. She has just stabbed a profiterole with such ferocity that the cream has gone flying on to my nice clean tablecloth.

'Well, I'm sure I'll know some things. Like when it is, I

hope,' says Mark. He is clearly trying to lighten the mood as a veil of tension has cloaked the dining room.

'I thought it would be a fun idea,' I say, with a nervous laugh.

'I think it's a great idea,' says Lou. 'Why don't we get the men to clear away the table and we'll go into the lounge and natter about it?'

I think that was Lou's way of creating some female solidarity for Phil's comments on the wedding. The boys, all of them, are now in the doghouse and I can see Mark and Russell giving Phil a 'way to go' look.

'Great,' I say. I don't actually mean it as I quite fancy hiding in the kitchen so that I don't have to talk about our soon-to-be non-existent wedding. But as the tension between Jane and Phil is practically suffocating us, escaping to the lounge seems like the only thing we can do.

'So what venues have you been to see?' asks Jane, clapping her hands together as she settles into the armchair.

'I haven't yet.'

'Oh, well Phil said that Mark told him the wedding was going to be in May.'

'That's right.'

'Surely all the good venues will be booked already?'

I almost do an air-punch. That is exactly what I am hoping for.

'I guess I'll have to see what's available,' I say.

'So you're seriously not going to tell Mark where the wedding is going to be? He gets no say in it?' asks Jane.

'Yeah, I think it will be fun.'

'It will be a lot of work. Weddings are very laborious and stressful.'

I happen to know for a fact that Jane had a wedding planner to organise her entire wedding, in true American style. That's what happens when you get married in a Four Seasons Hotel. They took care of everything, and I'm not just talking about the venue and the catering, but the flowers, the honeymoon, the hairdressers – *everything*.

I sneakily look at Lou and she is suddenly taking a great interest in my curtains. Her mouth is turned up at the side and I can see she is trying not to laugh.

'Well, I'm up to the challenge,' I say confidently, even though inside I am far from confident. They have no idea just how challenging it is going to be for me.

'I know, why don't we help you? Let's help you draw up a list of venues that you could go and see,' says Jane.

'Yeah, that would be a great idea. We could make appointments and go and see them,' Lou chips in.

'Um, I'm sure that we have better things to be talking

about. Besides, the boys will be back from the kitchen in a minute. It can't take that long to load the dishwasher,' I say in desperation.

'We'll send the boys off to the pub,' suggests Lou.

I want to go to the pub. Maybe I can leave Lou and Jane here to discuss the wedding without me, and I'll go and join the boys.

'Did I hear the word pub?' Phil asks as he walks back into the room.

'Yes, we're going to help Penny with the wedding,' says Jane, sounding like an ice maiden.

Phil is definitely in the doghouse. I would not want to be in their car on the way home. Phil scurries out of the room, presumably to tell the other boys, as before we know it they've said their goodbyes and they're off.

'Right, Penny. Get your laptop and some paper.'

I feel like I should salute Jane as I pass, but instead I go ahead and do as she commands. Within minutes I'm back sitting on the sofa, trying not to weep at the places Jane is Googling.

'Didn't you always want to get married in a castle?' asks Jane.

'Yes, a castle in Scotland, wasn't it, Pen? With a ceilidh band?' says Lou.

Why did I tell everyone about my fantasy wedding? We'd

barely be able to afford the flights and the accommodation now, let alone hiring an actual castle.

'We've decided to stay local you know – make it easier for the guests. We don't want everyone having to fork out for flights and accommodation.'

Oh, how considerate I suddenly am of other people. I'm a terrible person for telling such lies.

'Thank goodness for that. I was secretly worried about getting all the way up there,' says Lou.

'Right, local then,' says Jane.

The images of fairytale Highland castles are replaced with the Google screen again. Jane types in the Four Seasons hotel where she got married and I just manage to squeak the word 'budget' to her. I think Jane registers what I say as the screen is now back to Google and search results are for wedding venues in Surrey.

'Ooh, this looks promising,' says Jane, gasping.

'The Manor, Surrey,' I say, reading it out loud. It rings a bell but I've never been there before.

'They have wedding packages,' says Jane.

It's like she's saying to me, this place is cheap as they *actually* list their prices on the internet.

'Right, Lou, here are the figures.'

Jane starts telling Lou – who has been given the job of scribe – the figures. There is much too much money flying about for my liking. But it's hard to work it out as the packages are priced per head rather than giving separate prices for the venue and catering. But some of them do sound affordable.

'How many guests are you having?' asks Lou.

'Eighty.'

'Oh, I love a small wedding,' says Jane.

Eighty people is not small, is it? I thought small was just the two of you getting married on a beach somewhere, or only having your witnesses in attendance. Eighty people does not sound small to me, especially not at over a hundred pounds a head.

'Right, then. For the Diamond package, you're looking at £13,600. That's very good, isn't it?' says Lou.

'And it includes chair covers!' shrieks Jane.

Great. The chairs were going to be better dressed than me as with those prices I'd be in a bin bag.

'Um, yes. What about the other packages?' I ask.

By others I mean cheap, and Jane knows that.

'OK. Well skipping over the platinum, the gold works out to be £130 per head,' she says.

'Right, so that's £10,400,' says Lou, using her phone to do the calculation.

'Now, that is excellent value,' says Jane. 'I can't imagine you'll beat that in a hurry.'

A lump appears in my throat and suddenly I am finding it very difficult to swallow.

'So that's for the venue, the food and the drink?' I manage to say.

'Yes, what a bargain! I think you might have found your venue,' says Jane. 'Let's phone them and see if we can go and look around.'

'No! We can't!' I practically scream. Shit, I must think of a reason why we can't go and see it right now. 'I promised my sister and my mum that they could come with me to see the wedding venues. And I've been drinking wine. I wouldn't want to get too carried away now, would I?'

'Of course, I totally understand,' says Jane. 'Well, let's see, what else can we help with? What about florists? I know a darling little florist. Let me see . . .'

The website loading on the screen looks beautiful and, oh my, there are examples of bouquets that they've made for weddings.

'Now, look, here's a guide price list.'

'Holy crap! Is that how much a bouquet costs? For a few flowers?' I shout in horror.

Jane looks alarmed that I've sworn. I think I might need to up my budget for flowers. A bouquet just for me alone looks like it is going to be £300. No wonder no one throws them any more.

'Penny, are you OK? You're looking kind of pale,' says Lou.

Now that she's mentioned it I don't feel very well. In fact, I think I'm going to faint. I suddenly can't breathe and I think I'm dying. No, I don't think I'm being dramatic. I actually cannot breathe.

Aren't they going to help me? Surely they can see I can't talk. I start flapping my arms around.

'I think she's having a panic attack,' says Lou, running out of the lounge.

Great, some help Lou is! She's supposed to be my best friend and here she is allowing me to die in front of Jane, of all people. Before I know it Lou's back and she's shoved a paper bag into my hand; it looks suspiciously like the one that the bottle of fizz she brought came in.

'Breathe into the bag; it will help you,' says Lou.

Funnily enough it does seem to help, but even when my breathing returns to normal, I still can't imagine how I am going to pull this wedding off without giving myself a massive coronary.

However inventive I was, or even if I moved it to a Monday when no one would want to come, there is no way that I am going to be able to get my dream wedding on my meagre five thousand pounds.

'Perhaps you're feeling a little overwhelmed by the wedding. People get like that,' says Jane.

I'm about to give her a mean look but then I remember that she practically had a nervous breakdown during hers. Maybe she is right; maybe I'm just overwhelmed.

'What about getting some help? You could get a wedding planner like I had,' she says.

A list of wedding planner websites appears right before my eyes. I had no idea that they existed in the UK. I could have my very own JLo organising my wedding. But then I remember in that film she stole the groom. I wouldn't want anyone stealing my groom.

But then again, maybe a wedding planner would be able to make my wedding budget stretch even further and it would reduce the necessity for me to carry a paper bag to cope with my hyperventilating.

'So how much do you think one of those would cost?' I ask. Surely it's got to be worth a go.

'I think usually you pay about ten to fifteen per cent of your budget.'

Ten to fifteen per cent? That would be five hundred pounds straight away. And that's if they don't laugh at me down the phone.

Lou must have seen the face I've pulled about the wedding planner.

'Why don't you start with a wedding checklist?' says Lou. 'It'll show you all the things you need to plan.'

'Good thinking, Louise,' says Jane, Googling it. 'Gosh, I envy you, Penny, getting to plan your wedding. It was one of the happiest periods in my life.'

'Just like being happily married is?' I say before I can stop myself. The look that Jane gives me back tells me all I need to know. Perhaps what happened at the table was only the tip of the iceberg.

'I think we've done enough wedding planning for the day,' says Lou. 'Jane, why don't you tell us how your extension is going?'

I smile at Lou in relief. We both know that we'll be in for a long report on the latest update of their house renovations to make a larger office and add an extra bedroom to their already five-bedroom house. But, to be honest, right now I'd listen to anything that doesn't revolve around the disaster that is my wedding.

Although the afternoon with Jane and Lou had utterly terrified me, it had started to make me think about how much I love Mark.

Seeing Jane and Phil snipping and snapping at each other not only made for an uncomfortable dining experience but also started to make me wonder.

I poke my head underneath Mark's armpit.

'You OK there?' he asks.

'Yeah, I think so. You're always going to love me, aren't you?'

'I wouldn't be marrying you if I wasn't.'

'No, I mean people change, and what if you fall out of love with me?'

'I'm not going to. Where has all this come from?'

'I was just thinking about it. And about how things seem to change when people get married, and you know we're so happy not being married. Sometimes I just wonder if we should just stay unmarried and happy.'

Stay with me, people – this is my latest genius idea.

'What, and spend the money on a fuck-off big holiday instead?'

Damn it. I hadn't thought of that. If there is no wedding then Mark will still find out that the money's gone.

'No, I mean . . .' God, what did I mean? 'It's just that I don't think I want things to change.'

Mark sighs. 'Is this about Jane and Phil?'

'A little bit.'

'Yeah, that's been on the cards for a while. To be honest, I don't even know why they got married in the first place. You know that Jane issued him with an ultimatum and told him that they had to get married or break up?'

No, I did not know that. I can't believe that Mark has never told me.

'Is that why they got engaged so quickly?'

'Yeah, although he didn't tell us until the stag do. By then it was too late to talk him out of it.'

Wowzers. I always thought I was desperate to have a wedding, but that takes it to a whole new level.

'Look, Pen, you're nothing like Jane, thank goodness. For starters, if you were we wouldn't be getting married. But look, don't get stressed about the wedding or our future. It's just about us, OK? Just me and you. And it will always be just you and me.'

'And our zillions of kids.'

Stage six! I use any opportunity to squeeze that in, just to see Mark's eyes pop out of his head.

'We'll take it as it comes.'

I lie back against Mark's arms. Perhaps it will be all right after all. I just need to get some perspective. So it isn't going to be a spectacular extravaganza wedding like Jane's, but she isn't even happy. At least I know that whatever wedding Mark and I end up with, we'll just be as happy as we are now.

chapter five

'My name's Penny, and I'm a gambling addict.'

I can't believe that I've actually just said that out loud. But, as much as it pains me to admit it, it's true. I gambled again last night as I was so convinced that I was going to be able to win back some money and increase my wedding budget a bit, but I lost.

I lost £56. In the time it took Mark to go to see the latest comic book movie adaptation with his brother, I'd lost one per cent of my wedding budget. That's pretty much a drop in the ocean considering what I have lost in total. But when you have a budget as low as mine, you can't afford to lose any more.

My eyes are still scrunched closed as I couldn't bear to look at the rest of the group members whilst I confessed. I did think that they'd break out into rapturous applause, or at least parrot back, 'Hi, Penny', like they do in the movies at AA meetings. But there's no noise at all.

I open my eyes slowly to see the men sitting in a circle looking at me curiously. Maybe they're not used to having a girl in their group.

'Um, Penny, thank you for sharing that with us. This is actually the unemployed men's group. I think the room you're looking for is next door.'

My cheeks are burning and I'm suddenly mortified. Next door? With all my nerves and the effort it took for me to actually get my legs to cooperate and walk from the car into the community centre, I'd not paid much attention to the room number. I'd just seen the group of men sitting round in a circle and assumed that was the gamblers' group.

'Oh, I'm awfully sorry,' I say, dipping into my terribly polite, terribly embarrassed British mode, and I hurry out of the door as quickly as I can.

I don't feel like I can go through that again. Is it enough that I've admitted it out loud? Maybe now I've declared it to a room full of strangers it will have magically flicked some switch in my brain and I'll never gamble again. Maybe I don't need to go to the group after all. But as I'm walking towards the main exit of the community centre, I catch sight of my sparkly engagement ring and feel a pang of guilt about Mark. I owe it to him to sort myself out.

I take a deep breath and walk into the room next to the one I'd been in. But as I walk in I realise that this doesn't look like a gamblers' group either. The people in the room are all looking at me: the businessman in his suit, the woman who looks like she's walked out of an advert for White Stuff.

'I'm sorry, I must have the wrong room,' I say, sighing in frustration.

'What were you looking for, dear?' asks the woman standing up with a clipboard in her hand. She looks like a French teacher with her blue and white stripey top and red scarf tied around her neck; maybe this is conversational French. I can't tell *her* what I am here for. Whatever would she think of me?

'I'm looking for . . .' Shit. Think, Penny, think. Why am I so bad at this? I'm just panicking that I'll say I'm here for an introduction to pole dancing and this woman will tell me that's what this class is.

'Let me help you. This room is for online gamblers. Is that what you were expecting?'

My mouth drops open. This room and the people in it are definitely not what I was expecting.

'I'm sorry. I'm Penelope Holmes.'

'Welcome, Penelope. Take a seat. We're just about all here now, so we can get started. My name's Mary, and I'm a gambling addict, just like all of you. These meetings are your first step to controlling your addiction, so well done for coming.'

I feel a swell of pride that for the first time in weeks I've done something right.

'What we're going to do tonight is introduce ourselves to each other, introduce you to your one-on-one mentors, and then we'll give you some time to get to know one another. Usually we'd have a talk from one of our mentors to inspire you about their road to recovery. These two-hour sessions could literally change your life,' says Mary, beaming.

Blimey, two hours? I had this thing down for an hour max. I'm never going to make my body combat class. Maybe I should leave now. After all, Mark doesn't want a bride with a fat arse at the wedding. But then I remember, if I don't get this bingo addiction under control there won't be a wedding.

'So we'll just start nice and gently and go round and talk about what we've done and why we've come here today,' says Mary.

I can feel myself having one of those panic attacks like the other day. I sort of thought I was going to an AA meeting where you'd just sit and listen to a talk. Maybe introduce myself by name. But the fact that I'm going to have to share my horrible secret with people is practically bringing me out in hives.

'Right, then. I'll start. My name's Mary and I became a

gambling addict playing online bingo. I started playing when I retired and I was bored, and now as a result my husband's had to keep working to pay off my debt. I've been free of gambling for a year now and I've also gone back to work part-time to help my husband.'

Wow. I instantly feel like I'm not alone. Mary's just like me. And worse, she's caused her husband to delay his retirement.

As we go round the room I realise how far I am from being alone. The sharp-looking businessman is addicted to buying and selling on the stock market. He'd once fallen asleep waiting for the Asian markets to open and as a result lost £10,000.

Then it's the turn of the woman dressed in the White Stuff outfit. It turns out she is a librarian and she'd become addicted to the lottery and the daily play games on their website.

There is another bingo addict, two men obsessed with sports betting and another man who does all forms of gambling on the internet. I had no idea this went on behind closed doors. I thought you had to be trackside or at a bookies' to be a gambler. How dumb is that? Before I checked my bank balance a few weeks ago I didn't even think I gambled, and yet here I am, one among many gambling addicts.

Oh, crap. The guy next to me has finished speaking, and now it is my turn. What am I supposed to say? I'm so used to bottling it all up and telling lies that I don't think I can physically get the words out of my mouth.

'And you, dear?' asks Mary, motioning her hand at me.

I open my mouth and close it again. If I am not careful the other people in the group will think I am doing an impression of a guppy fish.

'I'm Penelope.' Was that a stutter? My hands are so sweaty that I'm having to sit on them for fear that they'll leak on the floor. And my armpits feel so wet that I bet I look like those guys in the Lynx adverts.

'My fiancé and I have been saving for a wedding. Or at least we were before we got engaged. I checked our savings account to see how much we had and we had ten thousand less than we should have done. I'd spent it on online bingo. I actually thought that I'd been topping up the fund rather than taking it out. Stupid, huh?'

'It's not stupid, Penelope,' says Mary.

Looking around the room, I see that everyone is staring at me sympathetically and nodding. I've been so scared about telling my story but no one is throwing rocks at me or chanting to have me burnt at the stake. They really do understand.

'That's great,' says Mary. 'I'm so pleased everyone was able to share about their problems. That is one of the hardest parts: admitting it to yourself. But as we go through the weeks we'll cover all sorts of things. How to get to the root of why you gambled.'

Mine is easy. It can be answered in four little words: Vera Wang wedding dress.

'We'll also talk about how we can try to quit our habits and how we can tell those around us what is going on.'

My blood suddenly runs cold at the thought of Mark knowing I was here. Mark can't know. It would end our relationship.

'Sometimes group members have found that it is easier to tell someone else close to you before you tell your partner, but we'll get to that.'

Great. Now that's made me think I should tell Lou. Of all the people in the world, apart from Mark, Lou is the person I want to tell. She always knows what to do in any situation. We tell each other everything. Well, *almost* everything. We do a lot as a foursome and there are some things I just don't want to know about her husband. But I couldn't imagine telling her about this. Lou struggles with money as it is. Perhaps struggles is the wrong word, but she and Russell are definitely not as comfortable as Mark and me.

In fact, Lou is the reason why we started our stupid savings account for the wedding. She let slip to us one night that she was still paying her's off her credit card. Lovely as their wedding was, it was not worth the tidy sum it was still costing them each month, three years later.

I've done it again. I've started thinking about other things and I've got no idea what Mary's been saying. What if she's told me the key to kick my gambling habit and I've missed it? I have *got* to start paying attention.

'Right, then. Time to introduce you to your mentors. This is someone who is going to be there, within reason, twenty-four seven for you. Someone who has been through it themselves and understands you.'

I turn round and there, sitting behind us, are a group of strangers. Oh my God, have they been there the whole time? Did they hear everything we said? I guess I really was too much like a rabbit in headlights when I walked in, and I missed them.

They look like a random bunch, just like we do. Again it's a mixture of men and women and different age groups. Oh, hello. There is one man who is to die for. Too bad I'm getting married or else I'd have been over there in a shot.

'Now, I've paired you up on the list, based on the information you gave me over the phone. It always works out best if people have similar lifestyles. You don't want a buddy who's working the night shift when you're a day worker,' says Mary. 'Right, I'll read out the names.'

I start praying that I get the sexy guy. Not that it matters, I don't think I need a mentor anyway, but it is always good to get the sexy guy.

Suddenly I'm transported back to school where you had to be in pairs and the teacher's picking random names and you're chanting in your head the names of the cool kids that you desperately want to be with. Of course at school I'd inevitably get one of the losers. They say like attracts like.

'Penelope, you're with Josh over there. Josh, wave your hand.'

I'm scanning the line of people, desperately looking for Josh, and then I get to the sexy man and see his hand is waving. Oh my God, I actually got the cool guy. I beam with pride and then I realise that it makes me look fifteen and I'm suddenly back looking down at the floor. Which in my defence is a very cool parquet floor which would look lovely in our Victorian terrace.

'Hi, I'm Josh.'

I resist the temptation to say that I know and instead I go into business mode and stick my hand out.

'Penelope, but you can call me Penny.'

Or anything else you like. What is wrong with me? I keep having a mental block that I'm engaged. It is just that he is so tall with dreamy blue eyes and he's wearing a leather jacket. Yep, I'm fifteen. And still a loser.

'Nice to meet you, Penny. I heard your story.'

'Pretty shameful, huh?'

'Yeah, but I've heard worse.'

I try not to think what could be worse; it is far too depressing to think about.

'Come on, you can at least smile. Hey, it's not like you stole from anyone,' says Josh.

No, that's true. I have not stolen from anyone. Except myself and, well I guess, Mark. It was his money, too.

'Well, I sort of did. It was mostly my fiancé's money.'

'Oh yeah, that's true.'

That's just great. I'm a gambler and a thief. I hadn't thought of it that way before. This is getting off to a swell start. I really hope that my mentor has other tips and wisdom to make me feel better about my gambling addiction.

Oh no, here come the tears. I just can't control them.

'Whoa there, don't cry. You're getting help. You're doing the right thing.'

He rubs my arm with his very manly hands. It is times like this that I wished my diamond weighed down my hand a little more, just to remind me about my fiancé, Mark. *Mark*. Focus on Mark and not Josh with his dreamy blue eyes.

'So what's your story?' I ask before I start to drift into a wedding fantasy, and this time Josh is in danger of making a star appearance at the altar.

'I was addicted to online poker. I won almost twenty thousand pounds.'

'Holy crap, that would have paid for my dream wedding.'

Maybe I could get Josh to play a few hands for me to help me.

'Yeah, but in the end I lost fifty thousand pounds. My partner, Mel, found out and gave me the "it's the gambling or me" ultimatum. And at that point I realised that I had a problem and I got help.'

Partner. God dammit. Of course Josh has a girlfriend. I bet she's perfect and wouldn't gamble away their wedding fund.

Mark. Mark. Mark. What is wrong with me? I have a fiancé.

'And now you don't gamble at all?' I ask, trying to concentrate on what is going on.

'Nope. I barely use the computer outside of work. It's just easier that way.'

Imagine not using the internet out of work! I don't think I could cope with that. It would be one thing to go cold turkey from the bingo but it would be another not going on the ASOS website for a little shopping every so often.

'How does this work then, with you and me? I mean, you being my mentor.'

I don't want him to think I mean 'you and me' in a couply

way. I'm just going to play with my hair so he can clearly see my engagement ring and then he'll know I'm not trying to flirt with him.

'So, OK, we swap numbers and you call me or text me if you want to play bingo. We'll chat or arrange to meet.'

'And if I'm not tempted to play bingo?'

'Then we'll check in with each other at the meetings on Tuesday. Just think of me as a safety blanket. You don't want to have to use me, but you know I'm there if you do.'

I like Josh. I like him a lot. I take back that I got cross with him when he called me a thief.

'Great.'

'So get your phone out and I'll give you my number.'

Putting Josh's number in my phone suddenly freaks me out. What should I put him under? Anything like 'mentor' might seem just a bit suspicious. And I can't put 'Josh' in case Mark sees his name and wonders who he is. I know, I'll put him down as Glinda, like the helpful witch in *The Wizard of Oz*.

'Well, you should mingle with some of the others. Like Mary said, it helps to get to know the group.'

'Thanks, Josh.'

I look around the room and everyone else still seems to be talking to their mentors. I can't go back and talk to Josh as he is now deep in conversation with Mary. The trouble with this mentor thing is that everyone is in personal conversations and I can't just go up and butt in.

I'll go and pour myself a nice cup of coffee instead. And just when I think I'm going to die of awkwardness by myself the White Stuff woman comes up.

'Penelope, isn't it?'

'That's right.' I'm trying to smile and make myself look as friendly as possible.

'I remembered because it was like Penelope Pitstop.'

'That's who I'm named after. Something to do with my dad's crush on a cartoon character.'

'That's sweet. I'm Rebecca.'

'Nice to meet you, Rebecca.'

'It's strange this, isn't it? I was terrified I was going to come here today and bump into one of the mums from the school run.'

Up to that point I hadn't considered that these people here have proper families and children. What are we all doing?

'I wasn't too sure what to expect either,' I say.

'I'm glad I came, though. I've got a nice mentor. I think I'm going to try and go cold turkey.'

'That's great, Rebecca. I'm hoping to as well. I just need to figure out how to stick to a budget for the wedding.'

'Oh, that's right, you're the one that's getting married. How exciting.'

'Yeah, well, it would have been. I haven't got the money any more and I'm terrified that Mark – that's my fiancé – is going to find out.'

'You haven't told him?' she asks.

I shake my head. 'I keep hoping I'm going to fix it somehow. You know, plan it with five grand and make it our dream wedding.'

'You still could.'

I almost laugh at her, but then I realise that, just like the woman from the Citizens Advice Bureau, she's serious.

'I know things are a bit different from when I got married. But you know, it isn't all about the money. I'm sure if you got creative you'd figure out a way. And no matter what the wedding is like, it will still be the best day of your life.'

I wish that was true. All the brides I've known have said it was the best day of their lives, but then all the brides I've known have had the wedding of their dreams.

'Anyway, I'll see you next Tuesday. I've got to get home to the babysitter.'

'Good luck with the cold turkey,' I say, realising I've got my fingers crossed together in some cheesy motion.

Luckily Rebecca must have taken it to be sweet and she does the same.

The rest of the room is starting to thin out and I have the familiar feeling of palpitations rushing over me as I realise the magnitude of the task I have ahead of me. I decide to quit while I am ahead.

I wave at Josh and his beautiful eyes as I leave. He waves back and I hope I'll have a reason to call him. No. I must stop thinking like that.

I do not want to call him this week or else that means I'll have been a dirty little gambler.

No, I will not call Josh.

At all.

No matter how blue his eyes are.

Now I'm going to go home and see my fiancé. Wonderful, wonderful *Mark*. And I'll try not to look too guilty as once again I tell him nothing about what is going on in my life.

chapter six

Today is the day that I am sorting out the wedding venue. I am. Really. Just because I've now been engaged for almost a month and I haven't booked anywhere, despite it being three months to the potential wedding, does not mean I've been burying my head in the sand.

No, I've been sorting myself out. I've deleted the bingo apps from my phone, yes, *occasionally* I used to use them. And I've also put parental locks on my laptop and put all the bingo sites I could remember the names of on the banned list. The bingo sites were already banned by our firewall at work, along with Facebook, external mail sites and Net-a-Porter. I made IT add the Net-a-Porter site, telling them one of our workers had an addiction to it. In reality it just means that I now actually leave my desk at lunchtimes and don't drool over handbags and clothes I can't afford.

So far blocking bingo out of my life has been working. I haven't lunged for the virtual dabber pen and I've managed to stay on the straight and narrow. Although I did nearly go and play actual bingo when I took a trip into town this morning. I had a moment of weakness as I walked past the bingo hall and then I saw an old woman with a blue rinse and it scared me that Mark's nan Violet might be there.

I also had a bit of a moment on Thursday when I nearly gambled but that was more to do with remembering how blue Josh's eyes were and I just wanted to see them again. But then I remembered that with only five thousand pounds left I couldn't risk losing any more.

'You surfing for wedding stuff?' asks Mark, sitting down in the armchair. I have a quick smell under my armpits just to make sure I'm not smelling really bad, as why else would he choose to sit on the opposite side of the room from me?

'Uh-huh.'

'Thought so; you've got the furrowed brow look. Don't worry, I'm not looking. I just wanted to watch the footie. Is that OK?'

'Yeah, fine.'

Phew. I don't smell after all. He's right about the furrowed brow, though. I've got to make sure that the wind doesn't change or else I'll have a permanent state of confusion plastered across my face.

I'm looking at those lovely, gorgeous wedding venues that Jane found. I've been trying to be all sensible and do my sums but the only way we could afford to spend £125 a head would be to only have forty guests. And the venue has a sixty-guest minimum. And then we'd have no money for anything else other than the venue and the food.

There has to be a cheaper way. Perhaps I could do some inventive Googling:

CHEAP WEDDING ABROAD

Oh, abroad. Just me and Mark. How romantic, just us on a beach at sunset. I'm starting to get so swept up in the fantasy that I can feel the sand beneath my toes, the warm water lapping at my feet. But the daydream stops after the ceremony. What would we do after? I know what we would do *later* – I have a lot of fantasies about that. But I'm talking immediately after. Would we have dinner, just the two of us?

'How open are you to the idea of a wedding abroad?' I ask as nonchalantly as possible, so that he doesn't think it is our only option.

'Where?'

'I don't know. I was just thinking, you and me on a beach together. Just the two of us.'

'What about our parents? And Nanny Violet? I don't think that's a good idea.'

Stupid family ruining everything. Mark is of course, right. I do want our family to be there. Or else imagine what my mum would write about me in the Christmas card. Not to mention I'd probably get written out of the will if I deprived my mum of the opportunity of being able to buy a new hat for the wedding.

Time for a change of approach. I Google:

BUDGET WEDDING IDEAS

Bingo! Oh, that is a poor choice of words. I just wanted to express that I seem to be on to something. There are absolutely loads of forums full of suggestions.

BRIDGETJ123

I'M GETTING MARRIED IN OUR LOCAL REGISTRY OFFICE AND THEN WE'RE HAVING A PARTY AT OUR VILLAGE HALL. MY MUM'S DOING THE FOOD AND MY AUNT'S MADE MY DRESS. TOTAL COST £1,500.

This is more like it. Although I don't think the community centre where I'm currently going to my gambling meetings would really cut it. For that to work I'm imagining a twee village hall with bunting and fairy lights. Croquet on the lawn. Afternoon tea. Make that champagne afternoon tea. With a barbershop quartet.

Nope. I can't imagine that I could get all that for five thousand pounds, especially not around here.

CASEYGOGO

I'M GOING TO GRETNA GREEN WITH MY HUBBY TO BE AND A MINI BUS FULL OF MY NEAREST AND DEAREST!!!! HOPE WE CAN HAVE A MEAL OUT AFTER. OUR BUDGET IS £1,000.

See, there are loads of people doing this kind of thing on a budget. I just need to start thinking outside the box.

'What about Gretna Green for our wedding?'

'Too tacky. Look, is the pressure getting to you? Do you want me to help you organise this wedding?'

'No!' Oops, that was practically a scream. 'No, I'm fine thanks, honey. I was just trying to throw you off the scent.'

There we are, there's the side head-tilt that is fast becoming Mark's signature move. He's been doing it a lot lately. He thinks I'm deranged. Who can blame him?

Perhaps the budget wedding search term is taking me down the wrong path.

UNUSUAL WEDDING VENUES HAMPSHIRE SURREY

I'm amazed at how many sites are popping up in the Google listing. There are a number of blogs alone that are dedicated to unusual venues. Seems from my scan reading that doing something unconventional is the trendy thing now.

Maybe that's what I can say to people. I didn't want a princess wedding as I thought it was all a bit too clichéd. I'm just uber trendy and ahead of my time.

The website I've landed on is perfect. There are loads of suggestions about where you can have the wedding reception. Old discarded railway stations, steam trains, boats. Sensing a theme here at all?

There's even a whole tab for museums. Who would want to get married in a museum? What with all the scary mannequins and old stuff? I click on the tab anyway, just to see what kind of a wedding you can have among the glass showcases.

Hello! I've spotted a massive website fail. I secretly love spotting errors on things like this. It's a bit of a howler as next to the text about the Surrey Military Museum, which sounds like a stuffy old museum, there's a picture of a beautiful old manor house.

Where is that manor house? It looks lovely. Maybe if I click on the picture it will take me to the right website.

There must be some sort of broken link as I've ended up on the website for the Surrey Military Museum.

This is a museum dedicated to telling the diverse and interesting military history of Surrey, including the story of those regiments stationed in the county during the Second World War . . .

Yada, yada, yada. Where's the bit about weddings? Ah, here we are.

Housed in an old officers' mess, the museum now caters for exclusive wedding receptions.

Oh, my goodness. The museum is the place in the picture. That place is gorgeous. Nearly as gorgeous as The Manor that Jane showed me.

I just want to find out how much it costs, but it's one of those annoying websites where there are only two pages and all it really tells you is how to get there.

'Hot lead?' asks Mark.

I look up and he's laughing at me. I guess my furrowed brow has turned into a look of desperation mixed with happiness. I'm just hoping this place is cheaper than The Manor.

'Possibly.'

I look down at the museum's 'find us' map. It is probably only about twenty minutes away by car, and they are open on Saturdays. I could go today. I could go right now. Who knows, maybe I could even have this wedding venue booked by this afternoon.

'I'm off to see a venue.'

The excitement in my voice must be evident as I'm rewarded by a lovely smile from Mark.

'Want me to come?'

'Nope, I'll be fine. I've got a good feeling about this.'

And I have; a *very* good feeling.

Pulling up outside the museum, it is every bit as pretty as it was in the picture. You had to go over a little moat to get on to the site and through a narrow set of gate posts that I have to hold my breath to get through in the car. Not that I drive a tank, but my Beetle is wider than I think it should be.

It reminds me a little bit of the family outings we had to go on as kids. Parking on a makeshift stony grass car park. Walking past the little museum shop filled with rubbers and pencils. I never could resist stocking up my pencil case with museum shop stationery. And my mum would always buy it for me as it was practically educational. It had come from a museum, after all.

This place would be perfect for the wedding. Please, please let it be in my budget.

There's a staircase at the front of the building which I can imagine walking down in my dress, the train trailing behind me. Oh, wait. I probably won't be able to afford a train. I can just imagine walking down here in my dress, swishing away. I'm sure I can still afford a dress that swishes.

I'm not entirely sure what is going to lie beyond the entrance. I hold my breath and pray that it is equally stunning on the other side.

'Hello, there,' says a beaming woman as I step over the threshold. She's just a little bit keen to see me.

'Hi.'

So far, so good. The reception desk is an old mahogany wooden desk and the rest of the inside looks . . . well, it looks like a National Trust Property.

'Something tells me that you're here to talk to us about weddings.'

The woman is pointing at me; I hope she's not pointing to my belly. We did have a massive fry-up for brunch this morning. I hope she isn't mistaking my pot belly for a baby bump. This isn't a shotgun wedding.

But then I realise she is probably looking at my engagement ring. Yes. That's where her finger is pointing. Phew.

'Yes, I was just wondering if I could talk to someone, you know, about costs. And maybe availability.'

'OK. I can help you with that. I'll just get Ted. Ted?'

An old man appears who looks like someone's granddad. He's so cute and smiley that I have to resist the urge to go and give him a hug and sit on his knee. Although that makes it sound pervy, like I've got a granddad crush. I'm just trying to say that he looks cute.

'I'll show you the room first then, shall I?'

'OK, that would be great. Thank you.'

In all my giddiness at the outside of the venue, I'd forgotten that there would have to be a reception room too. What if this is the room that is full of the showcases and scary mannequins?

But as the woman opens the door any doubts fall away from my mind. This is *the* room. It is perfect. It is wood-panelled in a nice, not cheesy seventies, way. There is a long mahogany table and chairs running along the centre and oil paintings adorning the walls.

The windows look out to the Surrey downs and I can't believe that anywhere this beautiful exists, and especially not in a museum. That will teach me for not going to anywhere vaguely cultural.

'We reserve this room for weddings and events. It's how we keep the museum going,' says the woman.

'It's just wonderful. Oh, look at the ceiling!'

There are chandeliers! This place is so going to be out of my price range.

'Now, depending on how many guests you have, you can either have the long table – that seats thirty – or, for a bigger wedding, we can move it out and you can have round tables. How many guests were you planning for?'

'We did have a hundred, but I think eighty is more realistic.'

'Eighty is fine in here; a hundred gets a little cramped for the sit-down meal. But for the evening anything up to one hundred and fifty is fine. Now, this is probably where the stage would go for a band or a DJ.'

A swing band would go really well in here. It would just fit the whole tone of the place. Maybe we could have a vintage wedding. I could put my hair in rags the night before to give me a curl and I could get a vintage wedding dress. A vintage *couture* wedding dress. I'm sure that would be lots cheaper than a brand new dress.

'Are you OK, dear?' she asks, interrupting my thoughts.

'Yes, sorry, just planning it in my head.'

The woman is smiling at me and nodding.

'Of course, if you want anything like a string quartet during the wedding breakfast then we have the little balcony up there. It also makes for a wonderful photograph if you get the photographer up there and your guests down below.'

I'm nodding like the nodding dogs I hate. I bet it would also make an excellent point to do a bouquet toss from. Although it could be a bit lethal if it hit someone from that height.

'It's perfect,' I say. 'But I'm on quite a tight budget, so I think before I get too carried away we should talk costs.'

'OK, that's very sensible. Take a seat.'

There's something unnatural about sitting at the table. I don't know whether it is because we're in a museum where you're usually barked at if you even breathe on an object, or whether it is because it looks too old and beautiful to disturb. But either way I'm terrified of sitting down, even though the woman told me I could.

'Right. I'll just get straight to the figures, then.'

For once in my life, I had listened to the little voice in my head that sounds an awful lot like Mark, and I've brought a notepad and pen. Getting it out, I feel like a journalist as I hold my pen over the pad eagerly.

'The room hire, which is this room and the museum grounds for the day, is £3,000.'

Hooray, this sounds like it might be in my price range.

'Then you've got the catering. We've got a number of different caterers you can choose from, which range from a cheaper option to the more expensive.'

'Can you tell me roughly what their costs are per head?'

'Yes, the cheapest option is about £35 per head and the most expensive is £50.'

I start to take deep breaths, because this is actually affordable. Now, I admit maths has never been my strong point.

That's usually where Mark comes in handy. But I think we may be able to afford it, if we don't buy anything else and we have no entertainment and no wine. But people would like that, right? It could be a theme wedding, the theme being no fun.

If only I hadn't gambled away the money then we could have afforded to have had a lovely venue like this which is half the cost of the other places and with tons more charm and character. I know that I can't go back in time and change what I did, but right now I'm furious with myself.

'Are you OK?'

The woman has a very concerned look on her face. I'm not sure whether she can see actual steam coming out of my ears.

'That all sounds very reasonable. It's just I'm still not sure that we're going to be able to afford it. I don't suppose . . .'

No, I can't do it. I can't get the words out of my mouth.

'You don't suppose what, dear?'

'That you offer any discounts on the hire fee. You know, if we got married on a Monday or something?'

There, I've said it. I'm officially mortified.

'I'm afraid not. And we're closed on Mondays. I know it probably seems steep but if you go round the other venues in the area I'm sure you'll find that they're much more expensive.'

'Oh no, I know that. I know this is an absolute bargain. It's just me. I had the money and I don't have it any more. Or at least I don't have enough for this.'

I prise myself out of the chair and stand up. I don't want to leave this place. Now that is the first time I've ever said that in a museum.

'I'm sorry, dear. I'm afraid we have to charge what we do or else we can't afford to run the museum.'

'Of course, I totally understand.'

'The only people who get discounts here are the staff.'

'I don't suppose you've got any jobs going, have you?' I ask, laughing.

I meant it as a joke, but that would kill two birds with one stone. A discount and some extra pennies to put towards the big day.

'Not paid ones. We only have a few members of paid staff.'

'Shame.'

We are back out in the lobby with the lovely mahogany desk and Ted, who I would like to adopt as a granddad.

'Thank you ever so much for your time. I'm sorry that I'm not able to book.'

'That's OK, dear. Would you like to go round the museum while you're here?' she asks.

I shake my head. Museums, in case you haven't already guessed it, aren't my thing. But just as I'm about to leave something hits me like a little light bulb going off in my head.

'You know you said that you didn't have any paid jobs? Does that mean you have unpaid jobs?'

'Oh yes, we have volunteers who help run the museum and help out behind the scenes.'

'And do they get a discount?'

My mind is racing a million to the dozen. Even a tiny bit of a discount would mean I'd be that little bit closer to maybe having our wedding here.

'They do. But . . .'

Uh-oh, there's always a but, and the woman's finger is pointed up to the sky, meaning this 'but' doesn't sound good at all.

'To get the discount our volunteers must attend regularly and they must have volunteered for at least three months.'

'I can do that!'

I *could* do that. It is three months until the potential wedding. I'm sure I could volunteer between now and then.

'Would you be able to give up two hours a week to come and volunteer?'

'Could I do it at the weekend?'

'Yes, we have Saturday-morning volunteers.'

Perfect, just when Mark plays golf.

'Great. How do I sign up?'

'You'd need to have a chat with the curator. She's not here today, but you can give her a call on Tuesday.'

The woman hands me a piece of paper with a name and telephone number on it, and I clutch it to my chest as if it is the most precious possession on earth.

'I will do. And what type of discount do the volunteers get?' I ask.

'You would have to pay the cost price, which is about five hundred pounds.'

That is some discount. Even I can work out that saving. Two and a half thousand pounds. Amazing.

'That's great. Thank you so much for all your help. And I'll phone the curator on Tuesday.'

Waving goodbye to the woman and Ted I walk out of the main entrance and down the sweeping staircase.

I feel like I am gliding down it. Not because I am imagining myself as a princess bride, but because I feel for the first time in weeks that this wedding could actually come together. I'd better keep all my fingers and toes crossed that the curator says yes to me volunteering, or else I'm going to be back to square one.

chapter Seven

I'm starting to get a grip on this wedding. So I haven't booked the venue yet or even found out if they have any dates free, but at least I'm not putting off thinking about it any more.

I've got to go and volunteer on Saturday at the museum to see if I'm a suitable fit. But I will do absolutely anything to make sure I am or else the wedding is off. And I'll be off too, as I'd have to confess to Mark about the horrible gambling-induced mess.

You'll be pleased to know that I haven't gambled in a whole week. I didn't even buy a lottery ticket. I think Mark thinks I've lost the plot, as I practically rugby-tackled him to the ground at the kiosk at Tesco's when he went to buy a ticket. I told him that with the wedding coming we should save every pound.

It's week two of my online gambling support group. I've got that sick feeling in my stomach. The one I used to get when I was going back to school after being off for a few days. I always used to imagine it was going to be a whole lot worse than it was. I know I'll be fine when I get there. After all, it can't be worse second time around, can it?

'Penelope!'

I stop dead and desperately try to come up with a cover story that will explain why I am entering the community centre at 4.30 p.m. on a Tuesday when I should be at work. You'd think I'd have invented a story just in case, with this being the second week that I'm coming. But I haven't, I'm just not creative. I clearly would make the world's worst spy.

I turn round slowly, wondering exactly who is going to be standing behind me.

Oh, the relief. It's Rebecca from the group.

'Hi, Rebecca,' I say, with far too much gusto. I'm in danger of it sounding sarcastic and nasty, but I don't mean it to be. I'm just relieved that it isn't one of Mark's aunts lurking about the area.

'Back again then?'

'Yes. I'm just as nervous as I was last week. Isn't that silly?' I say.

'I feel exactly the same. I nearly called Mary and told her

one of my kids was sick. And then I remembered that I'd come here to stop the lying.'

I like Rebecca. Without kids myself, Rebecca probably isn't someone I'd usually come into contact with. I know I've only met her twice but when I talk to her I instantly know that she understands exactly what I'm going through. Well, not exactly what I'm going through. After all, she is married and doesn't have the whole wedding palaver to get through.

'I don't seem to be able to stop lying. What with not telling Mark about the wedding.'

Walking into our room in the community centre, suddenly I don't know why I was worrying at all. Mary is beaming at me and Rebecca, and everyone else is chatting enthusiastically together. There are back slaps going on and 'good for you's' being exchanged. Suddenly my mood has changed and I'm back to feeling like I can do this. I can kick the bingo habit.

'Hey, Penelope.'

'Oh, hi, Josh. I didn't see you come in.' Or else I would have made sure that I'd taken off my frumpy coat and smoothed my hair down. It's those bloody eyes of his. I wish he did a Bono and kept sunglasses on all the time. Then I wouldn't be so hypnotised by him.

'How's your week gone?' he asks.

'Good. I haven't gambled at all. Not even a lottery ticket,' I say proudly.

'Hey, that's great news. Well done you.'

When Josh smiles at me and tells me I've done well I feel a bit like teacher's pet and I'm all glowing inside.

'Right then, shall we get started? I think we're all here,' says Mary.

I take my seat next to Rebecca, and Josh goes back to hovering somewhere near the back of the class with all the cool kids. Or at least all the other mentors.

'Today, we're going to think about our feelings around gambling. Why do we do it and how it makes us feel.

'Penelope, why don't we start with you?'

My cheeks immediately flush red. This always used to happen at school. I'd get picked on first. I think it's because I have such a memorable first name that teachers always remembered my name first before all the other kids' names.

'Um, OK. What do you want me to say?'

'Well, let's start at the beginning. Why did you gamble? Was it the rush?'

I'm panicking, I'm *really* panicking. What am I supposed to say? Is there a right answer?

'I wanted a Vera Wang wedding dress.'

From the stunned looks around the room I'm guessing that this might not have been the right answer.

'A wedding dress?' repeats Mary, in a tone that suggests she thinks she's misheard what I said.

'Uh-huh. Well, I was playing bingo to get myself a dream wedding. We'd saved money for it, but I wanted the icing on the cake. You know, the Vera Wang wedding dress, the Jimmy Choos or Louboutins on my feet, the amazing tiara, the magician or the candyfloss machine.'

I'm almost back there at my dream wedding, watching my guests' faces with their look of surprise at how beautiful it is.

When I open my eyes I'm embarrassed that I'm baring my vain soul to all these near-perfect strangers.

'And why did you pick – what was it – bingo?'

I can't say what I'm really thinking. That I've been hooked on bingo since I was a little girl. Since my gran took us along to bingo at her village hall one Thursday afternoon. As an eight-year old I was transfixed by the bright colours of the dabber pens. From that moment on my sister and I would play bingo together, making my gran be the bingo caller. Only we changed all the rhymes so that it would be *two swimming swans: twenty-two* and *two fat hippos: eighty-eight*. But I can't say that as that isn't why I picked online bingo.

'I saw it on the TV a couple of times and I thought about it. Then one day there was a pop-up on the internet that said there was a ten-pound credit. I was bored as my fiancé was always upstairs in the spare room studying for exams.'

'Boredom, that's like so many of us. So are you happy when you win?'

'I guess so.'

'You guess so? What does it feel like for you to win?'

'It feels like I'm closer to my dream.'

Why did I have to go first? I'm dying inside.

'Your dream being your wedding? And what does it mean to you when you lose?'

'The silly thing was I didn't pay any attention to whether I was winning or losing. That didn't matter. It was just that by playing I felt I was one step closer to the wedding. Half the time I realised that I wasn't even aware of the game going on around me. I was so caught up in my dreams and my fantasies that the bingo almost didn't matter.'

'That's like me.'

I'm momentarily shocked to hear another voice. I look up and see that the voice came from the man who is addicted to online football betting.

'Half the time I realised that I didn't even watch the games or check the scores. For me it wasn't about the winning and losing, it was just the habit of doing it,' continues the man.

As he carries on talking, I smile at him for rescuing me. Before long the whole group has shared their feelings and I am slowly learning that gambling addiction isn't anything like what I imagined it would be. Instead of all of us celebrating and getting off on our win, for most of us it was more about taking part. Others in the group felt so guilty they'd won that they played again until they lost.

By the end of the session I am well and truly confused about my motivations. Surely there had to be more to the bingo addiction than the fact that I used to like playing with my gran's dabber pens?

As I walk over to the coffee pot I'm practically on autopilot. I'm trying to drag my memory back to what happened to me that day last summer when I first started to play bingo. I know I was surfing the net, looking at wedding dresses. Goodness, I really was desperate to get engaged. And I vaguely remember a little pop-up box saying about the ten-pound credit.

I clicked on it as I used to be lucky with Gran's bingo. I only meant to use the ten-pound credit; I didn't mean to get hooked. If only I'd read a book that night or done something productive with my time. If only I hadn't gambled, instead I'd now be drowning in my emails at work, rather than standing stood in a dingy community centre room with my fellow addicts.

'You did well there, to open up,' says Josh.

'Thanks.'

I don't feel I've done well. It has just pushed me deeper into the pit of realisation of what an awful person I am. There I was with my wedding on a silver plate and like a greedy child I still wanted more.

'I expected you to text me in the week.'

'You did?'

Could I have sounded any more desperate? Why does my voice go all high-pitched and idiot-like when Josh is around?

'I thought you might have wanted to talk. You know, needed a shoulder to lean on.'

I'm sure he said it deliberately so that I would look at his shoulders – his lovely big protective shoulders that would be excellent to lean on. To sleep on. To *anything* on.

What is wrong with me? I'm getting married. To MARK, not Josh.

'You know, you can call me about stuff. Like if you're tempted to gamble or if you just need to talk to someone who knows about what you're going through. I can't help you much with your dream wedding though; I don't believe in marriage.'

Such a waste. I hope I said that in my head and not out loud. I look up at Josh and he is still looking normal and he's not backing away from me in horror, so I think I only said it in my head.

'So how have you been this week?' asks Josh, helping himself to another Bourbon biscuit off the counter. That's four he's had. Not that I'm counting.

'I've been good. I've put parental locks on my laptop and I've deleted the bingo apps off my phone.'

'That's good. A good first step. Cold turkey is always hard. So have you thought any more about talking to your partner? What's his name?'

My head wants to scream 'Josh'. But I manage to get Mark's actual name out.

'Mark. And no, I'm not going to tell him. *Ever*.'

Josh is even sexy when he looks disappointed.

'I think you should reconsider. It's a big secret to keep from him.'

'I can't tell Mark. And anyway, what's the point? I'm never going to gamble again. I'm going to organise the wedding of our dreams and therefore he won't ever have to know.'

'Do you think that is the best way to start a marriage?'

'How do you know? Aren't you the guy who doesn't believe in marriage?' I snap.

I instantly regret saying that. I didn't mean to snap; it is just that Josh hit a nerve. He's so right. It isn't any way to start a marriage. But I have no choice. I can't tell Mark. There won't *be* a wedding if I tell Mark, I remind myself.

'I'm sorry, Josh. I didn't mean that.'

'Hey, that's what a mentor is for. Look, I think you and I should meet in the week. I think you need to talk more than this little bit we get at the end.'

'I don't know. This week is quite busy for me,' I say, lying. It's busy at work, but not so busy that I can't meet one evening for a drink. It's just that I'm carrying around so many lies at the moment I don't think I'd be able to meet Josh and think of an excuse to tell Mark.

'OK. Well, it doesn't have to be this week. But I think we should talk.'

I'm lost again in Josh's eyes. It is like he is hypnotising me. I feel myself nod and tell him yes, although I have no control over my reactions.

'I've got to go,' I tell him. I need to leave now. I don't want to see his eyes any more.

'OK. Well, remember, text me if you want to talk.'

I nod and wave at the others before I practically run out of the room. Today's session was all a bit overwhelming for me.

It's a good job that I'm off to the gym before I go home. I usually do body combat on a Tuesday night. Not that I can go now – I'm too late. The class starts at 6 p.m. and it's now 6.30 p.m. I found out last week my body combat teacher does not take kindly to latecomers. She shooed me out of the door before I even put a foot over the threshold. But I've still got time to make an appearance at the gym before I go home to Mark.

Just as I'm walking out of the door of the community centre something catches my eye. Flower arranging. No, I haven't suddenly become a retired woman in need of something to do, but just seeing the cost of florists practically brought me out in a rash. If I could do it myself, then surely that has to be cheaper?

It can't be that hard anyway, can it? It's just putting a few flowers together and tying them into a bouquet. In fact, I reckon I'd be quite good at it. Pulling out my new handy notebook and pen, I jot down the contact details for the course.

The gym was just what I needed to do after my mentally exhausting time at the community centre. It might not have been my longest workout but it was a good one. I managed to do ten minutes of fast running on the running machine and then I had an equally long shower. Those showers are amazing. They are worth my gym membership alone.

'Hi, Penny.'

Oh shit. I've timed it so that I'm getting dressed just when our body combat class is ending.

'Oh, hi, Kate.'

'I've missed you the last couple of weeks. Everything OK?'

Great. Another person to add to my list of those I lie to.

'Yeah, fine. Works' just crazy busy at the moment.'

Why did I feel that I needed an equally crazy hand gesture to illustrate it? This lying is causing my body to spasm in all different ways.

'Oh, I know how that goes. Well, maybe we'll see you next week?'

'Yes, hopefully,' I say, lying yet again.

'Great. Well, I'd better jump in the shower. I must stink after that class. I'll look forward to catching up with you next week and hearing all your wedding plans!'

'Can't wait.'

I wonder if there is a limit to how many lies I can tell in a day without my nose going all Pinocchio.

By the time I get home I'm exhausted. I can't even think about sorting out dinner. All I want to do is curl up in bed and go to sleep. I don't even want to go on any wedding forums. I am *that* tired.

But I'm the first one home so I should start dinner before Mark arrives.

'Hey, honey, I'm home.'

Speak of the devil. He sounds cheesy, so he's clearly in a good mood. At least that makes one of us.

'I'm in the kitchen.'

'Wow, you're actually starting dinner?'

I hit him playfully with a tea towel as I walk over to him.

Cooking dinner is a bit of a stretch as I haven't got out a single ingredient yet. But I was thinking about cooking dinner, so that's a start.

'Thai curry?' I ask, opening the fridge to see that we have chicken and an aubergine in there. My mind is still so foggy from the group therapy session that I can't think to be inventive.

'Sounds great. How was the gym?'

'It was good.'

'Well, don't you go becoming a skinny minnie for the wedding. I know loads of girls at work who tried to become size eights for their weddings and they looked all bony and horrid in their photos.'

Fat chance of that. Excuse the pun. What with group therapy on a Tuesday when I usually do body combat and the flower arranging class that is going to conflict with my body blitz, I'm going to be struggling to get to the gym.

At this rate I'm going to have to start going at lunchtime or else it isn't just a wedding dress that I won't get into. We're allowed to wear jeans to work most of the time, as long as I'm not interviewing anyone. Which used to be lovely until skinny jeans came into fashion, and now wearing jeans to work is the bane of my life. I had to start going to the classes at the gym rather than just poncing around on the machines to make sure that I didn't look like a beached whale in the skinny jeans.

'You OK? You look exhausted. Do you want me to do the cooking?'

I nod. Even though according to the rules that means I have to unload and stack the dishwasher. Which I absolutely hate doing. At this point in time I don't care, as right now

I would agree to anything if it means I can go and collapse in a chair.

'Thanks, honey. That would be lovely. So tell me about your day.'

I get cosy, or as cosy as you can on a wooden kitchen chair, and I listen to Mark describe his day in detail. From his clients who try to get him to minimise the amount of tax they pay to the banter that occurred during his squash match.

My eyes start to glaze over as I listen to him talking. I can't believe that I could have done something so stupid as to gamble away our future and to lie to him. Before I know it, I've got tears running down my face.

'Hey, hey, Pen. What's wrong?'

'Nothing,' I blub. I'm so close to telling him the truth. But I can't. He'll never forgive me. 'I think I'm just tired and hormonal.'

That's the great thing about being a woman – you can blame almost anything on hormones.

'Why don't you go and put your feet up in the lounge and I'll bring you a cup of tea?'

I am the world's worst fiancée.

'That would be amazing,' I say.

And then I start crying even harder. What did I do to deserve such a lovely man as my fiancé? And more importantly, what did he do to deserve a lying cow like me?

chapter eight

Typically, on my very first day volunteering at the museum it is raining cats and dogs and Mark decides to be a fair-weather golfer.

It took every inch of resolve to get out of our wonderfully comfortable bed. Which is even harder to do when you've got a naked man in it, giving the world's best cuddles.

He is now so impressed with my dedication to go to my new Zumba class that he says he'll cook me an extra special fry-up for lunch as a treat as I'll have burned off a zillion calories. At this rate I'm going to be at the gym every lunch break during the week. Hey, maybe I'll lose weight just by missing eating lunch at lunch-time.

I'm pleased to see that the museum looks just as pretty in the rain. At least it did when I was in my car driving down the long driveway. It's not so nice now that I've got out of the car and I'm making a run for it up the sweeping staircase. Images of me sweeping down the stairs in my meringue dress have been replaced by me wearing wellies and yellow galoshes. Please, god of the weddings, let it be sunny on my wedding day.

By the time I arrive in reception I'm a dripping mess. I take off my mac and hang it – as directed by Ted, the man I want to adopt as my granddad – on the coat hooks. I then make an excuse to head to the toilet where I quickly change out of my gym gear and into my jeans and smart jumper. I want to make sure I make a good impression.

All I need to remember to do is stick my head under a tap before I leave so I have the just-showered look when I get home. Or alternatively I could just walk home, and then I'd have the just-showered look all over.

Once I've managed to get as much frizz out of my hair as I think I'm going to, I leave the safety of the toilets.

Ted radios for someone to come and get me and soon I'm following another museum assistant behind the scenes of the museum. It feels a bit naughty to be allowed to go through a door behind a showcase. It almost feels like I'm going to end up in Narnia.

The museum assistant is in no mood for small talk and he whisks me quickly through the tunnels of faceless corridors.

If I ever find my way out alive it will be a miracle. I'm finally deposited in a surprisingly bright and airy room somewhere below the main part of the museum.

'Ah, you must be Penelope,' says a woman walking towards me.

'That's right. But you can call me Penny.'

'Penny. OK. Welcome. I'm Cathy, the curator here at the museum. And this is our Saturday morning volunteering club.'

'Hi,' I say, waving my hand at the other three ladies.

'There's usually a few more of us than this, but this type of weather tends to mean only the diehards turn out.'

'A little drop of rain never hurt anyone,' says one of the ladies.

I sit down next to a woman and the curator sits down beside me.

'Now then, Penny, have you done this kind of volunteering before?'

I shake my head.

'Right. Well, we tend to work on different projects. At the moment we're making padded hangers for our uniform collection. How are your sewing skills?'

My non-existent sewing skills, I want to say. I hung up my needles after Mark got me to mend a hole in his sock. When he went to put his foot into the sock it got stuck as I'd sewn through the middle of it.

The curator definitely didn't say anything about sewing on the phone. The chances of me having my wedding here are beginning to look as likely as me winning *The X-Factor*, and that would never happen as I'm practically tone-deaf.

'They're not the best,' I say, grimacing. Wow, it is quite refreshing to actually tell the truth for once.

'That's fine. You can do the pattern cutting if you like.'

'OK.'

That sounds more like it. Put me in charge of scissors. That I can handle.

The curator spends the next ten minutes explaining how the hangers are constructed and why we have to make them. It's a lot more interesting than I thought it would be. Who knew that underneath the museum they have a whole set of reserve stores with hundreds of items of uniforms? And that each one of those uniforms has to be delicately stored and preserved? This volunteering is proof that every day is indeed a school day.

Before long I've graduated from cutting patterns and I'm being shown how to wrap the foam on to the hangers to make the padding before they get passed to the ladies who sew. I've been introduced to Betty, Lilian and Nina. Betty and Lilian are both retired and Nina is a student who wants to go into conservation when she graduates.

We've managed to exhaust all of what I call the Blind Date

topics of conversation (who are you and where do you come from) and we've moved on now to my favourite topic of weddings.

'Some of the weddings here have been stunning,' says Lilian.

'Oh yes, some of them have been. That's the nicest bit about coming on a Saturday morning – you get to have a good shufti at all the layouts upstairs before everyone arrives,' agrees Betty.

'And of course you get the occasional shocking wedding,' says Lilian. 'Do you remember the pink wedding, Betty?'

Betty looks like she is trying desperately not to smirk. I've got to hear more about the pink wedding.

'The bride wanted everything pink: pink dress, pink shoes, pink cake. She even had a pink tint to her hair.'

Wow. There are no words for that.

'The funniest bit was when she turned up here and she was furious. Her mother-in-law had only turned up wearing red, and of course not only did she outshine the bride but she clashed terribly with everything,' says Betty, laughing with a full-on dirty man's laugh.

Where did that come from? On the outside she looks like such a nice old lady.

'Oh love, you're not having a pink theme, are you?' asks Lilian.

Betty stops cackling and she suddenly looks very serious.

'No, don't worry. Pink is definitely not my theme. I haven't really thought of a theme, to be honest.'

To be honest I've had more pressing matters like trying to have a wedding where the groom doesn't kill me beforehand.

'Well, weddings don't have to have a theme,' says Betty.

'I was going to have a princess theme,' I say as visions of a big dress with a long train and a hundred bridesmaids in tow appear in my mind. My thoughts tail off as I remember with a thud that that wedding is a far distant memory.

'And you changed your mind?' says Betty.

'I guess I grew up,' I say honestly.

'I think princess themes have been done to death. All that Jordan and Peter glass carriage stuff, I think it's tacky,' says Nina. 'When I get married I'm going to do it just me and the groom.'

'Oh no, love, that's not very fair on your parents,' says Betty.

Nina shrugs. *If only I could do that, Nina.* But Betty is right. We have too many family members who would disown us if I took that idea seriously.

'Right. Well, I think that's me done for the day,' says Lilian.

'Oh yes, look at the time. Time for a cuppa before home?' asks Betty.

I look at my watch and I can't quite believe that it is 11 a.m. already. Why don't two hours at my work go this quickly?

And then I remember that at work I don't get to talk non-stop for two hours unless I am delivering training. At which point I am parroting out stuff and taking in none of what I say.

'Penny, shall we have a chat about this wedding of yours?' says Cathy the curator.

'Yes, that would be great.'

I follow Cathy to her office. I almost feel like I need to leave a trail of breadcrumbs so that I can find my way back. This place really is a maze. I hope that none of our guests get too drunk and end up taking a wrong turn to the toilets or else they'll be stuck wandering the white passageways for years.

'Here we are,' says Cathy, unlocking a door.

Her office is amazing. One wall is full of bookshelves with an amount of books I haven't seen since I was at university. Cathy's desk is stacked with piles of paper and folders and there are odd objects dotted around. There are gas masks and rubber items that look like they belong at a fetish party rather than a museum.

'Sorry about the mess. It always gets like this near the end of the financial year. There's always spending reports on grants to write, and reports for trustees and the like.'

I nod as if I know. But to be honest, all I know about year end is we get a million phone calls in our HR department about end-of-year bonuses. They still call us, no matter how many emails or letters we send telling our office that we don't deal with pay or anything money related. That includes bonuses. We have a fancy head office in Sweden that does that for us. We get all the fun stuff to deal with, like making sure we're following British law and policies, and the local hiring and firing.

'Right then, let me see. You want to get married in May or June? And I understand that you are keen to qualify for the volunteer discount?'

'That's right. I'm more than happy to come in and help out.'

'Excellent. It's always nice to have a mixture of age ranges for our Saturday club. If you're not careful it can end up feeling like a day trip from a senior citizens' centre. And that isn't what volunteering is about. It should be about mixing generations and people coming together.'

To an outsider it might seem like Cathy has been brainwashed by the Big Society propaganda that the government are banging on about, but she actually sounds like she means it.

'Sorry, I digress. Now, to qualify for the discount you'd have to commit to working at least three months here with us as a volunteer, of course.'

'Yes, that would be fine.'

'And it would have to be pretty much every Saturday.

We're not going to make sure you give us exactly thirteen calendar weeks or anything that harsh, but you can't turn up to a few and still expect to get a discount. That wouldn't happen.'

I suddenly feel like I am back in the headmistress's office at school. Not that I spent much time in there or anything. Honest. It wasn't my fault that I had a few growth spurts that left my once knee-length skirts suddenly hovering precariously around my upper thighs.

'I understand.'

'Good. I just wanted to make you aware. We've had cases in the past where people have agreed to volunteer and then haven't. Then after the wedding they've been handed the bill and it can get quite messy. Small claims court, solicitors – you get the drift.'

Why do I feel like I'm making a deal with the devil here? I can't understand how it can be that bad to volunteer here every week. I get out of bed to go to work every day and I don't like that very much.

OK, so I get paid to go to work, but here you have biscuits. We don't have biscuits at work unless you bring your own, thanks to Trevor and Biscuitgate. I did bring a packet to work the first week post Biscuitgate and I ate the whole packet of Jammy Dodgers in one day. Since then I haven't trusted my willpower and I've been biscuitless.

'I thoroughly enjoyed it this morning. The ladies were really nice.'

'Yes, they *are* really nice. There are only a couple of battle-axes that come, and then their bark is much worse than their bite.'

I thought Cathy should be selling this volunteering to me, not putting me off. I'm still smiling though, only now it's through gritted teeth.

'Shall we look at dates for the wedding then?' asks Cathy.

Does that mean I've passed the test? I can now become a fully-fledged volunteer? I have to resist the urge to make Cathy do a high-five with me. This whole 'don't tell the groom' thing is really tough; Mark would have high-fived me over this news.

I nod, not wanting to mess it up by saying something stupid like thank you, thank you, thank you with a cherry on top. Cathy doesn't seem like the type of woman who would appreciate it.

'Now,' she says. She's flicking so quickly through the diary that I wonder how she can possibly take it all in. No wonder she has so many books if that is how quickly she reads.

'I'm afraid there isn't a lot of choice. We've got the third weekend in May free.'

'I'll take it,' I say, before I even register what has come out of my mouth.

'Do you need to talk to your fiancé first?' asks Cathy.

'No, no. I'm organising the wedding. It's going to be a surprise.'

'He does know you're getting married, doesn't he?'

Cathy is giving me one of those looks which makes me think she's suddenly scared to be alone with me in an office in the basement.

'Yes, he does. He did propose to me,' I say, trying to laugh in a non-maniac way. 'We're just doing the whole *Don't Tell the Bride* thing only we're doing "don't tell the groom".'

'They're not filming you, are they?'

'No, it's just for fun.'

I literally want to curl up and die. Cathy is like a proper serious adult and I just sound like I'm a child.

'OK. Well, I'll pencil you in. Now, we don't have a marriage licence so you'll need to get married elsewhere.'

'OK. I'll sort somewhere.'

How hard can that be? Everyone knows the reception venue is the difficult place to book.

'So I'll put you in here provisionally, and we'll hold it for a couple of weeks until you can confirm with the venue you're getting married at. Then, once that's confirmed, we'll just need your five hundred pounds. If you keep volunteering that is all you have to pay, but if you don't, that money will act as the deposit and you'll have to pay the balance of two thousand five hundred pounds.'

By hook or by crook I'll be volunteering here. I can't believe it. I could actually pull this off single-handedly. I could be the savvy saving bride and no one would be any the wiser.

'Thanks, Cathy. I'll sort out the ceremony and I'll let you know.'

'I'll show you back up to reception then.'

Cathy is a mind-reader. I was just starting to panic about getting lost in the basement and someone finding me in fifty years' time as a skeleton and thinking I'm part of a display.

By the time I get back to the house I'm practically skipping. Well, I have to burn off the calories I was supposed to burn at the imaginary Zumba class somehow.

'Helloooooo,' I call.

'Hiya, I'm in the lounge.'

I unwrap all my layers as quickly as possible, getting stuck in my scarf that I probably don't need today as it's fairly mild, but I've become so attached to it over winter that I can't go anywhere without it. I'm so excited I *have* to tell Mark.

'We've got a wedding date!' I say, bounding into the lounge. Then I freeze. I didn't realise that Mark wasn't alone. Nanny Violet is sitting in the armchair having a cup of tea. In our house. This is weird. She's never made a house visit to us unannounced before. Or at least not since she realised that we didn't keep cakes in the house for unexpected guests. Although secretly I have some mini Battenbergs lurking in the cupboard for such emergencies now. Hidden from Mark, of course. If I'm lucky, they may still be in date.

'A wedding date. How wonderful,' says Violet, clapping her hands together.

Now, don't get me wrong. Nanny Violet is not evil. She is a nice nanny. It is just that since we've got engaged she seems to be out to get me and I'm definitely not being paranoid, no matter what Mark says to me.

I perch on the sofa next to Mark, suddenly unable to relax in my own house.

'I'm allowed to know the date at least, aren't I?' asks Mark, laughing.

'Of course you are, silly. You need to know when to turn up! It's the 18th of May.'

'Wow. Just under three months before you become Mrs Robinson.'

Here comes The Lemonheads again.

'I know, I can't believe it.' I give Mark a little peck on the cheek, forgetting that Violet is there.

But as I turn back into the room she's giving me the Look. The one I can't decipher.

'Anyone want tea?' I ask, jumping up. There's something going on with Nanny Violet and I can't work out what.

I know she doesn't approve of the whole 'don't tell the groom' principle, but I'm convinced there's more to that look than meets the eye. I am not being paranoid. I think Nanny Violet is out to get me.

chapter nine

'Pen, can you come in here for a moment?' calls Mark.

I'm being summoned to the lounge while I'm cooking dinner. This has to be serious as Mark knows that if he interrupts me there is always a danger that I'll never go back into the kitchen and finish cooking.

'What's up?' I ask, sitting down on the sofa next to him.

'We need to have a serious chat.'

'OK,' I say.

My heart starts to beat faster and I want to reach for a bag as I can feel a panic attack coming on. I'm getting clammy and a full-on sweat is beginning to break out across my brow. I am certain that he has found out about the wedding account and my dirty little gambling habit. What else would he have to tell me?

He takes my hand in his and starts to massage it. This isn't going to be good. He is obviously softening me up before he breaks up with me. What if it isn't to do with my gambling habit at all? What if Mark has met someone else and he's leaving me? I just couldn't take it.

'What's wrong, Mark?'

'It's about the "don't tell the groom" thing.'

Oh no, please don't tell me he's changed his mind. He was doing so well.

'What about it?' I ask cautiously.

'Well, Nan was talking about it when she came over at the weekend.'

Oh, I should have known Violet would be involved in this. I know she has it in for me at the moment.

'What did she say?'

'She was just talking about us getting married and she was voicing her concerns.'

'I knew it. I know she doesn't like me.'

'Pen, it has nothing to do with her not liking you. I've told you, you're imagining that.'

I am definitely *not* imagining it.

'Well, if it isn't that, then what?' I ask.

'She was disappointed that I won't be picking where we're getting married and I think it has really upset her.'

'But you don't mind not knowing, do you?'

'No, I do trust you. It's just that I think Nan is worried about what the ceremony is going to be like.'

'Hey, it's not like I'm going to book us a pagan wedding ceremony or anything.'

Hang on, that isn't such a bad idea, thinking about it. I would make an excellent pagan bride. I could grow my hair and have it in loose curls with a garland of woodland flowers on my head. I could have a flowing dress with bat-like sleeves and I'd be a cross between a fairy and an earth mother goddess. I wonder if Mark would like that as a theme?

'Penny, are you OK?'

I've done it again. I've gone into my wedding daydream. As I have said many a time before, this wedding planning is dangerous, taking away your concentration without notice.

'Sorry, I got lost in the moment. You were saying about Nanny Violet.'

'Yeah, she was sad that we're not getting married in her church.'

In her church? I want to scream. Does she have any idea how much weddings in a church cost? Not that I have any idea myself, but they *have* to be expensive. It is like hiring a whole separate venue. It isn't like a quick five hundred pound registry office affair.

'Her church,' I say slowly.

'Yes, St James and St Thomas. We went there once, you remember, for my granddad's funeral.'

I stroke Mark's hand in recognition of the memory. I do remember. It was a beautiful old-fashioned church.

'Is that what you want?' I ask.

'It would mean a lot to my family, and to me – I suppose.'

'I guess I hadn't given it much thought.'

Looking at Mark's face is killing me. I'll have to book the church. There's no way I can let him down on his one request. Even if it means I have to walk to the church and forgo my fancy car.

'OK, Mark. I'll pop in and see the vicar.'

'Thanks, Pen. I'm so sorry to ruin your "don't tell the groom" theme, but I think this is just too important.'

'Don't worry, Mark. There's still plenty that you won't know,' I say, trying to smile.

There is also plenty that I don't know either. Like how the hell I am going to pay for a church wedding.

The next night I am sitting in a freezing cold church hall waiting for the vicar to come in and see me. The nice lady who was flower-arranging in the main part of the church said he'd be along any minute now. On reflection, perhaps I should have just followed the woman around the church to pick up some tips as I start my first flower-arranging class on Thursday.

'Ah, Penelope, is it?' says the vicar as he walks into the hall.

It's nice when people wear such distinctive uniforms that they are instantly identifiable.

'Call me Penny.'

'Well then, Penelope, nice to meet you. I'm Reverend Phillips.'

'Nice to meet you too,' I say, shaking his hand. Penelope it is then.

'So I understand that you want to get married at St James and St Thomas?'

'That's right.'

'And where's your fiancé? Usually we have a meeting with both of you. Unless he's serving abroad? We have a few military weddings here.'

'Oh no. He's at home.'

'Well, it is usually better to have these discussions with both of you. We need to check whether this is the right type of wedding for you both.'

'Oh, it is. His nan Violet is one of your parishioners and Mark really wants the wedding to be here.'

'And yet he is at home?'

'Yes, but it's not like that.'

The vicar must think Mark is the laziest man around.

'It's just we're doing a "don't tell the groom" wedding.

Which is a bit like the BBC programme *Don't Tell the Bride*. Have you seen it?'

'No, but I have heard of it,' he says. He doesn't sound impressed.

'Right. Well, it's like that. I'm not telling Mark what I'm planning.'

'I see. And it is being filmed, is it?'

I somehow think people don't actually get that it is an analogy. It is *like* the TV programme but it isn't *actually* a TV programme.

'No, it isn't.'

'So why are you doing it?'

'Because we thought it would be fun.'

The vicar is scratching his head and I think I might be losing him. This is the only part of the whole wedding that Mark has insisted on and I'm in danger of it not happening.

'Penelope, marriage between two people should not be entered into lightly.'

'And it isn't with me and Mark. We've been living together forever and I've been wanting him to propose to me for years.'

Hang on, that didn't come out right. I didn't mean to announce to the vicar that we are living in sin. That wasn't going to count against us, was it?

'Let me rephrase this. I won't agree to do a wedding unless I meet you both. You'll both have to attend a marriage preparation class here, as well as attending services when your banns are being read.'

Marriage preparation class? Flipping heck. How much was that going to cost?

'So what you're saying is that Mark needs to come and meet you for us to get married here?'

'That is exactly what I'm saying. As fun as it must seem with you organising this thing on your own, the actual marriage is a sacred vow and should not be part of the fun. That is the part of the day that your wedding is all about. That half an hour will change your life. Not the dinner you eat afterwards or the amount you dance. That half an hour and those vows you take are what starts your whole journey of marriage.'

I feel about the size of a two-year-old.

'Can I call Mark and get him to come?'

'If he's quick. We've got an Alpha course here at eight.'

'OK, I'll make him hurry. Before I call him, can I just check that you're free on our date? I don't want to get him all the way here and be disappointed,' I say. I would hate to see Mark be upset about the one part of the wedding he's actually chosen.

'Very well,' he says, opening the large black book he had wedged under his arm. 'What date were you looking at, Penelope?'

'The 18th of May.'

'Next year?' he asks.

'This year,' I just about squeak.

Reverend Phillips is not very good at hiding what he is thinking; his disapproval seems to be written all over his face.

'Right. Well, you seem to be in luck. We have a wedding at 1 p.m. and then the rest of the day is free thanks to a cancellation at 3 p.m.,' he says.

'Perfect! I mean, not perfect that someone had to cancel their wedding, but great news there is space for us!' Blimey, does anyone have a shovel to dig me out of this hole? This is all too good to be true. Both the church and the museum have the same date free. It couldn't possibly be this smooth-running, could it?

'Can you tell me how much it is going to cost?' I ask.

'It costs three hundred and fifty pounds. Then by the time you've added the wedding licenses and the charges for an organist, it will probably come to about four hundred pounds.'

Wow, that was a lot less than I was expecting. My mouth is agape in surprise. A good surprise, for a change.

'And what about the marriage classes and the reading of the banns?' I ask. Surely they have to get you somehow.

'The marriage classes are free and the banns certificate costs twenty-five pounds.'

'That's such a bargain.'

Oh, I didn't mean to say that out loud.

'Yes, it is,' says Reverend Phillips, sighing. 'Now go and call your fiancé and we can talk about this seriously.'

I nod and run out of the church as quick as my little legs can take me to find a mobile signal to call Mark.

The next night I'm so excited that we have the church and the reception booked on the same day. Now I'm into full-on wedding planning mode.

If only I'd known sooner that it was cheaper to get married in a church than at a registry office. And we get a marriage preparation class thrown in for that, which makes it an absolute bargain. So with the seventy-five pounds we've saved by getting married in a church, I've decided to plough on with the invitations. We've just got the teeny tiny matter of sorting out the guest list first so that I know how many invites to order.

Mark and I are currently sitting on opposite sides of the room. It's like pistols at dawn. We're on about round three of drawing up our lists. We're both writing down the guests that we want to invite and then we swap pieces of paper. From there we get to challenge and veto each other's choices.

It's going pretty well so far. I've told Mark that we're only having eighty people as that will give the wedding a more intimate feel, and we've managed to shave fifteen people off our first attempt at the guest list. Now we've only got to get rid of six more people.

'What about Sheila and Tony?' I say, reading Mark's almost indecipherable handwriting.

'They're my godparents.'

'Yes, but do we ever see them?'

'We see them at my parents' house on Christmas Eve every year.'

'Oh, that's *those* people.'

So that's who they are. I'm not usually that rubbish with names, but Mark thought it was a good idea to take me home to meet his family for the first time on Christmas Eve five years ago. There were just so many of his relatives and family friends there that I couldn't take everyone in. And Sheila and Tony, as I now know they are, had introduced themselves to me and of course I promptly forgot what they'd told me. And now every Christmas Eve they embrace me like I'm their long-lost daughter and I have no clue who they are. But now I do. And so I suppose they'll have to stay on the list.

'What about Kate and Sylvie?' asks Mark.

'They have to come. I lived with them at university.'

'And when was the last time you saw them?'

I wriggle in my chair. So I haven't seen them for a few years, but that's not what counts, is it, with old friends? I'm sure they'd invite me to their wedding, wouldn't they?

'If you can't remember when you last saw them then they can't come.'

Gosh, Mark is being bossy tonight. It's quite a turn-on. I wonder if instead of the invitations we could go upstairs and, you know, practise for when we want to start stage six.

'I know! They came to our Halloween party, when they were dressed as sailors.'

'That wasn't Halloween. That was the nautical-themed birthday party you had for your twenty-fifth. So four years ago.'

Bugger. So it looks like Kate and Sylvie are off the invite list.

'OK, what about NV I've never even heard of a friend called NV,' I say.

'That's Nanny Violet. You're not suggesting we don't invite her?'

'Of course not.' Stupid Mark and his stupid abbreviations.

'Look, we've only got four more to go. And don't forget some people might not be able to come and then we'd be able to invite these people in reserve.'

'OK,' I say, looking at the list. 'What about Pam and Ben?'

'Ben's an old family friend.'

'Did you go to his wedding?'

'No, but his wedding was in Scotland.'

'Doesn't matter. If he didn't invite you, you don't have to invite them.'

Mark wrinkles his nose. Ha, I had him there. It seems he's met his match.

'Fine,' he says. 'Just two more to go.'

'What about Mike and Amanda?' I ask, looking at his list. I'm quite surprised that he even put them down. They're his boss and his wife. 'Can't you just invite them to the evening? You know he always makes you nervous.'

'I guess that's true.'

It was. They came round to dinner once and Mark was so nervous that he developed a funny little laugh that sounded like he'd inhaled a helium balloon. It was not a fun evening.

'Great. Then that's that. Eighty guests.'

Wow, we did it. At this rate we are going to be well within my budget.

All I have to do now is design the invitation. I've already bookmarked a cheap-as-chips online printer. They have these handy templates, so I just need to make a few personal tweaks, and *voilà*, we have invitations. Although we don't have actual invitations yet as I'm being tight and we have to wait for twenty-one days for delivery. But hey, sometimes it says they'll ship faster, so fingers crossed. And they will still be here more than six weeks before the wedding.

I might send everyone a quick little email to let them know the actual date, just to be on the safe side.

I look at the PDF version of the invitation and I can't help but smile. To be in keeping with the 'don't tell the groom' theme, they've only got the church details listed. It simply says 'Reception to follow'. I'll pop a little printed card in with it, with the details of the nearest hotels to the museum (once I've researched them), and I'll let them know that it is only a fifteen-minute drive from the church to the reception.

Somehow seeing the time and location of our actual marriage ceremony underneath our names is making it all seem so real. In three months Mark and I will be husband and wife. It's so close now that I feel I can reach out and grab it. I've just got to make sure I don't do anything else stupid to mess it up.

chapter ten

I can't believe that two whole weeks have gone by since I booked the wedding venue and the church and made the invitations. That is *all* I have done. But those are the most important bits, right? We are actually getting married and we have somewhere to go after and our guests will know about it thanks to the invites, all for the princely sum of £932. I'm going to gloss over the fact that we don't have anything to eat, to listen to, or for me and Mark to wear. But that's fine. I've got well over two months to deal with those little details.

'Bye, Betty. See you next week.' I wave as Betty walks off to the bus stop. She's got her son and her grandchildren coming to lunch at her house today so she can't stop with the other ladies for coffee after our Saturday club.

For once I'm not rushing off to make it look like I'm back

from Zumba. I've told Mark that I'm taking Lou to see the venue and for the first time in ages, when it comes to the wedding, I'm not lying.

It has taken me a long time to get Lou to come and see the venue. We've both been very busy lately, me with my 'work' aka secret wedding plans and Lou with . . . well, she has been really vague with what she has been up to.

I've been very secret squirrel with Lou. I haven't told her anything about where she's coming to meet me. I sent her a text with the postcode an hour ago in the hope that she'd just put it in her sat nav and not Google it first.

I want her to be as blown away by the venue as I was without having any preconceived notions. I sort of want it to be a test of what the other guests will make of it when they get here.

I'm just keeping my fingers and toes crossed that she likes it as much as I do and that I didn't get carried away because it was the nicest place I could afford. I'm doubting my judgement more than I used to; after all, I did spend £10,000 on bingo to buy a dress that would have cost me maybe £3,000 and a pair of shoes that would have cost me £550. I know I've said that maths is not my strong point, but even I can work out that I could have practically bought three sets of shoes and dresses for the money I lost.

There's Lou's car now. She hasn't noticed me yet, which

is a bloody miracle as I'm waving like a Looney Tune. But I can see her mouth is agape. Like 'count the fillings on her teeth' agape.

Now she's noticed me, and I put more energy into my wave as if to acknowledge I've seen her see me.

I can't wait for her to come to me, so I bound over to the car park like an excited puppy.

'What do you think?' I ask before she's had a chance to get out of the car.

'It's amazing! However did you find it?'

'A lot of Googling. I was just trying to find something different.'

'Well, it certainly is. Mark will never in a million years guess this. I was saying to Russell earlier that my money was on it being a castle. That's a bag of Maltesers that I owe him now!'

If only I'd bet Maltesers rather than actual money. Knowing me, I probably would've eaten as many Maltesers as I'd gambled. I might have been a whole lot fatter but at least I'd still be able to afford a castle. I've got to stop thinking like that. This place is beautiful.

'Now, I'm meeting with the caterers after you, so I don't know what the arrangements are fully. But if it's a nice day we're going to have the welcome drinks out here on the lawn.'

I desperately hope it is an amazingly beautiful day for our

wedding. The lawn out the front is sheltered within walls of the former barracks, which almost remind me of a castle wall. There is a big oak tree in the corner that would provide shade for our frazzled guests and there's a rose garden in the other corner with trellises and benches which will make the perfect backdrop for our photos. If I ever book a photographer, that is.

'Oh, it will be great. Are you going to have any music out here? A string quartet? Oh, I know – a steel band. That would be fantastic.'

It really would. In my dream wedding that's exactly the kind of thing I would have had. I can't tell Lou I can't afford it.

'I don't think Mark likes that kind of music,' I say, and I practically shove Lou up the stairs.

'Now imagine that we will have pictures of us taken on the stairs.'

'Lovely, just lovely. This venue is so perfect, I can't believe it. What's it like inside? Is it all arms and armour?' asks Lou.

'It is in the main museum, but not where we're having the reception.'

'You all right, Penny?' asks Ted as we walk round the revolving doors into the reception.

'Fine, thanks, Ted. Just showing my friend the wedding set-up.'

'Oh, very good. They've just finished setting up for today's wedding.'

I'd almost forgotten that people other than me have their weddings here. I'm getting quite fond of the place already and I forget that it isn't mine.

I smile and link arms with Lou as I take her into the anteroom.

'This is where the bar will be set up.'

I can see Lou look up as soon as she gets in there. It was the first thing I did, too. The ceiling is ribbed and decorated in almost Masonic iconography. It reminds me that I must ask Cathy what it all means at some point.

'What a beautiful room,' says Lou.

'Just you wait.'

I open the door to the main dining room and even I catch my breath at how wonderful it looks. Gone is the large mahogany table and in its place are nine perfectly dressed round tables, each covered with white tablecloths and the most beautiful floral centrepieces. They even have white chair covers with turquoise bows and for the first time I actually mourn the chair covers I won't be able to afford. They look lovely.

'I'm speechless,' says Lou. 'This must be the best-kept secret around.'

'I know. Isn't it? Do you think Mark will like it?'

'Mark is going to *love* it.'

I beam at that. Maybe I'm not the world's worst fiancée after all.

'Oh, look at the top table,' I say. 'This is where we'll be sitting. Here, look. That's your place there at the end of the table.'

I turn to Lou but she isn't looking at the top table, instead she's looking up at the ceiling. It is a lovely ceiling but she could get more excited about being the maid of honour and where she is going to be sitting.

'So are you having a band or a disco?'

Whichever is cheapest, I say in my head.

'Not sure yet, I need to look around. I was half thinking of a swing band. You know, something vintage to fit the room,' I say.

'Oh, that would be fun. And vintage is *so* in at the moment. Everyone would love it.'

Everyone, that is, except my bank balance.

'The band slash DJ will go over here on the stage,' I say, continuing the tour. Lou has started to become much more interested again.

'Ah, look at that view! I didn't notice it at first. Are those the North Downs?' asks Lou.

'Yep, they are. Don't they look gorgeous?'

'They sure do. This must be costing you a fortune. Is it?'

I want to tell Lou the truth. I desperately want to confide in someone as I feel like I'm carrying round the world's biggest secret.

'It's in budget.'

'Of course, you budgeted for your wedding. You two are so sensible with your money. I'm sure that Russell and I could learn from you and Mark.'

Lou has practically stabbed my heart with a fork. Or at least that's what it feels like. I really want to tell her how irresponsible I am with money just to make her see that I'm a million times worse with my money than she is with hers. She looks so sad about it.

'But your wedding was worth every penny.'

'It was a great day. I'm not sure whether it's been worth the sacrifice of holidays abroad for the last few years though, but at least it is paid off *finally*.'

'Holidays abroad ahoy, then?' I say, trying to bring a smile back to Lou's face.

'Hmm, if only,' she mutters.

'What do you mean?'

'Nothing. So what kind of food do you think you'll have?'

Whatever is the cheapest, I say again in my head. Is that the wrong answer? Something delicious that is also in budget. Does that sound better?

'I'm not too sure until I've spoken to the caterers, but as

I said, I'm going to be meeting them in a bit. We've just got time for a coffee in the tea rooms, if you like. I can buy you a cake, fatten you up so that you don't outshine me in your bridesmaid dress on my wedding day. I don't want you doing a Pippa Middleton,' I say.

Lou isn't smiling. I was only kidding. Lou is absolutely stunning in that just-rolled-out-of-bed, I-don't-need-any-make-up way. Her hair is poker-straight and it never goes frizzy. And in the ten years that we've been friends I've never once seen her with bad skin. The cake comment was also a joke as no matter what she eats she is always a size ten. *Size ten*, even after the biggest of curries. If she wasn't my best friend in the whole wide world, I'd hate her.

'I'm kidding – your bum's way nicer than Pippa's, for a start. We can just go get coffee, no cake, if you want? It would be the perfect opportunity to talk bridesmaid dress styles. I've been bookmarking internet pages on my phone.'

'Actually, I can't. I've got to get back to Russell – we've got plans.'

'Oh.'

Is it just me or did that seem a bit abrupt? Have I upset her as she's only just finished paying off her wedding? There's something not quite right about Lou today and I don't believe for one minute that she's got plans with Russell.

I can usually tell when she's lying as she tucks her hair

behind her ear. I can see her right hand twitching as if she wants to tuck the hair. She knows I know it is her trademark lying signal and I think she is trying to resist it.

'Are you sure you can't stay for twenty minutes? We could talk about what colours might suit you as that would help with the flowers and the decorations–'

'No, sorry, I promised Russell and . . .' she fades off and there is the trademark hair-tuck-behind-the-ear move.

I suck in a sharp breath in surprise. She looks at me in panic. We both know that I know that she's lied. We stand there awkwardly in silence for a few seconds.

'Right. I've got to go, Pen.'

'OK then.' I start to walk her out of the venue. Cathy is standing at the front desk and I try to make myself as small as possible so that she doesn't say anything in front of Lou about me volunteering. That would take a lot of explaining and a whole lot of lies to clear up.

'See you later, Penny,' says Cathy.

'Bye,' I wave.

'Gosh, it's very friendly here, isn't it? I like that everyone knows your name. What excellent customer service,' says Lou.

I bite my tongue to stop myself blurting out the truth and just about manage to nod my head.

Out in the fresh air again I hope secretly that Lou has changed her mind and that she'll stay for that coffee.

'Thanks for showing me this, lovely,' she says, leaning over and kissing my cheek.

'That's OK. Shame you couldn't stay longer. But we must get together soon to sort out the dresses.'

'Yes, yes,' she says, as she's halfway down the steps. Is she running? Am I being the most narcissistic person on the planet or is Lou just acting plain weird?

With twenty minutes to go before my appointment with the caterer I'm too angry to sit down with a cup of coffee. Instead I decide to do what I haven't done in years in this country. I'm going to go round a museum without being forced to.

'Penny,' says Ted.

I look round to see Ted behind me. I'd got so engrossed in playing on the computer in one of the galleries that I hadn't noticed him sneaking up on me.

'The caterers are ready to see you.'

I look at my watch and realise the last twenty minutes have flown by. Museums sure have changed over the years. Gone are the dusty places full of old stuff, and here in their place are light and brightly coloured walls with objects that you can *actually* touch and play with. I know that most of it is for kids, but I couldn't resist. I mean, how often do you get the chance to try on a Victorian helmet?

I'm thinking of a new theme for the wedding. Well, military tailoring is in fashion, is it not? I could get Mark all dressed up like an old-fashioned sexy soldier and I could go all Regency with an Elizabeth Bennet dress. Yes, you're right, I did watch too much *Sharpe* growing up. But Mark could totally give Sean Bean a run for his money, any day.

'Penny, caterers,' says Ted. 'You're always away with the fairies, you are.'

This bloody wedding. I wonder if I daydreamed this much before. I follow Ted back to reception and make a mental note to finish my tour of the museum off next week.

'Hello, you must be Penny,' says a woman dressed in starched white chefs overalls with bright turquoise bottoms.

'Yes, that's right. Nice to meet you. I love your trousers.'

'Thanks. I try to match the colour scheme of the weddings where I can. Gives the brides a smile on their big day.'

I already warm to Jenny the caterer. It has nothing to do with the fact that they are the cheapest catering option or anything.

'Shall we take a seat? I've got about half an hour before I'm needed in the kitchen.'

'That would be great. Thank you so much for taking the time.'

I follow Jenny into the reception hall and we sit at one of the tables. I try to make sure that I focus on her and don't get distracted pretending I am a guest at whoever's wedding this is going to be.

'Right. So let's start with numbers,' she says.

'OK, so at the moment I'm working on about eighty guests for the day.'

'And have you had a look at our sample menus? Any favourites?'

'I like menu number two.'

Not because it is one of the cheapest but because it sounds delicious. Any meal that is finished with Toblerone cheesecake is a winner in my book.

'That's our most popular menu. It usually goes down very well. And don't worry, we always have a few extra dishes just in case you get a fussy eater. If you let me know the final numbers and the dietary requirements a couple of weeks ahead we can move the menu around if we need to.'

'Sounds great.'

'Now then, drinks.'

'Yes, we'll be having drinks.' Lots of them. In fact, if I know my guests they'll drink the bar dry.

'So there is a bar charge of £100, with a minimum spend of £500 behind the bar, or £200 bar charge with no minimum spend.'

'OK,' I say, as I try to be good and jot down the numbers.

'Then there's the corkage.'

The whatage?

'That works out to be either £5 per person, or if you buy our wine it's free.'

I suddenly wish I'd brought my calculator with me, but I have to admit I'm impressing myself with my quick maths skills. I'm going to be paying £400 for the privilege of people being able to drink. And that is before I've even paid for a single drop of alcohol.

'I know it sounds expensive. But it is the going rate, especially when our price per head is so low compared to others.'

'Jenny, it's fine. I just need to sort out my budgeting.'

'OK. It was just I thought I'd lost you.'

'No, no. I'm still here.'

Although inside I'm screaming. I'm trying to work out whether our guests would mind a bring-your-own-booze arrangement. They could sneak alcohol into the reception in hip flasks or water bottles just like I used to do when I was a student.

'Does the corkage cover the welcome drink?'

'Yes, it does. You can provide your own drinks for that if you like. Have you had any ideas for that?'

'Sangria.'

What? Everyone has Pimms, and Sangria always puts

people in a good mood. Maybe I could have a Spanish theme. Flower in my hair, dress with a flamenco-style ruffle. I could even a get a little mariachi band, or is that Mexican?

'Ok. Well, let's see, you'd probably need to allow for at least 120 drinks for eighty people as you find about half the guests have a second glass.'

Knowing my friends, it will be very likely that they will have two.

'I'll email you a quote for sangria as it won't be on the price list. I'll also email you how much wine and lemonade you'd need, in case you supply it yourself.'

'OK.'

'Right then. So you need to decide if you want our wine or you're going to supply your own. And then that's it.'

'That was simple.'

Simple in principle. Just how I am going to pay for anything else is beyond me.

'Great. Well, it was lovely to meet you, Penny. And don't forget to let me know your colour scheme when you've decided. I want to make sure I've got matching trousers!'

I smile. 'Thanks, Jenny.'

As she disappears off in the direction of the kitchen I do the sums on my notepad.

It works out to be £30 per head on the food plus £5 per head corkage, which totals £2,800. Add that to my £900 for the venue and the church and I'm left with £1,600 and whatever magic beans I can save between now and then.

Both Mark and I have still been direct-debiting fifty pounds per month into the account and we're going to do that up until the wedding. So that is another £300. So we have £1,900 left.

That sounds like a decent amount. All I've got to sort out is the transport, flowers, suits, my dress, bridesmaid attire, DJ/band, photographer and favours. Am I missing something?

I'm right back to needing the bag to breathe into again.

Looking around the decorated room I feel like I'm about to weep. Whoever's wedding this is, is one lucky bride. It really is the wedding of dreams. The favours seem to be lottery tickets in those fancy lottery ticket holders that I've seen on the internet. There are beautifully decorated table numbers and place settings that look like they've been designed and printed specially.

This must have cost a fortune. Or at least it probably cost what I lost.

This is the closest I've felt to wanting to gamble since I went cold turkey. I'm trying to ignore the little voice in my head that is trying to get me to steal all the wedding favours. This wedding must have over one hundred guests. That means there are one hundred lottery tickets here. What are the odds that somewhere in this pile of lottery tickets there is a winner?

My hand hovers over one of the favour envelopes and just as I'm about to take it, I'm snapped back into reality by my mobile ringing.

I pick it up and wave to Ted at the front desk as I walk out of the main staircase and away from the lottery ticket temptation, as quickly as I can.

'Hi, honey.'

'Hi, Pen. I was wondering if you're nearly done. I feel like going to the cinema. Do you fancy it? Thought we could grab dinner out after.'

'That sounds nice.'

'My treat. I just thought you've had a long day organising our wedding, which I'm sure is going to be amazing.'

My heart sinks. If only Mark knew the truth about my excellent organisational skills.

'What do you reckon?' asks Mark.

'Sounds perfect,' I say, trying to hold back the tears. 'I'll be home in half an hour.'

'Half an hour, you say? I'll just draw a radius on the map.'

'Ha, very funny, mister. See you soon.'

I hang up and stare at the phone. Even if I do pull off the wedding of our dreams by some sort of miracle, am I always going to feel this lousy every time I think about it?

chapter eleven

Getting engaged, aka stage four of our life plan, is much harder than I expected it would be. Before I was engaged I thought it was going to be the most wonderful time of my life. Going food-tasting at wedding venues and sipping champagne in bridal shops. But my stage four is not panning out that way.

This morning I went to the post office to post our beautiful invitations and it cost me a small fortune. Since when did stamps get so expensive? And I'm not even going to talk about the paper cut I have on my tongue from when I licked the envelopes last night.

I also know I have to go dress-shopping at some point soon. My mum keeps phoning and texting me, trying to get a date in the diary. It's funny as before I got engaged, the dress was the part of stage four I was most excited about, but now it is the bit I'm dreading the most.

What if I have a dress made of awful synthetic material instead of the bundles of lace and silk that my dream princess dress is supposed to be made of?

I can't bear to go through that trauma just yet. I'm telling my mum that I need a few more weeks to shift some pounds. But, as she keeps telling me, I'm leaving it far too late to order a dress from a wedding shop as that can take months. And it is now two months until our big day.

Even Lou's got in on the act of forcing me to get a wedding dress. I keep suggesting we go looking for her dress but she tells me that it would be much better for me to get my dress sorted as that will impact on the type of bridesmaid dresses I pick.

But enough about the wedding. I'm giving myself a weekend off. It's Easter and there's no Saturday volunteering club. The weather, considering it is a British bank holiday, is not atrocious so I'm going to spend the day in the country with Mark.

I've started to realise that I've hardly spent any quality time with Mark since we got engaged. I'm always at the gym aka gamblers group/flower arranging/the museum – delete as applicable. I'm also exhausted most nights as I've worked the full day at work, and I've had to squeeze the gym into my lunch break so that I don't gain too much weight and lose my alibi. Then, if I'm not too tired when I get home in the evening, I'm scouring the internet trying to turn myself into a budget bride.

But today, it is going to be all about Mark. We're going for a nice walk on the North Downs and then we're booked into this great little pub in a small village for a very late lunch.

It's going to be perfect. And the best thing about Mark knowing nothing about the wedding means that it won't be a topic of conversation and I'll be able to forget about it *all day*.

By the time I'm starting to climb the walls in the house, Mark appears from golf and after a quick shower and change, we're in the car. There was some whining from one of us that Man United were playing Liverpool, but that was pretty short-lived. And now we're on our way to the country. Where the air is clear and all that.

'My mum wants to know if you want any help with the wedding,' says Mark.

Aagh, the W word. Does Mark not know I'm taking a break from it today?

'You can tell her I'm fine. All under control.' I say it with such conviction that I almost believe it myself.

'OK. Well, she said nearer the time if there was anything she could do, you just have to let her know.'

'That's really sweet of her. Tell her I might need to take

her up on that. But no more wedding talk. Have you spoken to Phil lately?'

'I spoke to him on Monday.'

'Are things, you know, OK?' I ask tentatively.

'I think so. Apparently they're trying for a baby.'

'Well, I hope they keep their legs crossed until after the wedding, or all we're going to hear about is her pregnancy.'

I wouldn't usually be that mean about people announcing they're trying for a baby, but I can just tell what Jane will be like. Three hours we listened to her talking about her extension when she was round at our house last month. I could probably have built the extension for her in that time.

'I think that Phil is hoping it will give Jane something to focus on.'

Obsess about more like. I actually feel a little sorry for Phil; he's probably having to have sex with military precision until he impregnates her.

Looking out of the window, I'm surprised that we haven't hit the countryside already. Our town isn't that big and there are an awful lot of houses still.

'Where are we going?'

'Oh, I forgot to tell you. I spoke to my brother yesterday and when I mentioned that we were off for a walk he wondered if we could take Bouncer.'

Bouncer is the loveliest Labrador in the world. And yes, he is named after Bouncer from *Neighbours*. I should have thought about taking him before. This means we'll be going for a proper walk in the country.

When I said I loved Bouncer, I think I meant I love him when he's not splashing me with muddy puddles or dropping his ball for me every five minutes, like he has been for the entire walk. Not to mention what he's just done. Mark and I have been standing in the same spot on a path for the last two minutes and every so often we glance down at the pile of dog poo that looks like a Mr Whippy ice cream.

'I'm organising the whole wedding by myself, therefore you should pick it up,' I say.

'Hey, you offered to do that so you can't play the martyr card. I do all the cleaning at home.'

I open my mouth and close it again. Mark does do all the cleaning at home.

'But I do the laundry and the shopping.'

'Neither get your hands dirty.'

'Well then, I'm not used to doing this. You are obviously well practised and you'll be used to this kind of thing,' I argue.

'Maybe you need some practice in it.'

'You've got bigger hands.'

'What's that got to do with anything?'

'Well, your sleeves are going to be further away from the poop when you bend down to pick it up.'

Mark leans over and rolls up my sleeves.

'There you go. You're ready for anything now.'

'But, Mark,' I pout, using my little-girl voice.

'Stop pouting. Pen, you're going to have to get used to this when you have kids.'

'Hey, just because I'm the woman does not mean to say that I'm always going to be in charge of the poop. And it's when *we* have kids, not when *I* have kids.'

Mark sighs. 'As I see it we've got no other choice than to bring out the big guns. Thumb war or rock, paper, scissors?'

'Rock, paper, scissors.'

With Mark's mutantly strong thumbs I lose every time at thumb wars. With rock, paper, scissors there is an element of luck. Although I usually lose at that too. But at least I know that it will not due to my puny thumbs.

'One, two, three,' says Mark.

Scissors. We both have scissors. Now do I stick with scissors and hope he'll go for paper, and at the same time hope he thinks I'll go for rock, or do I go for rock? This game is so taxing on the brain.

'One, two, three,' says Mark again.

I put my hand out again for scissors only to have it blunted by Mark's rock.

'Ha, ha,' he says, and he plants a kiss on my cheek. 'You might be needing this.'

I look at the black plastic bag in his hand and remember just why we were playing the game. He has such an adorable smile on his face that if we weren't standing next to a pile of Bouncer's finest then I would give him a good long kiss in the woods.

'That's it. We're *never* having kids. That is *the* most disgusting thing I've ever done.'

'I think that baby nappies are going to be worse than that,' he says.

'Really? Nope. We're stopping at stage five.'

'Fine by me. Means I won't have to give up my Saturday-morning golf.'

'You'd give up golf when we have kids?'

'Well, not completely, but I'm not going to be able to do it every Saturday, am I?'

'But you love golf.'

'I know. But I also love you. And as long as the kids don't look like the milkman then I will probably love them too.'

This time I do reach up to Mark and pull him by the scruff of his hoodie and snog his face off. Bouncer whines in horror and goes bounding off into the bushes, and it is only when we hear the ringing of a bicycle bell that I remember that we're standing in the middle of the path.

'Maybe I'll be able to change the baby's nappies then. You know, if you're willing to give up golf.'

'Um, remember I said play *less* golf, not give up golf. It's a bit different.'

There we go. That's the Mark I know. But still less golf is just as big a sacrifice.

By the time we make it to the pub I am absolutely starving. We must have walked at least ten miles and even Bouncer is exhausted. I've definitely earned myself the right to have a big fat burger and a sticky toffee pudding for dessert.

Before we go into the pub, we wait for Bouncer to have the world's longest drink of water from the dog bowl outside. It seems to take him ages as every time he starts to slurp he gets distracted by people walking past him, in or out of the pub.

'Come on, Bouncer, drink,' I say, bending down and pointing at the bowl of water. That seems to have done the trick. I'm clearly a dog whisperer.

As I get to my feet I notice the feet of the person walking out of the pub. Those big Timberland boots look really familiar to me. It isn't until I've reached eye level that I realise I'm looking straight into the bluest eyes I have ever seen.

Josh.

My smile goes up in an instant and I blurt out a hello

before I realise what I've done. Mark is standing right next to me.

Josh looks at me and his eyes slightly pop out of his head; he looks unsure as to whether he should say anything.

I turn to Mark and he is looking between me and Josh like he is trying to connect the dots.

'Hi, Penny,' says Josh, finally breaking the awkward silence that has ensued.

I'm looking round to see if his girlfriend is here, but he seems to be with two older people. They have got to be his parents as the man has the same piercing blue eyes.

'Hi, Josh.'

Have I said hello already? I'm not too sure where I'm going with this. Bouncer has finally finished drinking and has decided to drip the surplus water from his mouth all over Josh's boots.

'Josh is one of my work colleagues,' I say to Mark.

I'm the worst liar but that is the only way I can think to explain him. How else would an engaged woman get to meet another man who is just a little bit too sexy for his own good?

'I'm Mark. Nice to meet you.'

At least Mark has remembered his manners, unlike me.

'Sorry. Josh, this is my fiancé, Mark.'

'Nice to meet you, Mark. I've heard a lot about your wedding.'

'Ha. Well, that makes one of us,' says Mark, raising his eyebrows at me.

'Penny is keeping it as a surprise for Mark,' says Josh to his parents. 'These are my parents, by the way. Penny works in HR.'

Well remembered, Josh. I'm glad I didn't have to do that the other way round. I still have no idea what he does for a living.

I put on my best 'I'm the nicest girl in the world' smile, which is my classic default parent smile. It seems to work as they grin back at me.

'No Mel today, then?' I say to Josh, more to keep Mark from thinking there is something suspicious going on.

'No, not today. Anyway, we really must be going. I've got to get Mum and Dad back to the station.'

'Lovely to meet you,' I say to them.

I notice that Josh and Mark are still looking at each other warily before I herd Bouncer and Mark into the pub.

Well, that could have gone a lot worse. Thank goodness that Josh was quick on his feet keeping up with the cover story.

Settling down into the pub, we position ourselves away from the roaring fire. It's one of those pubs that does roaring fire very well and we've made the mistake of sitting next to it before. We ended up looking like we were playing strip poker by the end of our meal, with us having to de-layer after each food course.

Mark comes over and places my cranberry juice in front of me. It feels only fitting after my mammoth walk that I have a drink as virtuous and healthy. I'm glossing over the fact it is probably full of sugar.

'So what department does that Josh guy work in then?'

Did that not finish when we left him outside the pub? Maybe he'll forget about it if I keep studying the menu really intensely as if I'm considering whether to have the garlic mushroom burger or the Stilton and bacon burger. Yes, I am aware I have an impending wedding. But the ten-mile walk means I get to have whatever burger I want.

'Hello, earth to Penny.'

Damn. The intense menu stare didn't work.

'Huh? Sorry, I was reading the menu.'

'Right. I was just asking you what that guy did at your work.'

'Oh, Josh?' I say casually, as if there are many people he could be talking about. 'He works in IT.'

I mean, I think from what I remember he does work in IT. Just not at my work. That's the great thing about working for a big multinational company. There are always loads of general departments.

'Oh, right.'

I know he's now wondering, how I would have come into such close contact with the IT department for Josh to know about the wedding.

'He had a bit of a personal issue earlier this year,' I say in a hushed whisper. It's the voice I use when I want to be discreet at work.

'Oh. Right,' says Mark, nodding. 'I don't remember seeing him at the Christmas do last year.'

Bugger. He won't let this drop. I hoped that the *personal issue* would have put a full stop to the conversation. After all, as it was a personal personnel issue he should know that I can't discuss it. At least not when he knows names. Of course I do tell him some things, but I always try to protect the people's identity.

'I don't remember seeing him either,' I say truthfully. 'Perhaps he didn't go. It's not everyone's cup of tea.'

'At least you finally admit that. Does that mean that we don't have to go this year?' asks Mark.

'No, you're not getting out of it that easily. If I have to go to your stuffy do, you have to come to ours.'

Mark hates our work Christmas parties as we have themes and fancy dress. I must make a mental note with the wedding themes: no fancy dress. Perhaps I'll have to rethink the whole Spanish theme and him being dressed as a matador.

'I wonder what the theme will be for this year's Christmas party? I heard there were rumours of it being something sci-fi like *Star Wars* or *Star Trek*.'

And before you ask, yes, I do work for a large engineering company. I don't really like to reinforce any sort of stereotypes, but let's just say a *Star Wars* theme would make everyone's year.

'I don't think that this whole secret wedding thing is a good idea,' says Mark.

This again. And before I've had something to eat after our practically all-day hike and the run-in with Josh. I'm too mentally and physically tired for this fight.

'But we've come this far and I'm only halfway through. It would be wrong for you to come in now as I've only half finished my masterpiece wedding. It wouldn't make sense.'

Mark doesn't look happy. I can't have him finding out about the wedding now. Not when I've worked so hard to get it all sorted on budget and with me trying to curb my little habit.

'I just don't like the idea that that guy knows more about my wedding than I do,' he says.

'But he doesn't.'

Finally! Some truth. Josh actually doesn't know any of the details of the wedding. OK, so he may know a few more of the background details than Mark, but he doesn't know about the actual wedding.

'He seemed to think he did.'

'That's because he's a boy,' I say. 'I talk about our wedding a lot at work, I'll admit that. But only how I used to talk to you about it before we got engaged. I daydream out loud about dresses and shoes and the perfect favours.

'He's a man, his eyes probably glaze over when I mention the "wedding" word. Like you would if you knew the details,' I say.

Mark is half smiling now. Some warmth has come back to his eyes and I actually might be getting through to him.

'You don't want me to turn into a Jane, do you?' I ask.

'Please, dear Lord, no. Jane was a monster in the run-up to her wedding. I'm sure that was why it took me so long to pop the question to you.'

'Well, I'm not like that. I'm going to be a level-headed bride, and I want most of all for you to enjoy the wedding. That's why I want it to be a surprise.'

The waitress interrupts our little talk by taking our order and giving Bouncer a selection of dog biscuits. All the biscuits have disappeared before she has left the table.

'Easy there, Bouncer, you should learn to enjoy your food,' I say. Bouncer is really super cute. I bend under the table and give him just a little stroke around the ears and he rolls right over and lets me scratch his belly.

Bouncer has it easy. I wish I was a dog. Guaranteed cuddles, people scratching your back for you. And most of all he has paws so he can't gamble online so he wouldn't have lost all of his money for his wedding. Not that he'd have a wedding. He is a dog, after all.

'You're really good with him. Maybe we should get a dog one day,' says Mark.

'After the Mr Whippy incident today, we're only getting a dog if you promise to pick up all the poop.'

Mark laughs. Finally, I feel like the cross-examination has come to an end.

'This has been fun. I feel like I haven't seen you that much lately,' I say.

'I know, what with your crazy gym schedule.'

'It will calm down once the wedding is over, I promise.' Two more months and counting.

'Well, perhaps we should make more of an effort to borrow Bouncer,' says Mark.

'I'd like that.'

And just like that we have our excellent date back on track. And the silly thing is, instead of feeling guilty about the secret wedding I'm planning, it has reminded me of why I am doing it in the first place. I love Mark more than anything. I've just got to man up, and anytime I get stressed I need to remember why I'm doing it.

'I love you, honey,' I say.

'I love you too.' he says, kissing me.

Yes, I just need to remember that I get to become Mrs Robinson and that makes it all worthwhile.

chapter twelve

I've been really good at going to my Saturday volunteering slots at the museum. So far I've been to all of them. Today is the first Saturday I haven't wanted to go. Not because I don't want to volunteer, but because I want to get as far away from here as I possibly can.

Today is the day I am going dress shopping. The day I've dreamt about since I was a little girl and I used to play dressing up. I used to wear an elasticated pink dress of my mum's and I would play bridesmaid to my sister, the bride, who always got to wear my mum's actual wedding dress.

Only instead of being elated about the dress-shopping experience, I'm thoroughly miserable. I can't tell my mum that my budget for the wedding dress is about two hundred pounds, so I'm going to have to pretend that I don't like any of the beautiful dresses I try on today.

It's going to be torture. Like going into the Häagen-Dazs factory with a spoon and being told that you can only stir the ice cream and not eat it.

'Hello, Penny dear,' says Betty, as I sit down at the table.

'Hi, Betty.'

'What's wrong with you? You don't seem your usual cheery self today,' she says.

'Just wedding stuff,' I say, shrugging my shoulders.

Cathy is explaining to us that today we're making tunic bags. I get to be in charge of the pinking shears and I'm cutting the fabric that Betty is measuring and marking up. Nina is then pinning Velcro to the fabric and Lilian and Marjorie are over on the other side of the room with what seem to be antique Singer sewing machines.

'I don't understand these modern weddings,' says Betty. 'In my day it wasn't like this. There wasn't as much fuss. We practically organised them overnight. In fact, in many cases during my sister's generation, during the war, they did. Their fiancés came home on a weekend leave pass and they went back to the Front married.'

They had it easy. Wait, not in the war they didn't. I didn't mean that at all. I just meant that maybe that is the best way to do it. Getting married in a short space of time. No time to fritter the money away or get sucked into deciding which made my forehead look bigger, a side tiara or a front tiara.

'What was your wedding like, Betty?' I ask.

'Well, my wedding wasn't very grand. My Malcolm and I didn't have a lot of money. We both worked at the aircraft factory. I was a secretary in those days, before we had children.

'We got engaged not long after Christmas and were married in the February. Valentine's Day it was, just by coincidence. We got married at the church and then we went back to my mother's house for sandwiches after and people popped round all afternoon.'

'So you didn't have a formal reception?'

'No, Penny. Not many did in those days. We put a bit of a spread on at my mother's house. People generally called all week in the run-up to the wedding and brought us presents. Then that evening we took the train down to Portsmouth and went to the Isle of Wight for our honeymoon.'

I didn't think it was possible for Betty to smile any more than she did normally, but now, talking about her wedding, she is positively beaming.

'He was so handsome that day. When I turned up at the church Malcolm was there in his National Service uniform. I tell you, Penny, I still catch my breath when I remember the look on his face when we first made eye contact as I walked down the aisle.'

'What were you wearing?'

'I had the most beautiful dress. It was a long white dress with lace sleeves. Not unlike the type of lace that the Duchess of Cambridge had. Of course mine didn't have a train like hers. It was just a plain white dress and my mum had stitched the lace on to it. Don't forget that clothing rationing hadn't long been finished. We were still into the "make do and mend" mindset. Not that I've ever really stopped.'

'It sounds perfect.'

'It was, dear. But it was only the start of it. Sixty-two years we've been married now. Can you believe it? And we're still as happy as we were then.

'Of course, Malcolm's not as fit as he used to be and his mind is often elsewhere. But I know we've been blessed with our marriage.'

I wonder if Mark and I will be happily married sixty-two years from now. I'm glossing over the fact that will mean that I'd be ninety-one and Mark would be ninety-two. I hope that we are. I hope that one day I'm telling the story of my wedding to some whippersnapper who will probably be getting married on a spaceship or something equally futuristic.

'That's incredible, Betty. You're really lucky.'

'I know. My Malcolm and I think so. But enough with the past. Tell me about your dress. Have you picked one out yet?' asks Betty.

'Not yet. Funnily enough I'm going shopping for one with my mum after this.'

'How lovely.'

'Just keep your fingers crossed for me, Betty, that I don't lose my mind.'

'Don't you worry. I have two married daughters. Believe me, when you try *the* one on, you know it's the one.'

I don't tell Betty that that is exactly what I'm afraid of. I'm scared stiff that I might actually try on my dream dress with my mum and, thanks to my new budget, never in a million years have any chance of owning it.

I think I severely underestimated just how excited my mum was about the dress shopping.

I'd agreed in the week that it was OK for her to go ahead and book appointments. What I wasn't prepared for was the military operation she's planned for us. We have three bridal shops to go to and she's worked on the assumption that I'll try on up to three dresses in each shop, which would take around forty-five minutes, and then we'll have fifteen minutes of travelling time between them.

I hope that I am like Jack Bauer in *24* and I don't need to take a bathroom break or do anything else that would require me to go off schedule. I've faced the wrath of my mother on many an occasion and now I am old enough, and wise enough, to try to avoid it at all costs.

'So have you had any thoughts on the style we're looking for? Or the colour?' my mum asks.

'I haven't given the style much thought,' I say, lying as I try to banish all thoughts of the latest Vera Wang dresses that appeared at the trunk show a few weeks ago. Not that I'd taunted myself by going on the Browns website looking at the event photos, or read the blog of a bride-to-be that had had an appointment, or anything. 'And I want a white dress, nothing too untraditional.'

I definitely don't want a red or black dress. That would probably see Nanny Violet off out of this world.

'White? I meant, did you want a white white or an ivory or more of a cream?'

Really? Is my mother actually going to describe fifty shades of white?

'I think it's probably best if I just start looking. See if any inspiration hits.'

'Good idea, Penny. Keep an open mind,' she says.

I hope she remembers those words when I take her to the high street later on to see what in reality I can afford.

I'm beginning to wonder what sort of shops she's picked and when we pull up outside the small traditional looking bridal boutique, I get my answer. One that I would have chosen if I'd had my original budget and one that I won't now be able to afford.

Just stepping in the shop I practically go weak at the knees. I am giddy with the sort of excitement that I used to get as a child when my mum gave me twenty pence to spend at the sweet shop.

'Hello there,' says the impeccably neat sales assistant.

'Hello, we're here to look for my daughter. I made us an appointment. The bride is Penelope Holmes.'

'Of course, we were expecting you. Why don't you have a browse around, Penelope, and let us know if there is anything you fancy? If you struggle, I'd be more than happy to suggest a couple to you.'

'Thank you,' says Mum.

It feels wrong to be let loose next to all these wonderful dresses. I reach out to touch the first one and it feels exactly how I imagined it would. It's like it's been woven by fairies. And the little studded diamantes sparkle in the light as I pull it out and have a look at it.

I'm fighting the impulse not to download a bingo app on my phone just to try my luck. Surely if it was fate, and I was supposed to have one of these dresses, luck would be on my side?

Who am I kidding? I'd probably shrink the two hundred pounds dress budget into a tenner.

'What about this one, Pen? This is lovely.'

I turn round and catch my breath. My mum is holding the most beautiful dress I have ever seen.

It's a strapless dress that is cut straight across the top and then it goes out from the waist like the layers of a tiered cake. It's perfect. A perfect princess dress.

'Try it on. I can see you love it,' says the sales assistant.

I nod, still too giddy to speak or to stop myself.

The sales assistant brings the dress in behind me. I want to wait for her to leave the cubicle before I strip and get into the dress, but she's just standing there looking at me. Not actually looking at me, but she's still standing in here with me.

I don't think she's going to leave. I think I'm going to have to strip in front of her. I start removing my clothes carefully, not to make it look like I'm performing a striptease. On the one hand I'm pleased that I'm not wearing my usual comfy underwear, aka Simon Cowell pants, as Mark affectionately calls them, but I'm simultaneously embarrassed that I'm only wearing a lacy thong and strapless bra. I feel practically naked. I only put them on as I didn't want my old, tired underwear to show through the sheer high-street dresses.

But the sales assistant doesn't bat an eyelid. She just holds the dress open for me to step into and before I know it she's pulling the corset strings tight behind me. If I'm honest it is just a little on the tight side and I can barely breathe, but that doesn't matter. I'm sure I'm going to have the most amazing cleavage ever as I can almost feel my boobs grazing my chin.

'There you go,' says the sales assistant, as she draws back the curtain. 'Go and stand on the podium,' she says, giving me a little nudge, as I'm frozen in the cubicle.

I walk slowly on tiptoes so that I don't trip over and I stand on the podium and look in the mirror.

I look amazing. I was so born in the wrong era. I was made for wearing big dresses.

'Oh Penny, you look stunning. You look just like a princess,' says my mum, crying. There are proper tears and everything.

'How much is it?' she asks.

'This one works out at nine hundred and fifty pounds and then alterations are on top,' says the sales assistant.

That is fairly reasonable for such a lovely dress. Looks like I was wrong to budget three thousand pounds for a dress – this would suit me perfectly at a third of the cost. If only I still had the old budget, the one that I flushed down the toilet.

'It is lovely, but this is the first dress I've tried on. I should look for more.'

'Of course. I've got one that I think would suit you perfectly.'

Ten minutes later I'm back on the podium and I'm in another equally stunning dress. This one is completely different. Instead of looking like a wedding cake, I look like . . . well, like a mermaid. This one is a fishtail dress, the type of dress I thought would make me look horrendous and fat-thighed, but you know what? It really looks great on me.

By the time we've visited all three dress shops, I've reached the conclusion that every wedding dress is designed to make you feel special and beautiful. I could have bought nearly all the dresses I've tried on so far. Dress number one is still my favourite, but there isn't much in it.

We're just stopping for a quick coffee – all in the timetable, of course. This has been scheduled in as a refreshment and comfort break before going back to one of the shops if we need to. I'm just trying to pluck up the courage to tell my mum that I think we should go and see what the high street has to offer. Maybe I should drop in the whole Money Saving Expert forum; my mum has a bit of a thing for Martin Lewis, which might just convince her it's a good idea.

'Which one was your favourite then? Have you seen *the one*?' asks Mum.

I had. But I wasn't going to tell her.

'Not yet. I think we need to keep looking,' I say.

'Oh, I was hoping you were going to say the first one. I thought you were glowing in that one.'

I was glowing. I knew it. It could have been me sweating

from hyperventilating over the fact that I am never going to wear that dress. But still.

'Well, I think I should explore all of my options. I was thinking that perhaps we could look on the high street. I know that department stores these days have some nice alternatives,' I say.

'The high street?' My mum looks like she is going to break out in hives at the suggestion.

'Yes, you know the Money Saving Expert forum posts all suggest having a look.'

I'm staring at my mum to work out if I've played my trump card too early.

'The high street? Well, your father would be pleased at the money we'd save but honestly, that first dress . . .'

I stop listening to my mother after the first bit. I think I might have been hearing things but I could have sworn that Mum was suggesting that she and Dad were paying for the dress. I just need to be clear about this before we go any further.

'I'm sorry, Mum, are you expecting to pay for the dress?' I ask.

'Of course. We bought your sister's and we'll buy yours.'

I want to reach over the table and hug my mother. I *am* going to be able to be a princess after all. It might not be Vera Wang, but I reckon dress number one is the next best thing. I'm going to look super amazing in my wedding-cake dress and Mark is not going to be able to take his eyes off me.

Then it hits me: Mark. I can't get the dress of my dreams when I'm compromising every single aspect of our wedding. I feel lousy enough as it is, but I can't have budget everything else, then waltz or float down the aisle in my princess dress.

I start to try to tell Mum that she can't buy my dress, but it takes me three whole swallows before I can get a single word out.

'You can't buy my dress, Mum. Mark and I always said we'd pay for the wedding ourselves,' I say.

'I know, and we've always respected that. But a dress is different; that is just like our last present to our daughter.'

This really isn't the time for me to start hoping that she means it metaphorically and that in reality I will still get presents from her at Christmas. My mum does the best stockings.

'It's really kind of you,' I say, hoping that I won't regret the next words for ever and ever, 'but I really can't accept the offer. I'd rather you put the money towards a present for me and Mark.'

Even though the dress would technically have been a present for Mark as I would have looked pretty damn sexy and hot in it.

'Let's just go and look at what they have to offer on the high street,' I squeak.

'OK. If it's suggested on MSE then it would be worth checking out.'

Yes! I knew the Money Saving Expert card would work.

'I can't believe how nice these dresses are,' says Mum, fifteen minutes later.

I can see that my mother is genuinely surprised by the range of dresses on offer. It's also much less stressful looking at the dresses without the sales assistants following behind you and offering to help you out of your clothes.

These dresses are different. For starters, they fit on normal hangers. They're also not meringue-shaped, and there isn't even a hint of a ruffle. But they are all pretty in their own right.

I end up taking three dresses into the changing room with me. All are a variation on a theme: straight-cut dresses with different details around the bust. One is a V-neck, the next has a cowl neck like Pippa Middelton's infamous bridesmaid dress, and the last is a simple dress with ivory lace detail on the straps and under the bust.

Luckily, each time I leave my fitting-room cubicle my mum looks at me with the same look of wonder that she had in the bridal shops.

When I come out in the third dress she visibly reaches up and clasps her hand over her mouth.

'Now, that one rivals the wedding-cake dress,' she says. 'It is absolutely gorgeous.'

There's no escaping the fact that it isn't a princess dress in the traditional sense. But it is understated, sophisticated and, above all, simple. It reminds me of how Betty described her dress to me. Elegant, yet functional. Did I actually need a dress that I could barely sit down in all day and that took three people to lift up while I peed?

I didn't have a podium to stand on but I spun round in the aisle of the changing rooms.

'That dress was made for you,' says a woman, as she walks out from behind a curtain.

I look up embarrassed; I'd forgotten we weren't alone in the shop like we had been in the bridal boutiques.

'Thank you,' I say, blushing.

'When's the wedding?' says the woman.

'Eighteenth of May.'

'Good luck for then. You'll knock him dead in that dress.'

The woman leaves the changing rooms and I take one final look in the mirror. I trace my fingers over the lace at the shoulders. It really is pretty.

With this dress I could carry the simple theme over to

my hair, tying it up in a side bun decorated with a few loose pearls.

'This is the one,' I say to my mum.

'My goodness, that was easy. It took us three months of looking with your sister. And the best thing is we'll get to take it home today.'

So we can; another advantage of the high street.

'Can I keep it at yours?' I ask.

'Of course you can, love. You don't want Mark to see it before – that's bad luck.'

That much I do know, and with all the bad luck we've been having recently we need all the help we can get.

Getting changed back into my jeans and jumper I feel so ordinary. If only I could live in wedding dresses, it would make every day feel so special. I take the dress up to the till and at the last minute my mum shoves her card into the card reader.

'I don't want to hear another word about it,' she says before I can protest properly.

I was going to put up a little bit of a fight, but in the end I don't bother. I vow to myself that I'll put the two hundred pounds towards something for Mark. He deserves it.

'Thanks, Mum.'

'You're welcome, love. Now all we need to do is find me an outfit.'

I smile. If only that was all I needed to do. I still have practically everything else outstanding on my list.

I might have ticked off the wedding dress, but I figure that was probably a walk in the park compared to how difficult the bridesmaid dresses are going to be. That reminds me, I need to get Lou and my sister Becky to commit to a date. Both of them are being as bad as each other by avoiding my attempts to pin them down on a Saturday. Anyone would think that I'm inviting them to a day walking on hot coals rather than a little retail therapy. But now that I have my dress there are no excuses left.

Time is running out for me to organise this wedding and with only six weeks to go I have to get a wiggle on.

chapter thirteen

Why is it that when you have the heaviest bags from the supermarket the only space you can park in is miles away from your home?

This is just one of the reasons why I hate living in our terrace; there isn't a drive for parking. Not that it is usually a problem. Ninety-nine point nine per cent of the time I get a space either outside or close to our front door. But today, because I'm carrying twelve bottles of wine, I'm practically parked back at the supermarket.

The lights are on when I get home which means that Mark has beaten me home for once. Either that or we've got some very dumb burglars.

'Hello,' I call suspiciously just in case. I quickly decide that even if they are burglars they can stay as whatever they're doing in the kitchen smells divine.

'Hey,' I say, walking into the kitchen.

'Hey, you.'

I'm loving the outfit. Mark is dressed in his new dark blue jeans and a T-shirt, but what has really caught my eye is my frilly Cath Kidston apron.

'You're looking pretty special tonight,' I say.

'I try my best.'

He walks over and gives me a kiss on the top of my head as he opens the cupboard next to me and takes out the pepper mill.

'Are those the meatballs?' I ask.

'Yep, I'm almost done.'

'Great. Can I have a taste?'

'Nope, you will have to wait for later.'

'Dammit.'

Tonight we're having Lou and Russell round for a wine-tasting evening. I came up with the idea as a sneaky plan so that we could work out what wine I should buy for the wedding. But when I mentioned wine tasting they all immediately saw through my plan and realised what I was up to. But who cares? It isn't like they know any more than that.

I was going to do a booze cruise to France to stock up on the wedding wine, only when I looked into how much it would cost me to get there and back and buy petrol and snacks and lunch, etc., it would almost be as much as the corkage. I went on my new favourite forum of Budget Brides-R-US and some of the brides recommended looking out for when supermarket wine websites have sales.

Having made a shortlist of six reds and six whites, I've bought a bottle of each from the supermarket and we'll rate each one. I'm just hoping that we don't have to drink a whole bottle of each to make the decision.

While Mark finishes off his meatballs, I get to work gluing paper on the wine bottles and writing numbers on them. I've got score sheets and everything for us, so people can mark each wine out of ten. I got a bit carried away when I was making them at work and I nearly laminated numbers like on *Come Dine With Me,* so that we could hold them up theatrically after each glass. It was a very slow day at work, may I add. I don't usually have time for all that fun.

I've also made sure that we've cooked a few tapas dishes that have the same food groups as our wedding menu, so that way we can see if the wine goes with them. Clever, huh?

'How many bottles of wine have we got? There are only four of us, aren't there?' asks Mark.

'Yes, but we don't have to drink all of the bottles. I mean, most of them are screw-topped, so we can save the rest of them for the weekend,' I say.

'Right, because we usually drink a dozen bottles of wine between us?'

'OK. If we find ones that we all really like, I promise we'll stop. But come on, this is going to be fun!'

I've told Lou that the food is at seven thirty, so at seven forty-five I decide it is time to go and put on some glad rags and change my make-up from daytime to evening. Loosely that translates as me adding darker eye shadow, some eye-liner and extra blusher.

At exactly eight on the dot, and half an hour late, Russell and Lou ring the doorbell.

'Hiya. So sorry we're late. And what's with the parking tonight?' says Lou, leaning over to give me a hug.

'Tell me about it. There must be something on. Hi, Russell.'

'Penny. We weren't sure what to bring seeing as you told Lou no wine. So we brought cheese and chocolate.'

'Yum, my two favourite food groups. Come on through to the lounge. I would say I hope you're hungry but tonight it's all about the wine. So I hope you're thirsty.'

Walking into the lounge I see Russell and Lou pull faces at each other. Oh no. I can see what is going on here. They've had an argument. Great. We didn't invite Phil and Jane round as last time you could have cut the atmosphere with a knife and now these two are at it.

What is it with married people? Why are they always

arguing? When Mark and I get to stage five, and I'm Mrs Robinson, we will not be like this. Hey, there was no Lemonheads playing when I thought of Mrs Robinson – maybe it's wearing off. Oh no, there it is.

'So what shall I open first? Red or white?' I ask, trying to change the tone of the evening. 'I've got scorecards for every wine we drink. It's going to be a bit *Come Dine With Me*.'

'Um, actually I'm not drinking tonight. I'm driving,' says Lou.

I look at Lou and I wonder if I need to clean my ears out. Lou is never the non-drinking one. Or at least whenever we get together she isn't.

'Lou, it's a wine-tasting evening. You have to drink.'

'I can't face drinking.'

I look at her sitting on the sofa and I'm wondering just who this impostor is, as she certainly isn't the Lou I know.

'How come?' I ask.

'Russell and I got ridiculously drunk last night and I can't face even a mouthful of wine.'

'What did you do last night?' I practically scream at her. She has known about this tasting for weeks. She should have been resting her liver as well as her palate.

'Nothing, we just stayed in,' says Russell. He looks guilty and remorseful. He is sitting with his arms folded and he's looking down at the floor.

'We didn't mean to get drunk. We just opened a bottle of wine and then another . . .'

I look from Lou to Russell, neither one of whom will look back at me. Lou must be hung over; there are bags the size of saucers under her eyes and she seems dog-tired.

'Just the two of you?' I ask in a whisper. Lou has been awfully busy lately. What if she's been cheating on us with new friends? I take a sharp intake of breath. She wouldn't dare. I know Lou better than that. Don't I?

'Just the two of us,' says Russell. He looks at Lou with what I think is a very conspiratorial glance. I knew it. They do have new friends.

'Right. Well, Russell, you're drinking, aren't you?' I ask.

'Yes,' he groans.

'Good. Well, then you'll have to drink all of your wife's wine too,' I say.

Ha. Take that as punishment. Lou drinks like a fish. If he thinks whatever he has is a hangover just wait until I'm finished with him.

I practically storm out of the living room into the kitchen. Mark is busy garnishing dishes. Since when does he garnish? I've got to wean him off watching *Saturday Kitchen*.

'Lou isn't drinking. She's hung over,' I say.

'That's OK, we can still have a nice night. We'll just drink her portion of the wine.'

Mark doesn't get it. It is so not about the wine. It's about the fact that she knew she was coming to this and she still got drunk last night. It's like she doesn't care about my wedding at all.

'I think they had other friends round and they won't tell us. They're acting really weird.'

'As are you. Just calm down and open the wine. Take it through and I'll be in in a minute,' says Mark.

Men. They just don't get what is right in front of their noses.

I pick up bottle number one of the white and the scorecards before doing as Mark says and going back into the lounge.

'Here you go,' I say, handing out the scorecards.

'Look at all the trouble you've gone to with these,' says Lou.

I KNOW! I practically scream. But I don't. Instead I sit down in an armchair and open the wine. I can see Lou out of the corner of my eye. That will teach her to go drinking with other people. I bet she feels guilty now.

I pour three glasses of wine and then pause at Lou's empty glass.

'Do you want something non-alcoholic?' I ask reluctantly.

'Why don't you just sip the wine, Lou, and do what you're supposed to do in proper wine-tasting – spit it out?' says Russell.

'What an excellent suggestion,' I say. Full marks to Russell. That is a great suggestion. I've got a little steel tub that will be perfect. So it's supposed to be an ice bucket for small bottles of wine, but it looks the same, doesn't it?

Lou and Russell are looking at each other really strangely again as I go out of the room to get Lou's spit bucket. I really do hope everything's OK there, despite them cheating on us; they're my favourite couple that we hang out with.

'Here you go, Lou,' I say, handing her the bucket. She looks peaky, but she takes the bucket. She must feel very guilty if she's willing to do this.

'You'll have to do better than this at my hen do. After all, I'm sure that we'll be drinking at least two nights in a row,' I say.

'Oh yes, the hen do,' says Lou.

'Yeah, there'll be none of this 'I'm too hung over to drink' malarkey then. I remember your hen do and that excuse definitely wouldn't have washed. Have you and Becky started planning it yet?'

'What?' asks Lou.

'My hen do. You know as bridesmaids that it's your job to sort out.'

Thankfully that's one wedding task I don't have to deal with, and for once I'll be the one kept in the dark with all the secrets.

'Remind me to phone Becky tomorrow,' says Lou to Russell.

That hardly sounds like a promising start for the hen do organisation. Perhaps I should have told them both before now that they'd be organising it. I just thought it was a given.

'Hey, guys, sorry about that,' says Mark, as he swoops in from the kitchen, minus the apron. It's a shame; I thought the apron brought out the colour of his eyes.

I wait for everyone to do their handshakes and kiss hellos and then I launch right into telling them the wine-tasting rules.

'Right, this is wine number one. We have to see what we think about it and then give it marks out of ten. There are going to be quite a few wines this evening, so you might want to make notes, like hint of raspberries or delicate bouquet.'

'How do you taste a delicate bouquet?' asks Mark, smelling his wine before I've officially said go.

'I don't know. I've heard them say it on posh programmes,' I say.

'Oh well, bottoms up,' says Russell.

We all take a sip of the wine and I actually feel like a proper adult. What a sophisticated evening we're having.

What is that noise? I look up from my scorecard where I'm writing *very strong flavour* and I see that it is Lou spitting out her drink into the bucket. I'm sure when I've seen people wine-tasting on TV they do it a bit more discreetly than that.

'I think I'm going to be sick,' she says, running off towards the bathroom.

'Pass me her bucket,' says Mark. 'That was pretty rank.'

'What, the wine or Lou practically throwing up in the living room?' I ask snidely.

'The wine,' says Mark.

'Yeah, I have to admit it was a strong taste to have without food. Have we all done our scores?'

Mark and Russell look at each other and nod. Time for the big reveal.

'That was a South African chenin blanc,' I say, peeling off the label.

'Great. Are they all going to taste as awful as that?' asks Mark.

'I hope not.'

Oh, God! What if they are? What if I have the worst skills in wine-picking ever? I usually just go for the prettiest label and be done with it. Only this time I actually read the backs of the bottles to see what they went with.

'That's better,' says Lou, as she comes back into the room.

She doesn't look better; she looks as pale as Casper the friendly ghost.

'Shall we go into the dining room and eat?' asks Mark, as if he's sensing the uneasiness of the evening returning.

* * *

Mark and I have really excelled ourselves in our tapas cooking. Or at least Mark has – I just printed all the recipes off the internet for him. Every dish tastes delicious. It's a pity we have no idea how to cater for eighty people or else we could roll this out as our wedding food, it's that good. And think how cheap that would be!

'This wine is definitely my favourite,' says Russell.

Not that I wouldn't have noticed – he's drunk practically the entire bottle of it. We've stopped going methodically through the bottles and in the end we've assigned Russell to be the white drinker and Mark and I were trying reds.

'Can I have a quick sip?' I ask. I think it's best I get in on the act before there is an empty bottle. I reach over and grab Russell's glass. 'You're right, that is lovely. OK, we have our white winner.'

I peel off my stuck-on label and see that it's the French Chablis. I carefully circle it on my wine list and make a note: *This is the one*. Just in case I have too many more wines and then don't remember tomorrow morning.

I couldn't face going through another painful evening like this. It's like the worst dinner party ever, except with maybe the best food. Lou and Russell are barely speaking to each other and Mark and I are having to hold court.

'So, Lou, you're the only one who knows about the wedding venue. Am I going to like it?' asks Mark.

'You're going to love it,' Lou says, smiling.

So she can smile after all; I was beginning to think she'd said something nasty and the wind had changed.

'It's going to be a beautiful wedding,' she adds.

'Ah, thanks, Lou, and I'm sure you'll make a beautiful bridesmaid too. Except not too beautiful as you're not allowed to upstage me.'

'No chance of that,' she says.

Did that sound sarcastic to anyone else in the room? Or have I had too much wine?

I'm just going to glide right over it. 'Now that I've got my dress we'll have to go and get your dress sometime. Maybe next week?'

'I can't, I'm busy,' she says.

'OK then, what about the weekend after?'

'No,' she says, wrinkling her nose up. 'I think I'm busy then too. I'll tell you what, when I get home I'll check my diary and tell you what date I'm free.'

WTF? Is this my best friend I spent months and months traipsing round every dress shop in the south-east with, looking for a bridesmaid dress that was the *exact* shade of pink she wanted? And now she won't even commit to a date to go and look at dresses?

I'm too gobsmacked to even respond. Lou is the only person I've let into any aspect of this secret wedding planning and yet she keeps running a million miles the other way when I try to involve her. Is she trying to distance herself deliberately?

She really has got secret friends. It is the only explanation.

'How about we have dessert?' says Mark.

'I'll get it,' I say, standing up. I manage to collect up our dirty plates and walk into the kitchen before I let a tear roll down my face. I don't want to go all bridezilla on everyone but I just feel that Lou, of all people, should be taking an interest in this wedding.

I'm practically on autopilot taking the chocolate cake out of the fridge. Maybe this 'don't tell the groom' is harder on me than I realise. Maybe I'm being too harsh on Lou. Maybe I'm just disappointed that Mark isn't able to take an interest in the wedding details and I thought Lou would pick up the slack. Perhaps that's the real reason I'm feeling upset.

I'll give Lou an extra big portion of chocolate cake and perhaps that will be my peace offering to her. I even add an extra scoop of vanilla ice cream as I know that is her favourite.

'There you go,' I say, as I walk back into the dining room.

'Actually, I think we're going to skip dessert,' says Lou. 'I'm really tired and I still feel really sick.'

Who is this impostor and where is Lou? This is Lou's favourite dessert. I've seen her eat this after an Olympic breakfast at the Little Chef. Nothing stands between Lou and a chocolate fudge cake.

'Thanks, Mark and Pen, for such a lovely evening,' says Lou, standing up.

Lovely evening? Have we been at the same table all night?

'We'll have to have you round to our house sometime soon,' says Russell.

Lou just shot Russell the filthiest look at the mere suggestion that we'd be going round to their house. Come to think of it, we haven't been round to their house for weeks. Months even. Are they phasing us out and we're just not bright enough to cotton on?

Before I've registered that they're leaving Lou is out of the door. I don't even get a kiss goodbye; she just waves as she walks towards her Ford Focus.

'We didn't open the cheese,' I call.

'You two have it,' says Russell. 'Enjoy!'

I close the door and rest my back up against it for a minute, trying to digest what just happened. It's only a momentary lapse as I soon remember that I've left chocolate cake and ice cream in the dining room.

'Don't you think that was weird?' I say to Mark.

He's sitting there finishing off the last of the contents of his bowl. He looks completely unfazed by the tornado of an awful evening that he just witnessed.

'What?' asks Mark.

I watch him lean over and take Lou's giant portion of cake. Well, I guess it would have been going to waste.

'Lou's behaviour. Didn't you think it was strange? The whole hangover thing and not drinking. Them leaving before dessert. Before Lou's *favourite* dessert. Her non-committal attitude towards the bridesmaid dress shopping.

'As far as I can tell there is only one logical explanation to all this: they have new best friends.'

Mark looks up from his half-eaten fudge cake and stares at me. I don't understand what he doesn't get. It is simple when you add up all the bits of information.

'Really? All that happened tonight and that's your best explanation for it?'

I rack my brains to try to work out what I'm missing, only it isn't easy when you've consumed the best part of two bottles of wine.

'Or maybe Russell and Lou are getting a divorce. Maybe they're living in separate houses and that is why we haven't been over to their house in ages. Maybe Lou needs to be sober so she can drop Russell off and drive to her new place,' I say.

I'm now offended that Lou hasn't shown me her new place.

'I don't think that's it,' says Mark, smiling at me.

He looks so bloody smug. Well, I'm not going to let him tell me what he thinks. I'm going to try and guess. Even if it does feel like I'm playing *Family Fortunes* and desperately trying to get the top answer.

'Why don't you examine the facts?' says Mark.

There is definitely a smugness in his tone. That will be the red wine; he always thinks he's right when he drinks it.

'She wasn't drinking, she didn't have her favourite dessert, she went home because she was tired,' says Mark.

I'm struggling here to connect the dots.

'And she didn't eat the prawns,' adds Mark.

I'm still blank. I must remember not to drink too much of this wine at the wedding or else my guests are not going to have the most scintillating conversation with me.

'She's pregnant,' says Mark, with a heavy sigh.

Suddenly it is right there in front of me. All the signs are there flashing in neon lights. She was even wearing a baggy top over her skinny jeans.

'But she can't be. She would have told me. She hasn't even told me they're trying for a baby.'

Mark goes back to eating his chocolate fudge cake.

'She can't be pregnant,' I say. But it is a far more logical explanation than anything I've thought of.

This wedding is going from bad to worse. Not only do I have a third of the wedding budget, but now my best friend isn't going to be my maid of honour. She's going to be all glowing and distracted by the little bundle of joy she is having. I really shouldn't drink wine. It makes me think the worst of things. But it's just that I can't imagine a wedding day without Lou by my side.

chapter fourteen

I've hit rock bottom. I really have. I'm sitting in a coffee shop and looking at my hands as they're visibly shaking.

'Are you OK?' asks Josh.

He sits down opposite me with his coffee and for a minute I just want to lean across and hug him. I'm sure it's the leather jacket that he always wears; it makes me think that he could wrap his arms around me and protect me from anything.

He said something, didn't he? I can't for the life of me remember what it was, because I'm too busy looking at his shoulders as he slips off his jacket. Focus, Penny, focus. He was just asking if I'm OK.

'I've been better.'

'So your text said that you gambled again,' says Josh.

I wince. There is something so awful about the *G* word

when it's said out loud. It makes me feel like I've done something truly, truly heinous.

'I bought five scratch cards yesterday. I hadn't planned to do it, but I was getting some milk from the corner shop and I thought that I could just do with a little boost. I'd wanted to buy a lottery ticket but it was past seven thirty.'

Josh is nodding as if he understands. See, this is why I texted him.

'I just felt so dirty. I mean, I bought a scratch card. I felt like I was having an out-of-body experience as I watched myself hunched over the kitchen table and desperately scratching off the grey boxes. And then I got really paranoid that Mark would see one of the grey specks that I'd rubbed off and work everything out. I ended up hoovering the kitchen table just to get rid of any trace of them.'

'Did you win?' asks Josh.

'What?'

What does winning have to do with it? Surely the focus here should be on the fact that I gambled?

'Did you win or did you lose?'

'I don't know,' I say.

'What, did you throw them away before you looked?'

'No, I couldn't work out if I'd won.'

I reach into my pocket and dig out five slightly crinkled scratch cards and I pass them over to Josh.

'You need a flipping degree to understand if you've won,' I say, to make myself feel better. I can't tell whether it was the scratch cards that were complicated or if I was flustered that Mark might come home and catch me, but I honestly couldn't work out if I'd won.

'You haven't won,' says Josh.

'Really? Not even a pound? What about the one with the diamonds?'

'Nope, your stones don't match.'

I don't know why I am surprised that I've lost again. It wasn't like I'd had a whole lot of luck in the first place with gambling.

'Well, there's another waste of five pounds. It just feels so much worse than the bingo,' I say.

'How come?'

'Because I could see the mess I'd made afterwards. I'd scratched like I was a fox savaging a carcass. I couldn't help it.'

'In the grand scheme of things a few scratch cards are no worse than your online bingo. You do realise you lost ten thousand pounds doing that? I don't think you should rank forms of gambling as better or worse than each other. It's all gambling.'

I don't know why I bother talking to Josh sometimes. He makes me so cross. He knocks me down so that I'm even lower than I was before I spoke to him. This wasn't the kind of thing I wanted to hear when I texted him. I wanted him to give me a little pep talk. Next he'll be calling me a thief again.

'What made you do it?' he asks.

'I was buying milk and I saw them.'

'No, I mean what made you do it? Were you having a bad day? Why did you want the tickets?'

'I wanted to win,' I say quietly.

'Why?'

I take a deep breath. I know that Josh won't understand.

'I found out at the weekend that Lou, my best friend, is having a baby. So I'm down a bridesmaid. Then I've got flower arranging tonight, which I'm terrible at. I'm never going to be able to do my own flowers for the wedding. And so I bought the tickets hoping I'd win enough to pay a florist.'

'That's it? That's why you were having a bad day?'

'I'm sorry that it's not bad enough for you. It seemed pretty bad from where I was sitting,' I say stroppily.

'How many classes of flower arranging have you done?'

'Tonight will be my seventh.'

'Out of . . .'

'Eight.'

'Well, you've got a quarter of the classes left. You may get better.'

'No, I think it's one of those talents you've either got or you haven't.'

'So don't arrange your own flowers,' says Josh, shrugging his shoulders as if it's the simplest decision in the world.

'But I can't afford all the flowers I want without buying them wholesale and putting them together myself.'

'Then have fewer flowers.'

I roll my eyes at Josh. He is such a man.

'I can't have fewer flowers.'

'Why not? Do the flowers conduct the service? Do the flowers say your vows? No, flowers may be nice, but they're not an integral part of what a wedding is.'

That's told me. I start to drain my coffee, wondering if I can make a speedy exit.

'Look, I don't mean to be harsh. I'm just trying to make you try to see how you're worrying about all these little things that aren't important in the grand scheme of things,' says Josh. 'Let's put it in perspective. You were gambling because you wanted a dress, yes?'

'Yes, originally.'

'Right, and now you have a dress?'

'Yes.'

'And did it cost as much as your dream dress?'

'No. It was two hundred and twenty-five pounds.'

'Right, then. Is it any less nice?'

'It's different.'

'But do you like it?'

'I love it,' I say honestly, and my heart skips a beat as I remember the lace detail.

'Don't you see? There are always options. You don't need to find a quick win to get what you're looking for. When it comes to life there are no quick wins. You have to either work for things in life or adjust what you want. Gambling to get what you want is never a good short cut.'

I will not cry, I will not cry, I chant desperately in my head. I can feel the tears rushing to my eyes and my vision is starting to blur. I know he isn't having a go at me and I know that he is trying to help me, but I can't help it that I want to cry.

'Hey, hey, Penny.'

He's grabbed my hand and he's stroking it. I want to scream at him to stop being so nice. I half laugh, half cough, and a few tears escape from my eyes.

'Don't cry, Penny. Listen to me. None of the details you're worrying about are important. Don't you see?'

I nod. I did see. I was just always trying to get the next wow factor thing for the wedding.

'You see, Penny, this is why I don't do weddings. At the end of the day if you love someone, you love someone and that love can just be enough. If I were ever to get married, which I'm not, then it would be the most basic wedding you'd ever need.'

'Would you never marry Mel?' I ask.

'No, that won't happen.'

I'm intrigued to know what Mel is like. I know that not every woman wants to get married, but it just intrigues me nonetheless. With a boyfriend like Josh I bet she's pretty enough to be a model.

'Look, Penny, I'm sorry. I have to leave now if I'm going to get back to work on time.'

I glance at my watch. Yikes, so am I.

'Thanks for coming to meet me, Josh. It's just so hard not being able to talk to anyone else.'

'I still think you should consider telling Mark. He seems like a decent guy. I'm sure he'd understand.'

'No, he really wouldn't. But anyway, I feel much better about everything. And I promise, no more scratch cards.'

'Or any other get-rich-quick gambles. No taking yourself off to the horse racing or anything.'

'No,' I laugh. 'I promise.'

We walk back to the car park and already my shoulders seem lighter. It is such a massive relief just to have been able to talk about what was bothering me.

'Thanks, Josh.'

The next thing I know Josh is hugging me. It is exactly what I needed.

'I'll see you on Tuesday,' I say, waving as I get into my car.

Now all I have to do is get through an afternoon at work

and then hope that I've magically sprouted green fingers by six o'clock when I go to flower arranging class.

By 7 p.m. I realise that I haven't sprouted the green fingers.

This week's task is buttonholes. Mine resembles something a clown would wear. Only it wouldn't squirt any water, it would just fall apart if you pressed anything.

I glance at Amy, the woman who sits next to me. Her buttonhole looks like something you'd find in a florist's shop. I'm desperately staring at her fingers, which are all nimble and delicate. I wish mine were like that.

'What?' asks Amy as she looks up at me. I think perhaps my staring was scaring her.

'I just wish my buttonhole looked as good as yours. I've got fat thumbs.'

That is the only excuse I can offer. They may not be as big as Mark's mutantly strong thumbs, but I think they are fat enough to be hindering my flower arranging.

'You just need to take a bit more time over them,' says Amy.

'Patience has never been my strong point,' I say honestly.

'You're good with the colours though. They at least complement each other well.'

She must be a mum. That is such a mum thing to say, looking for the positives in a bad situation.

'That's really kind, but don't worry, I know it's crap.'

'I mean it, about the colours,' she says.

'So have you done this before?'

'No, but I'm an art teacher, so I'm used to working with craft materials and a lot of the principles are the same.'

'Wow, then you are really good.'

'Thanks. So how are your wedding plans coming along?'

'Well, I think I've got my buttonholes down, don't you agree?' I say, laughing. Who am I kidding? The forty-five pounds I spent on this course was a total waste of money.

'Aside from your lovely buttonholes. How are the rest of the plans going?'

'I've got most of the big things now. Venue, church and the dress. I have a dress! I've just got to sort the photographer, DJ, transport, flowers and the little details. Favours and decorations.'

'Have you given the favours any thought? I always love those. The last wedding I went to had lottery ticket favours,' says Amy.

I wince as I remember how tempted I'd been a few weeks before to steal all the lottery ticket favours from the other person's wedding. I somehow doubt that it would be a good idea for me to have them at our wedding. Besides which, if any of my friends won a big prize I'd be forever pissed off about the one time I bought a winning ticket and someone else got the prize.

I'm not saying that I wouldn't be happy for a friend or family member if they won the lottery. I'm just saying that I wouldn't be happy if I'd bought them the winning ticket. There's a difference.

'Yeah, I was thinking of making something,' I say. Or reading between the lines I want something cheap.

'Oh, I know. I went to another wedding that had love hearts – you know, the little sweets? They had the bride and groom's name on them and they were in little organza bags.'

That was a cute idea, but I can't imagine that they'd come in at under £30, which is my current budget for favours. My preferred favours at the moment are an IOU coffee note that I thought the guests could redeem at some future date, when I had more than two pennies to rub together.

'Right, now time to make your feminine buttonhole,' says the teacher at the front of the class, clapping her hands together to get our attention.

We all stand up and go and select some more flowers. This is just what I need, to knock myself even lower in the self-confidence stakes.

'What about making something you can eat?' suggests Amy.

'Wouldn't I have to make it really close to the wedding?' I ask.

'Yeah, but if you made something simple.'

That is not the world's worst idea. I might be a terrible cake baker, but I'm sure there must be some recipe that I could use. I mean, if I actually follow the recipe word for word, and don't get a bit creative halfway through as I try to channel my inner Nigella.

I like the idea of something edible. After all, who doesn't like a tasty little snack when they've been drinking?

My feminine buttonhole is not looking any better than the masculine one. In fact it looks worse. Not even a clown would be seen dead in this.

I hold mine up, rotating it to see if it looks any better at different angles, but it doesn't.

'I'm going to have the worst wedding flowers ever,' I say sadly. I know when I'm defeated. I'm embarrassed for thinking that I'd be able to do this.

'Look, if you don't think your flowers are going to cut the mustard, why don't I do them? I mean, unless you'd rather get a florist to do them. I wouldn't be offended if you said no,' says Amy.

'I'd love you to do my flowers. That's really kind of you. But the thing is, I was doing this course as I can't afford to get a florist. I wouldn't be able to afford to get you to do them either.'

'Yes, you could, I'd do it for free. Or at least maybe a couple of bottles of wine. Listen, if you provide me with the flowers the day before the wedding, then I'll put them together.'

'Really?' I want to lean over and hug her, but having only met her a few times I don't think that is entirely appropriate.

'Just before I commit to it, you're not having wall-to-wall flowers, are you?' she asks.

'No, nothing like that. Just three bouquets and buttonholes, of course.'

'What about table centrepieces?'

'No, I'm not going to have table centrepieces.'

There, I've said it, and you know what? It's quite liberating. I'm not having table centrepieces. What happens to table centrepieces after the wedding anyway?

'Great, then it should be easy. Can I take photos of them for a website? I'm hoping to do this kind of thing on the side. I thought it might be a good little earner during the summer holidays,' says Amy

'Of course you can. And what a great idea. You've obviously got a talent for it.'

I feel fabulous by the time I get back to the house. I've swapped numbers with Amy and I only have one more flower-arranging class to go next week. Now that I'm not doing the flowers for the wedding I no longer feel under pressure and I don't think I'm going to mind going any more.

In fact, in the mood I'm in nothing can bring me down. I've ticked another big milestone off my list.

See, this wedding organising stuff is actually quite simple after all. Josh was right.

'Hello?' I call as I walk into the house.

'In the lounge,' comes the response from Mark.

'Hey, how's it going?' I ask, plonking myself on the sofa next to him and kissing him on the cheek. He seems deep into his channel surfing. It's a pastime that he takes deadly seriously and it makes it a nightmare to watch anything with him. He changes the channels during most advert breaks and you find yourself watching about ten minutes of a programme before he gets engrossed in something else.

'Fine. How was the gym?' he asks.

'Same as ever,' I say dismissively. 'How was your day?'

'It was OK. I just had the weirdest phone conversation with Nan.'

'Oh, what did she say?'

'Not a lot. It was just the way she said it.'

'Well, she has been acting weird with me. Remember I told you she was looking at me funny and you told me that I was imagining it?'

'Are you saying that there's something wrong with her? Like she's losing it?' asks Mark.

I stroke Mark's arm to reassure him. There's nothing worse

than your loved ones getting old and you watching them fade away. I lost my own gran last year and it was hell watching her slip further and further under the pull of dementia.

'She isn't like my gran, if that's what you're worried about. I think your nan has all her marbles. I just feel like she's being cool with me.'

'Hmm.'

That didn't sound like a good hmm. That sounded like the kind of hmm that means he has more information on that.

'She does like me, doesn't she? I mean, I've always thought that me and Nanny Violet got on well,' I say.

'You did. I mean, you do.'

'Then what's she been saying?'

I knew she was out to get me, I saw it twinkling in her eyes. I had thought that it was just a flicker caused by me looking at her through her varifocal lenses, but now it is clear that Mark knows something.

'Tell me,' I say, jabbing Mark in the ribs.

'OK. It's just she was asking me lots of questions about us. She was asking me if we were happy and whether I was doing the right thing marrying you.'

'She what?' I stand up and start to pace the living-room floor like a caged tiger. 'I've never been anything but nice to your nan. Where has this come from?'

'I don't know. I don't. But I think it's probably just that

I'm the last grandchild to get married and maybe she's a bit more protective of me.'

'But we've lived with each other for years and she's never said anything else about us, has she?'

Mark shakes his head and I scratch mine in frustration. Why would she suddenly hate me? I rack my brains trying to think if I've done anything untoward the last few times I've seen her or if I've accidentally sworn in front of her. But I can't think of anything.

'I'm sure it's nothing,' says Mark. His voice doesn't sound very reassuring.

'And what did you say to her?'

'I told her there was nothing to worry about, and that I wouldn't be marrying you if I wasn't sure that you were the woman I wanted to be with for the rest of my life.'

'Ah, you said that?' I love it when Mark says mushy stuff. He's usually so serious and manly, but every so often he lets his teddy bear side out.

'Come here,' he says. I sit on the sofa and he wraps his arms around me. They're the second set of male arms I've had round me today and it makes me realise that no matter how strong and sexy Josh's arms were, this is where I feel the most comfort and protection: in Mark's arms.

'I think it's probably the whole "don't tell the groom" thing that's bothering her,' says Mark. 'Why don't you go round and see Nanny Violet sometime soon and tell her the details of the wedding? I'm sure she'd appreciate that.'

Right now I'd rather crawl into a lion's den than go and talk to Mark's sweet old nan. There is just something not right there. I bury myself deeper in Mark's arms and wish that I could stay right here forever instead.

chapter fifteen

There seems something slightly wrong about going into the church. I feel like I'm going to melt, like the witch in *The Wizard of Oz*, or that everyone will point at me and tell me I'm going to hell. I didn't feel like this when I came to see the vicar before, but I think the dark passenger that is my gambling addiction is making me nervous.

I grab Mark's hand as we go over the threshold, just in case.

'Don't be nervous,' says Mark, laughing. 'I think it's going to be quite relaxed.'

I smile sweetly. If only I was nervous about the fact that we're attending our marriage class. I'm more worried that Nanny Violet will have told the vicar that Mark and I aren't destined to be together.

It's been a week since Mark dropped the V-Bomb, aka when Violet questioned whether he should be marrying me. I haven't been to see her. I can't face what she'd have to say. What if she was right? What if Mark would be better off without me?

'Welcome, welcome,' says the vicar as he sees us approach.

'Hi, Reverend Phillips,' says Mark.

I am so nervous, I can't speak. I just go with a nervous smile instead which flashes way too much teeth.

'Ah, Mark and Penelope,' says Reverend Phillips.

Is it just me, or is there a tone of disapproval in his voice?

'And how are you two getting along? Still not telling Mark anything?'

He knows. He has to. That was such a leading question.

'No, I'm still totally in the dark. Apart from this bit. Which is a relief. At least I know I'm actually getting married and not having to worry about Penny organising some pagan ceremony or something.'

I laugh along but I'm a little insulted. A pagan ceremony would have been a great theme. I've said before that my hair would work so well.

'Great. Well, take a seat. We've got one more couple to come, then we will make a start.'

Mark raises his eyebrows at me and we take our seats.

There are three other couples sitting in chairs whispering to each other. It looks like everyone is nervous.

The last couple come in and sit down, as if they're late, but in fact we're all five minutes early. The woman looks flustered and she struggles to take her cardigan off before realising the church hall is quite cold and putting it straight back on again.

'Right, then. Well, thank you all for coming,' says Reverend Phillips. 'Don't be scared about today. This isn't a test and no one is keeping score. We're just trying to give you tools to equip you as a couple for your happy marriage.

'Now, I like to think of a marriage as like two pieces of paper that get stuck together. Once stuck the papers are solid and strong. Only when you try to pull the paper apart the two pages are never the same again. They're damaged. Which is why marriages always work best if you're like those two pieces of paper. It isn't easy, and sometimes bits of the paper will peel away, but through hard work and above all love, those papers can stay together and the marriage can flourish.'

I'm a bit lost. I know he's only been speaking for a minute but I've already drifted off into thoughts of sticking paper together with Pritt Stick and how you always get lumps and bumps and bits of glue that squish out the side. It suddenly makes me pine for stationery.

'Penny?'

I look up and Mark is staring at me. I look briefly around the room. Reverend Phillips has stopped talking and the couples have started whispering to each other.

'What's going on?' I whisper.

'We've got to write down our five favourite things about the other person. Were you not listening?'

'I got lost in the paper analogy.'

'Right. Well, you've got to write down five things you love about me and then you have to tell me.'

'OK,' I say.

Huh. This isn't that hard a class. If only school had been all based around Mark questions, I would have had straight A's.

Right. Where to start? I write on my piece of paper *Things I love about Mark* and then I underline it.

Hmm. I love his hair and his smell. Oh, I love the way he looks at me all doe-eyed after we've had sex and he gives the best post-coital cuddles.

I can't write those down as they will make me look shallow and like I'm only with Mark because he's a tiger in bed. Which is obviously a good reason to be with Mark, but not the only one.

Mark looks like he's writing an essay. Can't blame him. I bet there are thousands of things about me that he loves.

Focus, Penny, *focus*. Five little things.

I love the way he laughs. Yes that's a good one. I love that he laughs when I do stupid things and he goes into a deep belly laugh, and occasionally if I've done something really silly, tears roll down his cheeks. He doesn't do it very often but when he does it's a treat to see.

I love that he's intellectual. That he can have intelligent conversations about politics and he can actually do the *Times* crossword without cheating. And it has nothing to do with the fact that he looks really sexy when he does the crossword as he has these little brown-rimmed glasses and he furrows his brow. Is it getting hot in here or is it just me?

'Just a couple more minutes to think, then you should start sharing,' says Reverend Phillips.

Blimey. That doesn't give us much time.

I love that he's thoughtful and caring. Like when he hides my Valentine's Day card in my glove compartment, which he knows is where I keep my driving glasses.

I love that he loves his family. Like taking Bouncer for a walk, or babysitting his niece and nephew to give his brother and sister-in-law some alone time. And he always visits his nan, despite her being an evil woman.

Don't worry, I didn't actually write that.

And lastly, I love him. *Everything* about him. Even though it drives me crazy that he has ketchup with my home-made lasagne that doesn't need it, or that he always, without fail, destroys my secret stash of chocolate, no matter where I hide it.

'Start telling each other,' says Reverend Phillips.

I grin at Mark. I'm waiting to hear what amazing things he has to say about me.

'You first,' I giggle.

'OK.'

He's nervous, bless him. He's got a quiver in his voice and everything.

'I love the way you make me feel,' he says.

I start humming the Michael Jackson song. I can't help it. I have music in my head. *A lot*.

'Stop it,' he says, laughing. 'You know you make me feel special. I love that you laugh so much and you're nearly always happy.'

'I've got that too. Except I've got I love the way you laugh,' I say excitedly.

See, people? We're meant to be. Meant. To. Be.

'I love that you always see the best in people.'

I do? It's a good job that Mark can't hear my internal monologue and therefore does not hear that I can be quite an evil, judgemental cow.

'I love that you're thoughtful.'

'I've got that too,' I say, flashing him a quick peek of my list so that he knows I'm not cheating.

'I mean this whole wedding thing. The fact that you're organising it as a surprise for me, that is really thoughtful.'

Oh no. Here comes the guilt. I can feel my eyes start to get hot, like they do before I start to cry.

'And lastly I love that you're so honest. I know I joke about how much you talk, but I love that I always know what's going on in your world.'

I'm staring at Mark and I can't say anything. If only he knew the half of it. The melancholy hits me out of the blue. I can't believe that out of everything in the world, he loves me for two reasons that lately haven't been true.

'What about me? Come on, Pen?'

Mark is grinning like the Cheshire cat; he's clearly relieved that he's got his sharing out of the way.

'OK,' I say, choking on my words.

I read him an abridged version of my list and I can feel my eyes prickle with tears.

'That was lovely,' he says. He kisses me on the top of my head and gives my hand a squeeze.

I catch a rogue tear before it gets loose and rolls down my cheek.

I'm such a fraud. How in the world am I going to get through today without crying or, worse, confessing the truth? Which would mean the end not only to the marriage class, but the marriage itself.

'Right. Well done. Everyone seemed to take that very seriously,' says Reverend Phillips. 'The value of this day is really down to all of you. I like to use that exercise to break us in gently, so that you can firmly fix in your mind *why* you love your partner and *why* you're going on this journey with them.

'We're going to look at three topics today, and we'll watch videos for each topic and have conversations. Our first topic is communication.'

Of course it is. This is going to be a gem.

'Now, we're going to watch a video segment that will explain all about effective communication with our partners. And then we'll do an exercise about something that is worrying each of us.'

It really is getting hot in here. I can feel myself breaking out into a sweat. And I thought going to gambling support group was bad. This has to be ten times worse. All the way through the video I'm panicking about what I'm going to say to Mark, what is going to be my worry.

By the time we get to tell our worries I'm feeling physically sick.

I make Mark go first. He's the man after all – he should take charge.

'I'm worried about Nan.'

Phew. I'm relieved that his worry isn't that his fiancée has a deep-dark secret that he can't figure out.

'What about your nan?' I ask.

'I'm worried that there's something wrong with her that she isn't telling me.'

'I'm sure that she's fine. Have you got reason to suspect anything, or is it just from what you were saying the other week?'

'She's just been different lately. She's been vague and she seems sad, like she's somewhere else. And she called me Geoffrey.'

'Who's Geoffrey?' I ask.

Apart from the giraffe at Toys Я Us, but I can't imagine Nanny Violet would have got him confused with Mark, as they look nothing alike.

'I don't know.'

'Well, that doesn't mean to say that there's something wrong with her. Maybe she's a bit lonely. Perhaps we should just go and see her more.'

Says me who has avoided her, or any mention of her, for the past week. I had no idea this was bothering Mark so much.

'Yeah, I guess. I know she's old, and I know that she won't be around forever. It's just that I wanted her to see our children and for them to know her.'

'And they still can.'

As long as we get a move on to stage six pretty sharpish,

then that could still happen. I can almost imagine the maternity leave now and the amazing elasticated jeans I've had my eye on in Mothercare for years. I expect they'll revolutionise my Christmas dinner eating experience.

'Now, as you're talking, think about how nice it is opening up to each other and listening to each other. Think about how you can incorporate this into your daily routine,' says Reverend Phillips.

I can just imagine. *Hey, honey, I'm a little worried today as you're going suit shopping and I've only given you fifty pounds as I've gambled the rest of the money away*. I'm sure that would go down really, really well.

Reverend Phillips is looking at me oddly and I'm suddenly wondering if he is psychic, or whether he's been told from up high what I'm thinking. I turn and look at Mark and do my sympathetic head-bob to try to encourage him to talk about his nan more.

'Your turn,' he says.

'What, really? Don't you want to talk about your nan some more? Haven't we just scratched the surface?'

I was sort of hoping we could focus solely on Mark's problems and then we'd run out of time for mine.

'No, I think you were right. I should spend more time with her.'

'Great.'

See, I'm an excellent problem solver for everyone but myself, it seems.

'My worry is . . .' I'm stalling I have a million worries and none of them I can tell him. 'I worry that we'll end up like Jane and Phil – you know, at each other's throats when we're married.'

It is true; I do worry about that. I worry that things will change and they won't be how they are now.

'Really? Jane and Phil, they're different. And I don't think they're that unhappy. I think that perhaps Jane put too much emphasis on the wedding. I don't think she had any hobbies or anything. Not like you. You're always at the gym and stuff. It's not like you're obsessed with our wedding or anything.'

'No, of course not.'

Oh dear. I have a whole internet history and dozens and dozens of posts on Hitched and Confetti, even from before we were engaged, that say otherwise. That makes me worse than Jane, as I was doing the wedding planning before we even got to stage four. I should have just been enjoying stage three. Stage three, the limbo stage where I started gambling while Mark studied for his accountancy exams. I never thought I'd miss it, but I am actually pining for it. Well, not all of it. Not the bingo. I just wished that I hadn't been in such a hurry to get away from it.

'Don't worry, Pen. If you look like you're turning into

Bridezilla or you start talking to me the way Jane talks to Phil, I'll tell you.'

'Thanks, honey.'

'Right. We're now going to look at how we talk to each other and what we don't say,' says Reverend Phillips.

Great. This sounds like it is going to be right up my street. Not.

By the time we make it through to the end of the day, I've learnt an awful lot about Mark and me as a couple. On the whole it looks like we're pretty compatible. Which is good, seeing as we're getting married and everything. The only thing that lets us down is me and my secrets.

I don't think Mark and I have ever opened up to each other in this way before or been so honest about what our worst faults are and what we think our future is going to be like. And it hurts me that I'm not being as honest with Mark as I should be. I'm so tempted to take him home and explain everything, but I just feel like I'm so close to making a success of everything that I can't risk losing him forever.

We say our goodbyes to the vicar and his wife, and the other couples. Not that we spoke to the other couples, but I do feel like I got to know the couple sitting next to us a bit better as I may have done a little bit of earwigging when Mark went to the toilet. I might just happen to know that the woman of the couple seems to think that the man has arguments with her just so they'll fight and have to have make-up sex. I was trying to make Mark drink lots of tea so that he nipped to the toilet during the bedroom section as I wanted to earwig the ways that the other couple kept their romance alive. But Mark and his camel bladder weren't going anywhere. Who knows what tips I could have got?

The keeping the romance alive was the most embarrassing section. There is something wrong about discussing sex in front of a vicar in his late fifties. I caught him raising suggestive eyebrows at his wife, who was sitting in the corner, when he talked about it. She spent the rest of the afternoon blushing furiously. That was one mental picture that I didn't need to imagine.

'Well, that was an eye-opener,' says Mark. 'I don't think I'm going to be able to look Reverend Phillips in the eye when we get married, now I know how he keeps his romance alive. Did you see the suggestive eyebrows?'

'I did.'

I link arms with Mark as we walk back to the car.

'I really enjoyed today, though. I thought it was really good,' I say.

'Yeah, it was. Most of it made sense too. I think we should do this more often.'

'What, sit in a room of strangers and talk about our communication styles?'

'No, do things just the two of us. Like quality time.'

'Like a date?' I say.

'Yes, we should have date nights.'

A date night? I used to think that we didn't need an actual date night as we would have one every night. But Mark's right. Maybe we do need to set aside some *us* time.

'OK then, why don't we have date night every Thursday?' I say.

'Don't you have body blitz or pump or whatever it is you have at the gym?'

Flower arranging, I add in my head.

'I do, but I think I should cut down on the gym. Spending time with you would be much nicer.'

'That sounds great. Although you're not allowed to turn into a heifer. I don't want a fat wife.'

'Hey, you can't say that!' I poke him hard in the ribs.

Mark presses the button to unlock his car and we both climb in.

'I'm just kidding. You know I'd love you any which way, don't you?'

I nod. I do know that. I think Mark needs to wear his glasses more than he lets on, as he doesn't appear to care how bad I look. Even when I'm wearing no make-up he still thinks

I'm beautiful. I reckon I could be the size of a house and he wouldn't notice or care.

Mark is beginning to make me nervous as he hasn't started the car and he is just tilting his head to the side in that pose where he looks puzzled.

'Pen, you would tell me if there was something else I needed to know, wouldn't you?'

My throat starts to close up and I feel like I'm going to choke from the lack of air. My heart is beginning to throb so loudly that I am sure Mark is going to notice. He's staring me straight in the eye.

If ever there was a perfect lead-in to tell him what's going on, this is it. I open my mouth but before I can utter a word there's a knock on the window. Mark and I jump round to see Nanny Violet standing outside the car. Mark switches on the engine and the electric window slides down.

'Hi, Nan,' he says.

'Hello, love, I thought it was your car. Hello, Penelope.'

Penelope? I thought we moved past that years ago.

I say hello and I smile, but it really is through gritted teeth as I'm mad about what she said to Mark last week. But then I remember how worried Mark has been about her and I try to force a smile on to my face.

'We've just been to our marriage class,' says Mark.

'Oh, I'd forgotten about that. I bet Reverend and Mrs Phillips are great at that. It really separates those that want to get married from those that don't. I've heard of several engagements that have been broken off thanks to that class.'

Is it my imagination or was she looking straight at me when she said that?

'Well, we found it very helpful and it just reminded me how compatible we are,' I say.

Mark shoots me a look and I shrug my shoulders. Well, if she is going to play the game, so am I.

'What are you up to, Nan?' asks Mark, not very subtly changing the topic.

'I'm just dropping off some shortbread for a funeral on Monday. I can't make it as I've got the doctor's.'

'The doctors? Is everything all right?' asks Mark.

'Oh yes, love. It's fine. Just routine. We have a lot of that at my age, dear.'

'Do you want us to wait for you and give you a lift home?'

'Oh no, that's all right. I've got to speak to the vicar about something and then the walk will do me the power of good.'

Mark looks like he is torn, as if he is wondering whether he should argue and wait for her, or whether we should go.

'I'll see you tomorrow, when you come to tea,' says Violet.

'Great,' I say. 'See you then.'

'OK, Nan. See you tomorrow,' says Mark.

We both watch her as she makes her way across the car park. She seems to be walking just fine.

'What do you think she's talking to the vicar about?' asks Mark.

'I haven't a clue. Doesn't she sit on different church committees? It's probably just church business.'

Mark doesn't look convinced. Neither am I. I can't help thinking that she knew we'd be here for marriage class and she is going to pump Reverend Phillips for the details. But that is me being just a little narcissistic.

'Mark, I'm sure she's fine and if she wasn't she'd tell you.'

'I know. I should get us home and then you can cook me tea. Like you're supposed to as my wife.'

I roll my eyes at him, seeing as I can't poke him in the ribs while he's reversing. Just because we worked out in the marriage class that we should balance our chores more evenly and that I should help out more with the cooking, does not mean to say that we need to start right away.

Perhaps I should go early to Nanny Violet's tomorrow to have a little chat and actually find out what's going on. Maybe I'm not being narcissistic after all; maybe Mark is wrong, she isn't ill and she just hates me. And I really need to find out why.

chapter Sixteen

I know I said that I was going to find out what was wrong with Nanny Violet but I've bottled it well and truly. And even though Mark had told her we were going round for Sunday afternoon tea I couldn't face it. His brother Howard and his family are going over later and I feel too awkward to be a part of it. I do need to speak to her on her own, but I'll pluck up the courage eventually. Honestly I will.

I've lied and told Mark that he should go and spend some quality time with Violet by himself and that I need to go and sort things out with Lou. Which is not a lie. I have barely spoken to her since she came round for the wine-tasting evening two weeks ago. I sort of thought I'd give her some space for a week, and let her come to tell me she is up the duff. But she hasn't.

With less than a month to go I need to start getting the wedding back on track, and at the moment the bridal party is in disarray and my maid of honour is MIA.

Mark was happy I was going to see Lou as he had told me off for not having gone to see her before now. He's reminded me that she's pregnant, she hasn't got a contagious disease, and that she could probably be a bridesmaid while pregnant. Although he did admit that he didn't know that for a fact as he wasn't an expert on pregnancy.

I could have perhaps called Lou to let her know I was on my way over but I haven't. I guess part of me still thinks that she might have secret friends and this way I'm going to catch her in the act.

Only one way to find out. I press the doorbell and my stomach starts to get butterflies. I don't know why I'm so nervous all of a sudden. I've stood on this very doorstep hundreds, if not thousands, of times before.

'Penny!' says Lou, as she opens the door. 'What are you doing here? Did we have plans? Did I forget?'

'No, no. I was just passing and thought I'd pop in. Unless now isn't convenient?'

I peer down the hallway, straining my ears in case I can hear the chatter of her exciting new friends, but alas it is all quiet on the western front.

'Um, I guess now is fine. Russell's gone food shopping.'

And yet I'm still standing on the doorstop. I can't just barge past her so I smile and raise my eyebrows.

'Sorry, come on in. Did you want a cup of tea?' she asks.

'I would love one, thanks.'

I follow Lou into the kitchen and I look subtly around for any clues that Russell isn't living here any more. After all, I still don't know she is *actually* pregnant; until she tells me, all my conspiracy theories could be plausible.

'So how have you been?' I ask.

'Yeah, fine. *Busy*.'

'Oh?' I say, trying to dig a little deeper. Lou has her back to me and is busying herself preparing the cups with tea bags while the kettle boils.

'Yeah, work and stuff. How are the wedding plans?'

'Good.' How long is it going to take her to tell me her news? Maybe I should try and hurry things along. 'I'm thinking of serving prawns for the starter, with Brie.'

'Sounds delicious,' she says.

Hmm. Is she trying to bluff her way out of it? I'm trying to get a sneaky look at her belly, but she's wearing a hoodie from our college days that should have been thrown out years ago. And just like we used to wear them to look cool and cover our puppy fat, it is doing a good job of being oversized and I can't tell what's hoodie and what's belly.

It looks like I'll have to try harder. She puts the cup of tea in front of me and sits down at the table. Now she has to look at me.

'I really could do with us going bridesmaid-dress shopping.'

She sighs and keeps stirring her tea. 'You know, things are quite busy.'

'Yes, so you keep telling me. Look, if you don't want to be a bridesmaid you can just say. I can always ask someone else,' I say in a tone that was not nonchalant like it was supposed to be. It sounded more like I was a stroppy five-year-old. The truth is I don't want anyone else and she knows it.

'Of course I want to be your bridesmaid.'

'Then what's the problem with dress shopping?'

Lou is looking very intently at her tea and doing a very good job of stirring it.

I look down at mine and then I notice it is a really odd colour. 'Why is my tea so funky looking?'

'It's Roobios.'

'Roobios? For goodness' sake, Lou, will you just tell me you're pregnant.'

Finally, for the first time since I arrived, she is looking me directly in the eye. 'I'm pregnant.'

'I knew it!' I say. I'm just going to gloss over the fact that I had a number of other theories too.

'I thought you'd guessed at the wine tasting. Was it the lack of wine or the chocolate cake?'

'Neither. I didn't put two and two together. It was Mark who guessed.'

'Mark did? Who knew he was so perceptive?'

'I know, go figure. But why didn't you tell me?'

'We were going to. We'd just had our scan and we'd planned to meet you for drinks and then you got engaged and those drinks turned out to be your engagement drinks.'

Oh no. I hijacked Lou's big news night.

'You should have said; it could have been a double celebration.'

'Russell and I both knew how excited you'd be that Mark had finally proposed. We couldn't steal your thunder.'

'But you were drinking that night,' I say, trying to turn my mind back to that night in January.

'Nope, I wasn't. You were though. You were drunk before we even arrived.'

Ah, the perils of drinking too much and not noticing anything around me.

'Well, you still should have told me,' I say, folding my arms defensively.

'I didn't want you to be mad at me.'

'Why would I be mad?'

'Because what if I'm the size of a whale at your wedding?' she shrieks.

'So, why would I mind that?'

'Because it's *your* wedding. You know, your wedding that you've been planning for years. I know how you've planned every little detail to a T. I didn't think a fat me would feature well in the plans.'

'Are you kidding? You can stand next to me and make me look uber skinny.'

'Ha, thanks,' says Lou, laughing. 'It's all your fault anyway.'

'Hang on, what have I got to do with it? You were supposed to be waiting until we tried for stage six at the same time so we could be preggo and on maternity leave together.'

'I know. That was the plan. I came off the pill last year as it kept giving me headaches and Russell and I thought it would be good for when we did want to try. And then Mark finished his exams and you were so convinced on that night out he was going to propose to you.'

'Yes, but that was stage four, not stage six,' I say, trying to keep up.

'Mark and his bloody stages. But don't you remember that night? You were so convinced he was going to pop the question that you bought bottle after bottle of Prosecco and you made me tell everyone how Russell proposed to me. And all the bubbles had gone to my head, and I was feeling all loved up. So by the time we got home one thing led to another and we forgot to use protection. Ha, me at thirty with an accidental pregnancy.'

I don't know if I quite want all the details.

I hate thinking about that night in November. It was so embarrassing. I was all dressed up, expecting Mark to ask me at any second. I kept making sure that my lips were freshly glossed and my make-up was flawless, so that the photos that came post-proposal would be perfect. But by the end of the night I was a sulking and crying mess. It was good to know that at least someone's life changed for the better that night.

'Well, that's pretty cool. Congratulations, by the way.'

'Thank you. I've been dying to tell you.'

'I wish you had – I was beginning to think you'd got new friends.'

'Don't be daft. You know if I was going to drop you I would have got rid of you during your purple hair phase.'

I shudder. Lou knows better than to talk about that. I've only just got my sister to stop calling me Vimto. Thank goodness that tragic hair choice was just before I met Mark or else I don't think he would have fallen for me and we wouldn't now be at stage four.

'So can you, you know, still be my maid of honour?' I ask.

'Of course I can, if you still want me.'

'Yes, of course I bloody do.'

Oh my God. Are those tears in Lou's eyes?

'I'm sorry,' she splutters as she wipes her eyes and laughs at the same time. 'Bloody pregnancy hormones. I used to think they were a myth, but they're really not.'

'Ah, come here and give me a hug.'

We hug and even I get a little choked up. Lou, my bestest buddy in the whole world, is going to give birth to a little person. There is going to be a mini Lou and Russell.

I can't believe that Lou would withhold this magical news just because of my impending wedding.

'I still can't get over that you were scared to tell me,' I say.

'Jeez, really? Don't you remember at my wedding when your sister got pregnant? You told her she was inconsiderate and that she should have waited as she wouldn't be able to drink on my hen do?'

'I said that? Wow.'

I have some vague recollection of something of a fuss with Becky about Lou's wedding but I'd forgotten what it was about.

'And then you said to her that she had better get her baby-making out of the way before you and Mark got engaged, as you didn't want her to ruin the aesthetics of your photos.'

I shift uncomfortably in my chair. I really have been planning this wedding for a long time. I can't even laugh this off like I was joking as I probably wasn't, not even in the slightest.

'I'm sure that's why she gave birth to Ethan and Lily so close together. She was probably fearing your wrath,' says Lou.

I look up at Lou and now it is me that is starting to cry.

'Hey, hey, don't cry, Penny. You're not pregnant too, are you?'

'No,' I say, shaking my head. 'I just can't believe that my best friend wouldn't tell me the biggest thing to happen to her because she was worried that I would be a complete cow about it. Lou, I'm so sorry.'

'Don't be. I haven't really told many people as even though it has been almost six months it's taken a bit of getting used to.'

'I can't believe you're going to have a baby.'

'I know Russell and me as parents – what a scary thought!'

'I think you'll be great parents.'

They will be too. I just know it.

'Ha, we'll see. So now we've got that out of the way. Tell me, aside from the bridesmaid dresses, how are the wedding plans coming along?'

Ah, the wedding. It always comes back to the wedding whenever I see anyone now. I don't want to tell them that I'm barely anywhere with it. I've done all the big things, but that is it. And it's always the little things that make weddings memorable.

'It's going OK. I've, um, oh I've sorted out the flowers since we last spoke,' I say.

'That's great. And you've got the wine sorted?'

'Yeah, kind of.'

I know which ones I want, I'm just currently stalking the wine website waiting for special offers. Fingers crossed it will be soon, as the closer it gets to the wedding, the more I'm starting to develop a nervous twitch about it.

'That's great. It's going to be amazing, I'm sure. I remember the last time I saw your mood board, and all that pretty fabric. Oh, you can tell me about your dress now that Mark isn't here. Is it huge and princess-like? Are you going to be able to fit in the toilet?' asks Lou.

A tear rolls down my cheek.

'Oh my God. You *are* pregnant, aren't you?'

'No,' I say, shaking my head. The tears are really coming thick and fast now. 'It's such a mess.'

'What is?'

'The wedding. It's all going so badly.'

'But I thought you'd done all the big things. And you always knew what you were going to get and you saved so hard for it.'

'That's the problem. I spent the savings.'

'Already? Well, how much more have you got to pay for? I'm sure Mark would give you a bit extra.'

'No, you don't understand. I spent most of the money before we'd even got engaged.'

'On what? Don't tell me you've been buying shoes and hiding them from me.'

'Ten thousand pounds would have got me a lot of Jimmy Choos,' I say, laughing. For a brief moment I'm lost in a walk-in wardrobe where I'm surrounded by ten thousand pounds' worth of Jimmy Choos, aka heaven.

'So what did you spend it on?' asks Lou. 'Pen?'

'Bingo.'

I close my eyes tight so that I can't see the look of disgust on Lou's face, but all I can hear is laughing.

'That's funny, Pen. Nice joke.'

'It's not a joke. I spent just over ten thousand pounds on bingo. I was trying to get the money for a bigger wedding, and now I'm organising our wedding on a shoestring budget. And I go to a gamblers' support group every Tuesday.'

I can't believe how good it feels to get that off my chest.

'Fuckity Fuck. Suddenly my bump at the wedding seems quite small in significance. I think you're going to have to start from the beginning.'

So as Lou puts on the kettle for another cup of funky-tasting tea, I tell her the whole sordid story from A to Z.

I tell her about the bingo rush, the bank account, how Mark doesn't know, and I tell her about the gambling support group and Josh. I tell her, I cry, I eat biscuits and she cuddles me.

When Russell comes home he gets banished to the kitchen and we go into the lounge so that we can talk more.

'I still can't believe it,' says Lou. 'I really can't. I've been so jealous of you with your sensible saving for your wedding. But hey, you're just as screwy as the rest of us.'

'Thanks.'

'Why don't you just do what me and Russell did and put it on the credit card?'

'Because Mark would wonder why I was eternally poor.'

'Well, it sounds like you're doing a good job so far coping with your budget. I would never have known that the venue was so cheap.'

'I know. It's amazing.'

'But what I really don't get is why you don't tell Mark. He'd support you through it.'

'I can't. He'd be crushed. He's so good with money.'

'What if he finds out, though? You're going to be married to him for the rest of your life. What if it just slips out?'

'It doesn't matter as we'll be married by then and he doesn't believe in divorce.'

Lou is pulling a face in horror at me.

'OK, so I haven't thought that far ahead. But if I do a good job with the wedding then he'll never know,' I say.

'I still don't agree with you not telling Mark, but I'll help you with the organising if you like.'

This is why I love Lou. She's not only fun to be with but she'd do anything for anyone.

'Thanks. I might have to take you up on that offer.'

'So what have you got left to do?' she asks.

'Favours, music, bridesmaid dresses, transportation, photographer, cake, suit hire.'

'OK. Wedding favours on a budget – yes?'

'Uh-huh. I'm not averse to making them. Amy, who's doing my flowers, suggested something edible.'

'OK, how about gingerbread hearts?'

'Gingerbread?'

'Yes, it's practically all I've been eating over the last few months. I've been making it too. It's pretty good.'

'And easy?' I ask, as gingerbread to me is just a little too close to the cake family.

'Uh-huh. We can make it a couple of days before.'

Done. Wow. If only I'd told Lou sooner, I bet we could have had everything ticked off by now.

'What's next?'

'Music. You don't happen to know a DJ or a band that will play for free?' I ask.

'Why don't you just do an iPod DJ? You can make a play list.'

I had thought about that. I didn't think my mixing skills would be up to it.

'I don't have anything against it, but I sort of feel like you need someone to get the music going. You know, react to the crowd. Drop a big one when needed.'

Yes, I still listen to Radio 1. I sometimes think I am down with the cool kids, and I know that I am not. I know I am too old for the target demographic.

'Oh my God. I have the best idea,' says Lou.

'What?'

'Do you trust me?'

Now, you'd probably expect me to say yes to this question. But I'll give you a little background. When Lou last asked me this question, I said of course; the next thing I knew I was waking up in hospital with my leg in plaster after Lou had pushed me down a hill in a shopping trolley. In her defence we were steaming drunk.

'You promised you'd never ask me that again,' I say.

'Ah yeah, I forgot. But it is different now. I'm all responsible. I'm going to be a mum. I promise there will be no more broken bones or shopping trolleys on the horizon.'

'OK then. I trust you. Why?'

'Because I've had *the* best idea for a DJ and I'm not going to tell you. You've got your "don't tell the groom"; I think we need a "don't tell the bride". Let's just say it will last about an hour and will fit in perfectly in the middle of two sets of something.'

'Should I be worried?' I ask, wincing.

'No, it will be awesome.'

'It doesn't involve you singing, does it?'

'No, I don't want to scare anyone.'

'Good,' I say. There are cats that can sing better than Lou.

'So all I need to do now is find a band that will play for buttons.'

'I'd play for buttons.'

'Can you play?' I ask hopefully.

'No. But there must be someone we know that has a band.'

'I've racked my brains and I can't think of anyone.'

'Ask around. Someone must know someone.'

'Yeah, maybe.'

'We'll think of something. Oh, this is fun. It's like *Challenge Anneka*. What else do we need?'

I smile at Lou. I can't believe how differently I feel from when I arrived over two hours ago. It's like a big weight has been lifted off my shoulders. Not completely off, it's still there, but my shoulders definitely feel lighter.

I've got that little kernel of hope back that with Lou on my side I may actually pull this off after all.

chapter Seventeen

In three weeks time I'm going to be getting ready to become Mrs Robinson. I'm starting to practise my signature. Perhaps a bit premature as I should be sorting out the remaining details for the wedding that I haven't organised yet, like booking a photographer, cars and a cake, but right now a new signature seems like a top priority.

To tell you the truth, I'm avoiding doing any more organising. I've got £1,200 left in my budget, and although Lou has been really great at suggesting ideas for the favours and everything, there is no escaping that I'm never going to be able to plan the rest of the wedding with such a small amount of money.

The only way that £1,200 sounds like a lot of money is if I was buying penny sweets. But even inflation has hit them since I was a child, and you don't get much change out of five pence any more.

So instead of trying to sort it out like an adult, I've gone back to primary school mode and I'm doodling my new signature.

'Are you ready to go?'

I look up to see Ted standing in the doorway. I'm so into my scrawling that I've forgotten that I am at the museum.

'Yes, ready,' I say.

I jump up from my chair and follow Ted out into the car park.

Today I'm helping out at a fête. All the volunteers are. Lilian, Betty and Nina are doing the afternoon shift and this morning I'm with Ted and Cathy. I volunteered to go with Ted, who is driving down there in one of the museum vehicles.

'She's a beauty,' I say as we get closer.

The green army jeep looks like it is out of an old war movie.

'She's all right. She's a 1944 Willy's Jeep, American,' says Ted.

'Wow, is it really from 1944 and it still runs?'

'Don't look so surprised, Penny. A lot of things made in the forties still run, you know.'

I smile at Ted; I'm guessing he was made before the forties.

I climb into the jeep and do up the seat belt, which is a small fabric belt that goes around my middle. I'm just hoping we don't crash as somehow I don't think this thing has air-bags.

'Hold on to your hat,' says Ted.

He pulls some levers and the jeep starts as if by magic. The engine is really noisy and it sounds like it is going to conk out at any moment. Instead of being phased by it Ted revs the engine and then suddenly we're away and I grab on to the door for dear life.

Who knew a vehicle over sixty years old could go so fast? Or at least it feels fast. It reminds me of being in a tuk-tuk in Thailand. Overexposed to the elements and vulnerable in a motor vehicle. But it sure is fun.

When we reach the field and pull to a stop, I clap my hands with delight and shout 'Again, again!', just like the Tellytubbies.

It was so much fun. The noise, the movement, the petrol smell of the engine – it was great.

'Thanks, Ted, that was ace,' I say to him as I climb out. My legs are a bit like jelly and I'm trying to make them go rigid so I can walk on them.

'You're welcome. It's nice to give the girl a good run.'

'Is this the only time you take her out?'

'Oh no, we do it about once a month. Usually around the block, just to make sure she doesn't seize up.'

A comedy cartoon light bulb pings in my head as I am

suddenly hit with a brainwave. I notice Cathy is busy setting up shop stock and I decide this might be a good time to help her.

'Need any help?' I ask as casually as I can, when all I really want to do is beg her to let me have the jeep on my wedding day.

'Thanks, Penny, that would be fantastic.'

She hands me a box of toy soldiers and I start laying them out on the table as artistically as I can.

'How was the jeep ride?' asks Cathy.

'I loved it. So much fun,' I say. I wasn't going to get a better opportunity than that to drop my hiring the jeep into conversation.

'In fact, I really loved it. I was just wondering. There isn't any way I could hire the jeep for my wedding, is there?'

'I'm sorry, Penny, we don't do that as we're not insured.'

'Oh, OK.' I'm gutted. The jeep would have been perfect for the wedding. I try to concentrate on unpacking the toys as neatly as I can, all the while racking my brains over how I'm going to beat the jeep with a cooler wedding car.

'You know, we do take the car out once a month for a test run.'

'I know. Ted was saying,' I say sadly.

'Well, let's say that we just happened to drive it to a church and happened to drive it back. Maybe picking you up along the way?'

'I'm listening,' I say.

'Now, we can have passengers in it, as long as no money changes hands.'

'I see. And if I was perhaps to give a donation to the museum?'

'Or to the *Friends* of the Museum,' says Cathy.

'OK, to the Friends of the Museum. Do you think that the little trip could be organised for the 18th of May?'

'I don't see why not. As long as Ted agrees. But to be honest, I don't see that being a problem; he really only needs the smallest excuse to get it out of the vehicle shed.'

'So a donation of how much do you think the Friends would like?'

'Thirty pounds to cover the petrol.'

'How about I say fifty pounds to include wear and tear?'

'Done,' says Cathy.

I look over at the jeep parked in the centre of the field and I smile. I can't wait to see our guests' faces when I pull up in that. I'm not going to think about how I'm going to get in and out of it in my lovely ivory dress, though. But beggars quite literally can't be choosers.

I spend the day in an old army surplus tent telling everyone how wonderful a day out the museum is, and I can't help coming over in a warm glow when I talk about the place.

It's been great volunteering there before the wedding as I already feel connected to the building. I'm finally starting to get excited about our wedding. I have a feeling that it is going to be absolutely perfect.

I'm still staring at the jeep, caught up in a daydream where I've got Mark to wear an old American GI uniform for the wedding day, when I see a distinctive blue rinse coming towards the tent.

Nanny Violet. What is she doing here?

OK, so it is a local fête, and technically Violet lives locally, but I just hadn't even considered she would be here.

I frantically look around the tent for a way out but the sides are fixed down and Violet is heading this way. I bend down. Maybe I can peel back one of the tent flaps and crawl out under it.

Dammit, I mutter under my breath. It is well and truly pegged down. I slowly make my way towards the trestle table at the front of the tent and sit under it. I'm sure no one will notice me underneath the tablecloth.

From my vantage point under the table I can see Violet's trademark red patent shoes. I love those shoes.

'Violet, how are you?' asks Ted.

What? Did I hear that right? Violet knows Ted. What the . . . ? I curl myself up into a smaller ball. There is no way that they can know I am under the table.

'Hello, Theodore. I'm very well, thank you, and how are you?'

'Can't complain, really. My hip is playing up, but at our age whose isn't?'

I can hear Violet laugh, or at least I think it is Violet as there are no other shoes that I can see. It just doesn't sound like her, it sounds almost . . . flirty. Oh no. I wrinkle my nose in disgust. They can't be flirting, can they?

'So you volunteer at the museum, do you?' asks Violet.

'Oh yes, every Saturday without fail. You should come down sometime, have a look round. I'm sure you'd enjoy it. We've got a whole section about this area during the war.'

Oh no. I really hope Violet doesn't come to the museum before the wedding. She'd definitely tell Mark if she saw me there; she'd not be able to help herself. She wouldn't understand why I'm volunteering. It's not like it's really in my character. And Mark would be confused about why I've been volunteering and not at Zumba. Then I'd have to tell him the truth.

'Perhaps one day,' says Violet.

Her voice has changed and there is no longer a flirty tone to it; now it just sounds sad and distant.

'Bye, Theodore.'

'Bye, Violet.'

The patent red shoes walk out of my line of vision and after counting to twenty I think it is safe to leave my little cubby-hole.

'What are you doing down there?' asks Ted as I make a very ungraceful exit from underneath the table. I am starting to feel every bit the twenty-nine years I am.

'I dropped a pencil,' I say, holding up a pencil in my hand. Luckily I'd been holding one when I'd ducked under the table.

'Was that a friend of yours?' I ask casually, hoping that I can get to the bottom of the flirty tone.

'Oh, Violet? She and I go way back. We were friends during the war. I was a friend of her husband's.'

I'm about to chip in about Mark's granddad Albert, but then Ted would know that I'd hidden from Violet and get suspicious.

'I see her around every so often and I think it makes her sad to see me as it reminds her of the war,' he says.

I've never spoken to Violet about her time during the war, but Mark says that she doesn't talk about it. My gran always did; she was a hairdresser and she had hundreds of funny wartime anecdotes. But not Violet.

'Why does it make her sad?' I ask.

'Her husband was shot and killed not long after they were married. He was in a unit that landed on the beaches in Port-en-Bessin, Normandy.'

I can't help but gasp. I'd met Violet's late husband, Albert. Who was this man killed on D-Day?

'Ever so sad it was. She was like a changed woman after that. She stopped training to be a nurse and went away to secretarial college.'

My head is starting to explode. Firstly, I find out that Violet was married before Albert and then I find out Violet was training to be a nurse?

'I didn't really see her much after that. She remarried, of course, but we still see each other every so often when our paths cross.'

I look at Ted and I wonder for a minute what those years must have been like. Your friends being killed all around you; families' lives torn apart. Yet those that lived coped and got on with their lives. I doubt our generation could do that with such humility.

I spend most of the morning pondering about who Violet's first husband was and whether Mark knew about him. It isn't really the kind of subject that would have come up between us. I don't think that even I could engineer it into a topic of conversation.

Maybe that's why Violet is suddenly acting so strange. Maybe all the talk of weddings is making her think of her weddings plural, and her two dead husbands. Poor Violet. It must be awful to have experienced such loss.

'Your afternoon relief is here,' says Ted, snapping me out of my daydream.

I see Betty walking towards us carrying a wicker basket with a flask sticking out of it. And after one cup of extremely strong tea and two delicious homemade scones I make my way home to see Mark.

It feels funny walking in and seeing Mark and knowing what I do now about Violet. I don't really think that I can let him in on my insight – there would be far too much to explain: who Ted is; why I'm volunteering in the first place. I just have to put it to the back of my mind like the rest of the 'don't tell the groom' information.

'Hey, you were a long time at the gym,' says Mark.

'I had to run some wedding errands.'

Technically that's true: we do now have transportation. 'We have wedding transport.'

'Interesting that you use the word transport. You didn't say car, which makes me think horse and cart.' Mark reaches up and pulls me on to his lap.

'My lips are sealed,' I say, smiling.

'Any way I can unseal them?'

He starts kissing me in a way that well and truly unseals my lips. Unfortunately for Mark though, I can't talk when we're kissing.

'The main question is, am I going to like it?' asks Mark.

'You're going to love it,' I say, smiling and sliding off his lap on to the sofa next to him.

'Great. Well, you'll be pleased to know I followed orders and got the suits today. Nice choice.'

Wow, men finding what they're going to wear for the wedding is far easier than it is for women. I'd given Mark a choice of three suits ranging from light grey to charcoal, and more importantly they were all in budget.

'Glad you liked them. Which ones did you go for?'

'The charcoal. You've just got to phone the shop and tell them what colour cravat you want us to have.'

I nod, but I'm too lost in the daydream where Mark is standing there in the charcoal suit waiting for me at the end of the altar.

'So how are we doing with the budget then?' asks Mark.

If ever there was a way to snap me straight out of a daydream, it is the word budget.

'We're in budget,' I say desperately, hoping to get off this topic quickly.

'Really? It's just that the way you always talked about what you wanted for the wedding made me feel that the costs would start to spiral out of control.'

'Well, they're not,' I say, a little defensively. Just because he is the accountant doesn't mean to say I can't budget too.

'I didn't mean it horribly. I just thought that once you started to realise how much everything costs we'd have to dig a little deeper. I guess I've been waiting for you to ask me for more money.'

Mark would have given me more money? Now he tells me. I wonder how much he could give me and whether it would be enough to cover the magician or the doves. Or even something as basic as a band or a photographer.

The more I think about how the money can be spent, the more I keep thinking what we have still to do. Wait, correction: what *I* have left to do.

'Don't worry, Mark, it's all under control.'

'Great. More to spend on the honeymoon, then.'

Oh, my God. I haven't even thought about the honeymoon. Well, not since before we got engaged. I've been so preoccupied with wondering how there's going to be a wedding that I've forgotten all about what comes next.

'Don't worry, I'm going to treat you to the honeymoon. I don't think our fifteen grand could have included that,' says Mark.

I wince. It would have done if I hadn't gambled it away.

'So where are we going to go?' I've always seen myself on a tropical beach somewhere, strutting around in my bikini, with a perfect tan, telling anyone who I met that I had a husband.

'Well, I was thinking that I could not tell you. You know, get you back for the "don't tell the groom" stuff.'

I suck my cheeks in. How would I know what to pack? I don't think Mark quite understands that a beach holiday can be so different depending on where it is. What if it was somewhere hot and humid like Malaysia, where I'd need a ton of anti-frizz products to keep my hair under control in the humidity? Or if it was more of a backpacky place like Thailand I'd tone down my dress and shoe collection.

'Don't worry, I'm going to tell you. I don't want you packing absolutely everything under the sun just because you don't know where you're going.'

Mark has clearly seen the look of horror on my face.

'So,' I say, tickling him so that he has to tell me quicker.

'Mexico.'

'*Mexico?* I have always wanted to go to Mexico.'

I have, honestly. I want to climb all the pyramids and the ruins of the Aztecs and the Mayans and I want to go diving with turtles. And the beaches. I'll need some more bikinis for the beaches.

'I know you have; that's why we're going.'

God, I love Mark. He really does know everything about me. Or at least everything I've let him know. Once the wedding is over, I am never keeping a secret from Mark again.

I lean over and kiss him in thanks.

'Mexico,' I say again. 'I'll have to dig out my Español phrase book.'

'I guess you will. Oh, by the way, we got an RSVP back from Michelle and Graham.'

I do a mental flick through my Rolodex of Mark's friends to remember exactly who they are. I think they're university friends or cricket friends.

'Can they come?'

'No, they can't come as they've got another wedding to go to.'

Yes, I scream in my head. I nearly do a victory lap with my arms in an aeroplane around the living room. That's what I want to do. At this stage in proceedings anyone who doesn't come is all extra money in the budget. That seventy pounds we've just saved means the difference between me buying my wedding shoes from a shoe discount shop or from Next. I'm so over the Jimmy Choos, I have resolved that they'll never be.

'But they have sent us £50 worth of John Lewis vouchers.'

'Blimey, that was nice of them. I don't even think I've met them.'

I wonder if it would be too cheeky to ask Mark for the John Lewis vouchers. After all, I do still need my wedding shoes and maybe that would be an option.

'I'm sure you'll have fun spending that after the wedding. That reminds me, quite a lot of people have been asking what we want for a wedding present, seeing as you didn't put a gift list in with the invitations.'

I hadn't put one in deliberately. With me having spent an awful lot of money it somehow feels wrong to get everyone to give us lovely presents.

'I forgot,' I say, lying.

'That isn't like you. I thought you had your china pattern picked out already in John Lewis?'

'I had.' It's a beautiful Jasper Conran for Wedgwood pattern. It was a classic design which I hoped would be classy and timeless. But somehow it doesn't seem important any more.

'Well, I had an idea about that and the holiday. I'm looking to book it through a company that can add extras to the honeymoon.'

I start to feel uncomfortable about people contributing to our honeymoon when I've blown so much money. It feels wrong. 'I don't think we should get people to pay for the honeymoon.'

'Oh, we're not. It's excursions on our honeymoon.'

'Excursions?' That could be interesting.

'Yeah, look.'

Mark reaches over and picks up his laptop and pulls up the window of a fancy-looking holiday company.

'What we do is when we've picked our resort we just choose

all the activities we want to do. They have the prices next to them and people can either pay for the entire excursion or part of it. Look, we can tick a candlelit dinner at the lighthouse restaurant.'

'Oh, that looks fabulous.'

'Or we could go snorkelling with turtles on a catamaran cruise.'

'I want to do that,' I say excitedly.

'Why don't you check you like the resort I've picked first and then we can look at what we want to put on the list. Then, if you're happy, I'll phone the company and book the trip. We can email everyone and let them know about the list.'

Just like that, easy peasy. See how organised my fiancé is? If he was organising the wedding he'd have dotted all the i's and crossed the t's by now. He wouldn't have a list as long as his arm still to do.

'Just three weeks and a day more and we'll be on the plane to Mexico,' says Mark.

It sounds so simple when Mark says it like that. If only he knew the truth.

chapter eighteen

I haven't looked at my mood boards for a long time. They're entangled in my head with the brightly coloured electronic balls flying across my computer screen. It was almost like I stuck something on the mood boards and then tried to make the dream come true by playing bingo.

It all seems so silly now. I've got mood boards and Pinterest boards full of enough stuff to make Kim Kardashian's wedding look like it was on a tight budget.

None of these details matter. Not the wedding favours from Jo Malone or the box of flip-flops for my female guests to change into for the evening, to soothe their tired feet. Well, maybe just the Swarovski crystal-emblazoned knickers with 'Mrs Robinson' sewn on the bum for the wedding night. But apart from those, it was all the puff that seemed important but in reality no one would ever remember. Or at least I can't remember it from any wedding I've ever been to.

The bit I always, without fail, remember about weddings is the first dance. It's my favourite part of a wedding. It's the first time the bride and groom are finally reunited after running around like headless chickens all day. After the first minute or so of awkward swaying and after other people flock to the dance floor, I always watch the looks the bride and groom give each other. You can tell a lot from those looks.

Now when I stare at my mood boards it doesn't make me lust in the same way it used to and my fingers don't get twitchy wanting to go in search of the bingo balls.

Maybe I've grown up over the last few months, or maybe I've just realised that a wedding is not about the day but a whole lifetime of marriage. Whatever it is, I actually feel like I've changed as a person. Cue emotional Westlife music that would appear if this was some cheesy segment on an *X Factor*-type show.

The worst thing about all these revelations is that I'm dying to tell Mark. He'd be so proud of me, his irresponsible fiancée all grown up. Only to tell him would mean telling him the whole story and he would be full of disappointment and frowns. Mark is not an attractive frowner.

I give the mood boards one last look before I pick them up and start ripping them to pieces. All the nights I spent carefully collating them and now I'm ruining them in seconds. It feels amazingly liberating.

I just about stop myself from burning them. It might be cathartic, but I'm sure that Mark wouldn't be too impressed if I burnt the house down.

The doorbell goes and I quickly pick up the little pieces of my fantasy wedding and put them into the bin where they belong.

I open the door and I'm comforted to see both Lou and the big box of chocolate fingers in her hand. I'm going to gloss over the bag of grapes she's holding too, as surely they're for a sick relative she's visiting afterwards.

'Hiya,' I say. 'Dinner is almost ready.'

By this, I mean that I've got the takeaway menu out of the drawer and I have put it on the kitchen table. It was ready to read as soon as Lou got here.

'Great, let's order. I'm so hungry. This eating for two is so difficult.'

Lou has come round to keep me company as Mark is off on his stag do, or stag weekend that it has become. He's gone pheasant shooting in Scotland. That is all he is doing, or at least that is all that I'm being told he is doing, as quite frankly I'd rather not know. I'm more than happy with a 'what goes on on tour stays on tour' mentality. Mainly because I know that Mark won't do anything dodgy, and I'd rather not know that he had some strange woman's breasts in his face. But pheasant shooting, that's all men in wax jackets and cigars. No boobs there.

After deliberating over the menu for a very long time, we settle on a variety of Thai dishes and I phone through the order.

'I hope it doesn't take too long, I'm worried that the baby will start eating me,' says Lou.

'Have some grapes,' I say, pushing the bag across to her. It still is weird bringing fruit to a girlie night in.

'Thanks. I know I broke the cardinal rule of nights in, in that they aren't carbs or chocolate, but I thought I'd better balance out the crap for the little nut's sake.'

I'm not the only one doing the changing around here. Since Lou shared her news with me I've started to notice changes in her too.

'Right then. Now I've got my vitamins in me again, what's on tonight's agenda?' asks Lou.

That's a very good question. I've had the foresight to write a list of what we needed to do. Or at least I started to write a list and it scared me as it didn't seem to be ending. Instead I'd decided we should just wing it.

I feel like we deserve to wing it as we've already had a really productive day. Today not only did I get Lou and my sister Becky to finally go bridesmaid-dress shopping but we also bought dresses. Gorgeous purple floaty dresses. I'm just slightly disappointed that Lou actually doesn't look like a whale in hers and instead she looks radiant. Maybe that's the problem with having a pregnant bridesmaid: the fact that they glow.

And this afternoon, Lou agreed to lend me her Polaroid-type camera so that guests can put their photos in the guest-book. Cool, huh? It might not be a photo booth that posts photos to Facebook, but I'm sure our guests will be pleased that I made the sacrifice as now they will have something to eat instead.

'Shall we start with the wedding cake?' I suggest.

'Good choice. Naturally you're having chocolate fudge cake?'

'I thought you weren't eating it?'

'Well, this trimester seems to be better for the cake. So that's a yes?'

'That's a hmm. I don't think my mum would approve.'

'OK, well, perhaps doing the whole flavour thing is a bit premature. Maybe we could start with the costs and stuff first?'

'Sensible plan. Now I can't afford to spend much on it, so that rules out every bakery and cake-maker. I'm left with two options: either I make one or I buy one from a supermarket.'

'Make one? You and baking don't mix. And don't you look

at me. I'm going to be up to my eyes in gingerbread-making in the run-up to your wedding.'

'It would definitely be the cheapest option,' I say, looking hopefully at Lou. She, at least, can bake a cake that comes out of the oven edible.

'Would it really, though? Do you have the right size tins?'

'No, but how much could they be?' I ask.

I swivel the laptop round and Google cake tins. Blimey. No wonder people charge that much for wedding cakes when tins are that expensive. When am I ever going to use the 15 cm cake tin needed for the top tier again? To justify that type of price I'd need to be baking a lot of those little cakes.

'OK, perhaps it isn't the cheapest option. Looks like it's a supermarket cake then.'

'What about cupcakes? Aren't they cheaper?' asks Lou.

'Nope.'

I had already Googled that and wished that I was blessed with the ability to bake cupcakes. For such a little cake they were surprisingly expensive, and if only I had a talent I could have made some money on the side for my wedding fund.

'Right, show me these supermarket cakes then.'

We surf our way through a number of different supermarket sites. The cakes are all pretty and some of them get really good reviews. It's just that theyr'e missing that little (as the French woman inside me would say) *Je ne sais quoi.*

'I think that the best option would be to get the plain ones from M&S and then we can decorate them,' says Lou.

'But how would we decorate them? And look, we can't stack them on each other.'

I'm exasperated. I know that half an hour ago I was singing the virtues of how much I'd changed, but you know what? I haven't. You see, the cake is one of the few things about weddings I actually remember. From Phil and Jane's profiterole tower to Lou and Russell's tiered chocolate fudge cake with fudge flowers all over.

Which means I have to come up with something equally fabulous. I sigh an overly dramatic sigh and Lou gives me that look. It's the look that says don't give up. She's given it to me a number of times over the years. From when we were trying to find a man to snog on Saturday night when were at sixth-form college to when we tried spinning at the gym.

'Perhaps you need some inspiration.'

Lou steals the computer away from me and starts tapping away furiously.

The Google home page transforms into large thumbnails of amazing-looking cakes. They aren't your average cakes; they are all weird and wonderful, unusual shapes. There is a cake in the shape of a mountain with hikers on top, one that looks like a Disney castle, and another in the shape of a giant guitar.

'Who has these cakes?' I ask in disbelief.

'I think they're kind of cool,' says Lou.

'Yeah, I'm not saying they're not, but I could never afford something like this.'

'Well, let's think about this laterally. What could we make? Let's think of hobbies you have.'

'Mark has golf . . . I have . . . well, I'm not having bingo balls.'

I can see Lou's trying not to laugh. A cake of hobbies wasn't really me or Mark.

'What about your honeymoon? We could make it Mexican.'

My head is suddenly confused with cakes made of rolled fajitas and topped with jalapeños. Or worse, tequila-flavoured cake in the colours of a bright poncho, with a sombrero on top.

I'm wrinkling my nose up in disapproval while Lou is hot on the keys again. The next thing I know she's brought up the M&S cakes website again.

'Here: this is my idea,' says Lou.

I look at the screen and all I see are the rectangular iced cakes used solely for cutting extra slices.

'I know they're cheap but we can't use them,' I say.

'Sure we can. We get a load of them and we stack them up

like a pyramid you know – like the Mexican pyramids. We'll get some edible gold icing dusting glitter and *voilà*. You'll have Mexican cake.'

I look at Lou and I look back at the cutting cakes. I turn my head sideways and squint my eyes. It could just work. Or it could be a disaster. But at least this way we can have lots of different-flavoured cake.

'OK, sod it. Let's do it. But you're in charge.'

'As long as I'm not baking then I don't care,' says Lou.

Taking back control of the laptop, I start adding the cake to my virtual basket. To make the pyramid I reckon that I will need six sets of cutting cake, and the bonus is that they are on three for two, so it only costs me £42. Bargain.

And ten minutes later I've bought the edible gold dusting glitter and two claydough figures that look vaguely like Mark and me.

We are on a roll.

By the time the Thai food turns up I've even bought a flower cutter so that we can make our own table confetti. I'm going to gloss over the fact that it means every night from now until the wedding I'm going to be punching cardboard flowers. But again, I need it to look like I've put some thought into this wedding.

'Now we just need to sort out the music for the reception,' I say, shovelling a spoonful of Pad Thai into my mouth.

'OK, how much money have you got for it?'

'About five hundred pounds.'

Lou has her game face on. Which is a bit like the 'don't give up' face, only with a more furrowed brow.

'What about reggae?' she asks.

Thoughts of calypso drums and brightly coloured shirts pop into my head as well as the unmistakeable smell of ganja. Lou and I went to the Notting Hill Carnival in our early twenties and the three have never been separated in my head since then.

I've decided the wrinkle nose is very handy. It means that I don't have to say anything any more and Lou knows exactly what I'm thinking.

'What about this woman?' she asks.

'She's a wedding singer? I don't think I like the idea of just one person by themselves. I think if I'm going to do it, it has to be a full band.'

Lou's brows are getting ever more furrowed and I'm worried that I am causing stress to her unborn baby.

'How about this? They're a swing quartet. They're six hundred pounds. Is that too much?'

'What do they play?' I ask, my ears pricking up at something being within budget.

'Let me see. Here you go. "Fly Me to the Moon", "I Get a Kick Out of You", they even do stuff like "Twist and Shout".'

'They sound perfect! Have they got a phone number?'

'Yep,' says Lou, nodding her head. 'And they're not booked the night of your wedding.'

'Read it out to me!'

I'm so excited I might wee myself. I never thought we'd actually find an affordable band. And to think I was going to pay two thousand pounds for the full seventeen-piece band when I could have booked these guys. We are streaming their sample songs online and they sound pretty good.

Lou reads me out the number and I hit Call.

Please, please let them be in. Although if they're any good I guess they'll probably be out playing a gig tonight. Please, please let them be out. Answerphone. *Yes,* I smile. They're clearly good. Or people love them because they're cheap.

'Hi. Um, my name is Penny Holmes. I'm getting married in two weeks' time and I know it's ridiculously short notice, but I see from your website that you're free and I wondered if I could hire you?'

I start waffling on about where the wedding is being held and how excited I am, and I only just manage to fit in the number before the second beep. If they ever call me back it will be a miracle.

'What's left on the list?' asks Lou.

'Aside from presents, which I'm planning to get tomorrow, I've mainly got stuff for me to sort out. Wedding shoes, who's going to do my hair and make-up.'

'I can do your hair for you if you like. And I'm sure your sister can do your make-up. She's still the only person I know who can apply liquid eyeliner.'

'That's true,' I say.

My sister has got off quite lightly with the whole wedding planning. Mainly because I haven't been able to tell her what is going on. I'm sure she would be quite relieved if all she had to do was do the make-up.

'Have you looked at shoes on eBay?' asks Lou.

'I might be broke, but there's no way I'm going to put my feet into other people's shoes when they've been worn.'

Yuck, imagine that. You'd never know where those sweaty feet had been.

'You do get new shoes on eBay too,' says Lou.

'I don't really like eBay, though. It all gets a bit too tense for me, and at the last minute I find myself panic-buying and bidding way over what it's worth.'

And I don't say it to Lou, but it is too much like online bingo for me. For some reason bidding on an online auction doesn't feel like I'm spending real money and that, as we all know, is extremely dangerous for me.

'OK, what about Amazon?'

'I need shoes, not books,' I say, in exasperation.

'Amazon sells shoes. Look.'

I stare at the computer screen in disbelief. There, in all

shades of ivory are pretty wedding shoes, and – *Wow!* – at an amazing price to boot. Twenty pounds for a pair of shoes. How did I not know about this before?

I don't really care if they're last season's wedding shoes. At this rate I'm just pleased I'll be getting married with something on my feet that isn't my favourite Converse (and my mum has already forbidden me from doing that). Too bad I didn't have the giant princess dress as then she would never know what was under it.

'Those ones. I want those ones,' I say, pointing at the screen like a small child. They're beautiful peep-toes with not too high a heel. They are a dark ivory colour, just like my dress, and they have a small glittery bow above the peep-toe.

I mentally add 'Get a pedicure' to my list of ever-increasing things to do before the wedding. It would be just my luck if I forget and slip my foot into the shoe the day of the wedding and see my half-and-half nail situation. Half real nail, half old nail polish from the last time I wore open-toed sandals, which was for my work Christmas party.

Feeling suddenly decisive for the first time in this whole wedding-planning process, I click Purchase. With one-click Checkout, the shoes are now winging their way to me. I'm not even going to think about the possibility that they won't fit; I'll leave that drama for when the postman knocks on my door.

The sound of The Lemonheads fills the room as 'Mrs Robinson' starts to play. I don't think I was even thinking about becoming Mrs Robinson; perhaps it is tapping into my subconscious mind. Scary.

'Are you going to answer your phone?' asks Lou, passing it to me.

It is then that I realise that The Lemonheads is coming from the phone and not my head. I don't have time to worry about my new ringtone as the caller's number isn't in my phone and my first thought is that there has been a terrible shooting in Scotland. Overly dramatic, me? Never.

'Hello,' I say cautiously.

'Hello, is that Penny?'

Oh my God. It's a proper man's voice. He sounds just like a policemen.

'Yes, this is Penny.'

I'm so nervous that something has happened to Mark that I almost drop the phone in surprise when the man introduces himself as Chris from the band.

'We're just on a break at a gig, so I can't chat for long. But we are free on the 18th of May – we recently had a cancellation. Bride pulled out of the wedding. So we'd be delighted to play for you. Did you want to come and watch us before you confirm?'

'I would love to, but I don't think I've got any free time between now and the wedding, so I'll just have to trust what I saw on the internet. There is just one thing. Would you be able to play "Mrs Robinson"?'

'The Simon and Garfunkel song?'

'I was thinking more like The Lemonheads' version?'

'I'm sure we could put something together.'

'That would be amazing,' I say.

'OK, great. Well, in that case I'll pencil you in and I'll give you a ring in the week to talk deposits and song lists.'

'Great! I'm so happy I could kiss you!'

Did I just say that out loud? I'm going to die on the spot when I meet him now.

'Don't do that. That's why the other bride had to cancel her wedding. Not that she kissed me – it was some other fella. But anyway, I'll give you a ring in the week.'

'Thanks, Chris.'

I put the phone down on the table and just stare at it.

'Get you and your new ringtone,' says Lou, laughing.

'In my defence, that must have been Mark. But at least it reminded me to ask the band if they could play that song.'

I can't believe it. All the pieces of this wedding puzzle are falling into place. And so what if it doesn't look anything like my extravagant mood boards? It is still going to be the best wedding ever.

chapter nineteen

Waking up the next morning feels strange for a number of reasons. Firstly, I'm not hung over. Which in all the years I've known Lou has only happened on a few occasions after a night in with her. Pregnant Lou, and soon-to-be Mummy Lou is going to take a *lot* of getting used to.

It's also strange as when I roll over to Mark's side of the bed it's empty and cold. There isn't the head-shaped dent in the pillows and there isn't the smell of his aftershave on them either. Not that I smell his pillows or anything. It's just that sometimes when he gets up and showers first, I roll on to his side of the bed as I'm convinced it's more comfy, and the first thing that hits me is the smell of Hugo Boss. It's the second nicest thing to wake up to, the first being actual Mark.

I know it sounds stupid to say that I miss Mark as he only

went yesterday morning. But I do really miss him. And I don't think it's because he's away; I think it's because I haven't been able to open up to him lately, which is making me miss him more.

But this is the last-ever secret I'm keeping from Mark. Once the wedding is out of the way there will be no other secrets that I keep from him. I mean it. I will even tell him about my secret shoe stash in the spare room. I will, honestly.

Without the excuse of a hangover to legitimise my lie-in, I really should get up. I don't want to get out of bed, but I have to as I promised Mark that I'd go and chat to Nanny Violet.

I haven't seen her since the time we were at the fête, and then I only saw her bright red shoes. And with the wedding only two weeks away I really want to get to the bottom of why she's acting so strangely around me. It was her insistence that we get married quickly and now it seems like she's getting cold feet.

Maybe I'll just go back to sleep for ten more minutes; after all, she'll be at church for hours yet.

By the time I finally summon the courage to go over to Nanny Violet's house it is after two o'clock in the afternoon. I found lots of important things to do at home like tidy out the kitchen cupboards and deep-clean the fridge. All things that really needed doing two weeks before I got married. And Mark says I can't prioritise tasks properly.

I ring the doorbell and the first thought that pops into my head is 'Please don't be in'. Followed by my second thought, that I'm the meanest woman alive for thinking that. This is an old widow who looks forward to her relatives visiting her at the weekend and I want to be anywhere but here.

'Ah, Penelope. How nice to see you. Do come in,' says Violet, opening the door.

I smile at Nanny Violet, but she's turned and is racing up the hallway to the kitchen before I can do my usual air kiss. Something is definitely not right.

I follow her into her kitchen. The kitchen is always roasting hot, no matter what the outside temperature is, as the Aga is permanantly on. Usually there's something comforting about sitting in Nanny Violet's kitchen but today there seems to be a chill in the air, and with the Aga on it has to be coming from Violet.

'Did you want a cup of tea, love?'

'Yes, that would be great. Thank you.'

I'm hovering in the doorway, not too sure whether I should sit down at the little breakfast bar or whether we're going to go into the formal lounge that Violet keeps for Sundays and visitors. It is Sunday, I suppose, and I am a visitor, so I just continue to hover.

'Why don't you go and take a seat in the sitting room and I'll bring it through.'

'Are you sure?' I ask.

'Yes, yes. Go and sit down.'

It sounds a bit like an order and I go into the lounge.

I obviously haven't been here for a while as everything seems just a little bit different. I can't put my finger on it at first but then it dawns on me; the floral wallpaper has been replaced by a deep yellow paint. It suddenly makes the room feel warm and homely.

And look at those photos. Along the wall behind the sofa are a series of framed pictures of Violet's grandchildren and great-grandchildren. Phew, I'm even in one of the photos. I'm sitting on Mark's lap and we're gazing lovingly into each other's eyes. I have no memory of the photo being taken.

I know the photo must have been taken on Christmas Day as I'm wearing my ridiculously lovely reindeer jumper that everyone in the world, apart from me, hates. Mark says he takes offence to it as the red nose on the reindeer hovers where my left nipple is in real life, and he says that he has difficulty not just reaching out and giving it a squeeze. I think he's worried that other men might follow suit.

I must have had one Bailey's too many on that Christmas Day as I wasn't even aware of anyone with a camera. Except maybe Mark's brother, Howard. But surely he couldn't have taken these wonderful photos, could he?

'There you go,' says Violet, entering the room. She places

my cup of tea on the coffee table before she takes up her normal position in the armchair.

'I love the new decoration,' I say, as I sit down on the rigid sofa. You can always tell when a sofa isn't sat on very much as your bum doesn't mould properly into the seat.

'Thank you, dear. Howard did it for me. I'm afraid he had it forced on him as little Rose drew on the wallpaper with crayons. To tell you the truth I'd always hated the wallpaper anyway. My husband had a number of talents, but hanging wallpaper straight was not one of them and the more I sat in this room the more I noticed.

'Have a cake, dear,' she says, taking the plate of cakes off the tray.

Oh, I really am in the doghouse as far as Violet is concerned. She's only gone and bought in Viennese Whirls. I hate them with a passion and she knows it. I just find the cream so sickly. But not taking a cake in Violet's house is a sin in itself, so I reach over and take one anyway.

'Did Howard take the photos?' I ask.

'Yes, he's quite good, isn't he? Ever since Caroline bought him that fancy camera at Christmas he's been inseparable from it. You should see the photos he shows me of the children. Poor little loves. I bet being at home for them is worse then being a celebrity on the red carpet.'

The whole Howard and camera thing had passed me by. I

guess we haven't seen them a lot lately. Maybe I'll pop round and see them after this. Not that Howard will be there though – he'll be doing goodness knows what with my husband-to-be. I wonder if I can ask his wife about him taking the photos for the wedding as she wears the trousers in their relationship anyway, from what I can tell.

I bite into the shortbread that would be so delicious if that was all that was in it, and then the taste of the warm cream and jam hits me. They're wrong, wrong, wrong.

'So how are the wedding plans going? Getting any last-minute jitters?'

I'm ignoring the hopeful tone in Violet's voice like she is willing me to be having second thoughts.

'No. No jitters. I'm just really excited. I can't believe that I'm going to get married in two weeks!'

'I know. It will come round before you know it.'

'I hope it doesn't come round too quickly. I still feel like I have loads to do before the big day, and I've got the hen do next weekend.'

'It wasn't like that in my day. We didn't even have a hen do. Well-wishers just popped in for a cup of tea. Now it's all Blackpool and Vegas. I watch the telly. Big waste of money, if you ask me.'

I guess things were really different then. You didn't know, like Violet, if your husband was ever going to come back from the front line. I guess hen parties would have seemed too trivial back then.

I desperately want to ask Violet about the conversation I overheard with her and Ted, and what he told me after. But I can't think of a clever way to manipulate the conversation.

'Mind you, weddings are a big waste of money too these days, if you ask me. They don't seem to last five minutes before they ditch each other and are on to the next.'

'I agree with you that people do spend too much on weddings, but not everyone gives up on their marriage. A lot of people still have long happy marriages.'

I see Violet raising her eyebrows. Does she honestly think that Mark and I won't be together this time next year?

'You don't have anything to worry about with me and Mark; we're like two peas in a pod.'

'Are you, now?' asks Violet.

She holds my gaze as she drinks her tea and it makes me shiver like someone has walked over my grave.

'Violet, have I done something wrong? It's just you seemed so excited about the wedding and now you seem to be encouraging Mark and me to break up.'

'I'm not doing anything of the sort.'

Great. Now Violet is pouting. I'm not letting her get away with this. Just because she is nearly eighty-eight, it does not mean to say that I'm going to drop it.

'Yes, you are. You've been giving me funny looks ever since we decided on May for the wedding. What's wrong? Are you ill?'

I promised Mark I'd be subtle and not come straight out with this, but it just sort of slips out.

'No, I'm not ill. Whatever gave you that idea?'

'Mark was worried as you called him Geoffrey.'

'I did? Oh,' she says.

Perhaps I should have kept that to myself. Nanny Violet has gone very pale – the colour has completely drained from her face.

'I'm sorry. I shouldn't have told you,' I say.

Mark is going to kill me. I was supposed to subtly see whether his nan was ill, not cause her to have a heart attack. She didn't look ill when I first walked in, but now she looks positively peaky.

'No, dear, you were right to tell me. I don't want Mark worrying. He has enough to worry about with your upcoming wedding without thinking I'm about to keel over.'

'Just because he doesn't know any details about the wedding does not mean that he has something to worry about,' I say.

'Oh, Penelope, it isn't the actual wedding I was referring to; it's your little secret.'

Now, if my life was actually an *EastEnders* episode then this is the moment where the duffers would go off and viewers would be left hanging, wondering what's going to happen next. But as this is my actual life there is no dramatic music playing. Instead it is my turn to go pale and lose all the colour from my face.

'How did you know?' I say in practically a whisper.

I mean there was no way of her finding out. I've been so careful.

'I saw you in the community centre. I go there sometimes, and I saw you.'

Oh, I had been careful, but I'd also gone to the gamblers' support meetings at the community centre. She would only have had to ask at the front desk what the room was rented out for and she'd have been told.

I can't speak to Violet. I'm so ashamed.

'I thought you had a secret. You looked so shifty when you were setting the wedding date. I recognised it. I, too, had a secret on my wedding day.'

'You did?'

I'm barely listening to Violet as my mind is racing ten to the dozen. Thoughts of whether she'll tell Mark or his family are buzzing around my mind.

'Not to Mark's grandfather, but I was married before.'

If she had started this story five minutes ago I would have been delighted that she'd almost read my mind and answered the question about her first husband. But now I can't get excited that she's opening up.

'Geoffrey?' I say as a guess.

'Yes, his name was Geoffrey. Lovely fellow he was. All tall and dapper. I knew him a bit from our childhood and then we started courting when I left school.

'Then one day, not long after we started stepping out, he signed up for the war and off he went. We wrote to each other, of course. How I loved to get those letters. After his basic training he asked me to marry him. We decided that when he was next on leave we'd set a date.'

Violet pauses and it makes me realise how sucked into the story I am. I've momentarily forgotten about the pain and mayhem that's about to ensue and instead I'm hanging on every word.

'Then what happened?' I ask.

Of course I ultimately know the ending, but for some reason I don't think that is why Violet is telling me this story.

'He was away for a long time. He went off to North Africa and I didn't hear from him as much. I tried not to think about him as I couldn't bear the worry. It was after the first year of our engagement, and I hadn't seen him in all that time, that I started to become friendly with one of his friends. Theodore had been invalided out of the war after he was shot in his shoulder and he had started working at one of the factories. He often accompanied me to the dances – not that he could dance. At first it was so that he could look out for his friend's girl. But as we spent more time together, we started to realise how much we had in common. And one night when he walked me back to my mother's we kissed. Not just a kiss of friends, but something more.

'I felt awful the next day. I'm sure you know all about that feeling. All loss and regret and wishing you could go back and change how it happened.'

I can feel myself welling up at Nanny Violet's story. That is exactly how I feel with Mark. I do desperately want to go back into my very own DeLorean time machine and rip up my mood boards sooner and then I never would be in this very sorry post-bingo mess.

'Geoffrey sent a telegram later that week and told me he was coming back on leave the next weekend. I didn't have time to wonder whether I should cancel the wedding or not. I just booked the church and told my relatives. By the time Theodore found out he was livid, and he told me that I should be marrying him, not Geoffrey. But I had made my promise; I was going to marry Geoffrey.

'And I did just that. I felt guilty *every* day of our short marriage. I felt that I'd let him down by not being honest with him. I decided that I would tell him when he came back, when the war was over. Only he died on the beaches of Normandy. Twenty, he was.'

Violet stops talking and I see her wipe a tear from her eye. Every instinct in me is telling me to rush up to her and give her a massive hug, but I know that she wouldn't want me to. She's far too proud for hugs.

'And what about Theodore?' I ask. Even though I know that Violet didn't end up with him.

'Theodore felt just as guilty as I did when Geoffrey died. He did try to take me out after, as friends again, but I wouldn't let him. I couldn't spend time with him as he just reminded me of how awfully I'd behaved with both of them.'

'But you must have been so young.'

'I was sixteen. But sixteen in those days was mature, mind. I'd left school at fourteen and been working for two years by then.'

'And so you met Albert after?'

'A few years after. I met him when I was nineteen. Because of my relationship with Geoffrey I'd learnt how important it was to be honest with one another, and I never, even in the sixty-five years we were married, kept anything from him.'

I can't help wondering what would have happened if Violet had picked Ted instead of Geoffrey, and how if that had happened I wouldn't be marrying my lovely Mark. If I wasn't feeling so awful that Violet knew my secret I'd be thinking deeply about fate and what life throws at you.

'You see, Penelope, I could see something in your eyes. It was the look I had when I was married to Geoffrey,' says Violet.

'But I can't tell Mark; it would crush him.'

'Is it still going on?'

'No, it stopped ages ago. It really did. Mark means too much for me to lose him. Please, Violet, don't tell Mark. I love him more than anything in the world and I know now, more than ever, that I never want to do anything to hurt him.'

'It's a bit late for that.'

Oh my God. She's going to tell Mark and then he'll know my deep, dark secret. There is absolutely no way on this earth that he will marry me if he finds out what I've done. I've dug myself a massive pit of lies and I can't explain my way out of it.

'Please, Violet, please don't tell him.'

I'm so far off the edge of the couch that I'm practically on the floor begging her not to tell Mark.

'It's not my place to tell him, dear. But if you want to learn from my mistakes then you'll tell him yourself. You may be surprised with Mark. He has a big heart.'

'No, he'll never forgive me,' I say, shaking my head.

'Well, I'll leave it up to you, dear. But know this, when you get him down the aisle it won't change things. That secret will eat away at you. You mark my words.'

I put my cup of tea down on the coffee table. It is suddenly making me feel really sick.

'I should be going,' I say. I know I've barely been here half an hour but I just need to get some fresh air.

'Penelope, look, I'm not going to tell Mark. You don't have to tell him either. If you say it is in the past then I believe you. I can see that you sincerely regret it.'

'I do, I do,' I say, agreeing with her.

Maybe she understands after all. Maybe she won't make me tell Mark.

'You know, you're putting me in a difficult position, Mark being my grandson. I only want what's best for him.'

'And so do I, Violet. *So do I*. I may have made a mistake, but I want to move forward with my life, with Mark by my side.'

'I really hoped that by telling you my story you'd confess to Mark, but I'm not going to force you. If I've learnt anything from living as many years as I have it's that everything works out for the best in the end.'

I'm not entirely sure what Nanny Violet is trying to say, but all I know is I have to get out of here as soon as possible, before I faint.

'I'll see you at the wedding,' I say to Violet as I dash out of the living room and towards the front door.

'I'll be there,' she says after me.

Far from giving me the fresh air I need, the warm air hits me as I leave the bungalow.

I know that Violet doesn't agree with me not telling Mark, but this is completely different from her situation. She fell for her husband's best friend. It's not like I'm having an affair or anything.

I'm sure once the wedding is over the guilt will fade and the wedding will just be one of many magically memorable days for us. That's just as long as Violet is true to her word and doesn't tell Mark.

chapter twenty

This time next week I'll be waking up a picture of peace and tranquillity as I glide through my preparations as the calmest bride ever on a wedding day. Or more likely, I'll wake up in a blind panic wondering how I'm possibly going to be ready on time for my big day with the biggest spot you've ever seen which, knowing my skin, will have popped up overnight on my nose. That is how my life works out.

It has been almost a week since Nanny Violet revealed she knew my secret. Despite being on tenterhooks for the first few days when Mark got back from his stag do, I'm now convinced that she is as good as her word. The bonds of sisterhood seem to be tighter than those of blood at the moment.

Coming to the museum today feels odd. I'm suddenly not sure how I'm supposed to act around Ted. Now that I know his secret and I know that at one point he wanted to marry Violet, it is all too much to take in.

I know that Ted did get married, as his wife died a couple of years ago. That's why he volunteers here, so that he gets out and about and mixes with other people. It's weird to think that he could have been married to Violet; their lives could have been so drastically different.

Looking at my watch I realise I've only got half an hour left before Lou picks me up for the hen do. I can't wait.

I know that I'm going to have much more fun on the hen do than Mark did on his stag do. From the little snippets I've found out about, it seemed like the stag do was a form of cruel and unusual punishment.

I also hope with Lou being pregnant that I don't come back looking as rough as Mark did. Although unfairly he's bounced back quickly; I'm not sure I'd do the same.

Today at the museum we're supposed to be making tunic bags, but there has been a bit of a halt in the production line as we've run out of Velcro. Lilian and Betty have gone off for a cup of tea in the tea rooms and Nina seems to have passed out in the corner. She looks how I imagine I will tomorrow morning, like she's had no sleep and has been dragged through a hedge backwards *and* forwards.

I decide to pass the time by texting Mark, who should be just back from his Saturday golf.

PENNY

Are you missing me already? x

He's clearly assumed the position for watching sport and is tucked up in his armchair as he texts back almost instantly.

MARK

No more than normal. You've only been gone two hours. x

That might be true but Mark obviously failed the first test there. He's supposed to say of course he misses me, and that he always misses me when we're apart.

PENNY

What are your plans for the day? Lots of sport? x

MARK

I was thinking of tidying the spare room. Don't forget my cousin Liz is going to stay there the night of the wedding.

I *had* forgotten that. She is a student and she can't afford to stay in the hotel where we are all staying. Mark's mum thought it was a good idea to have someone in the house. Something about wedding announcements in the paper and wedding gifts in the house.

I make a mental note to make sure we have enough clean sheets as my mum will be staying the night before to keep me company, and then I make a mental note to get Mum to change the sheets after she gets up. It's not like I can do it. I'll have far more important things to do as the bride.

Once I've made all the mental notes a slight sweat breaks out across my forehead as I realise the enormity of the situation. Mark is going to clean out the spare room. The spare room where I keep my secret shoe supply. Surely he'll twig that I bought them in secret if he sees all the boxes and the shoes?

PENNY

Don't bother with that. She's a student, she's used to mess.

Stereotyping students? Me? Never.

MARK

Well, it will need to be done at some point soon as I'm sure we'll be looking at stage six after the wedding.

My stomach does a tiny somersault as it always does when Mark hints about babies. There is something so sexy about it. I can just imagine Mark with a baby resting on his shoulder, topless and suddenly in black and white. Oh, whoops! I've put Mark into an Athena poster of the late eighties. Ah, my first real love.

PENNY

Just leave it. We'll have plenty of time to worry about that after the wedding x x

I put an extra kiss on that text to make him realise that I didn't mean to be harsh. I just wish he wouldn't do sorting out stuff when I'm not there to supervise. And by supervise, I mean hide all the stuff I don't want him to see.

MARK

Don't worry, I know about your secret shoe stash. I've always known. I don't have that bad a memory, you know, Miss 'These are old, I've had them years'.

Oh bugger; I'm busted. I can't believe he's known all this time. For years I've been buying shoes and trotting round the patio in them before he gets home from work, just to scuff the bottoms up a bit. And he's known all along. I can't believe he didn't say.

PENNY

Oh, in that case bring on the cleaning spree! x x

I can now relax once more and my shoulders are no longer rubbing the bottom of my earlobes. My phone buzzes into life. Lou is calling; she must be early.

'Hello.'

'Hey, I'm here at reception!'

'Be up in a second.'

It's not like anyone is going to miss me with the Velcro drama that has unfolded.

'Nina, can you tell Cathy I've gone?'

Nina doesn't answer me back. I'm about to lift her head to see if she is still breathing when her fingers scrunch together and she forms a thumbs -p motion.

I grab my bag and run upstairs. As I've been volunteering here for three months I've learned there is a sneaky way to reception that avoids the maze of corridors. It does involve me appearing out of the back of a Home Guard tableau and getting quite intimate with one of the mannequins. But Captain Mainuring, as the mannequin is known, has never complained. You just have to make sure there are no visitors in the vicinity or else they think the mannequins have come to life and you scare them off.

When I get into reception the small area is full of pink helium balloons.

'What the . . .?' I mutter before I see underneath all the pink foil is Lou.

'Happy hen night!' she says, thrusting three helium balloons into my hand. Each balloon is bright pink and has a different cheesy last-night-of-freedom type motto.

Before I know it, Lou has dressed me up in the tackiest of outfits. I'm still in my jeans and jumper, but I now have a tiara, a veil and LED-flashing L-plates.

Lilian and Ted are standing there and I give them a look that says 'Please help me'. But they take it to mean I'm fine and they give me a little wave before bundling me and the balloons out through the revolving doors. I'm sure that the flashing L-plates aren't good for the low levels of lighting needed at the museum.

'So where are we going then? Or do I not want to know?'

'Relax, relax,' says Lou. 'Here.'

She passes me a blindfold as we get into the car.

'No way. I'm not being blindfolded. I know what your driving is like. I want to be able to see.'

'Really? I would have thought you'd find it preferable to the eye-scrunching you usually do.'

The woman has a point. I take the blindfold and put it on over the veil. Please, dear Lord, do not let us break down.

By the time we reach our destination I feel thoroughly sick. It turns out wearing a blindfold while in the car with Lou is a lot like seasickness. Speaking of seasickness, is that the sea I can smell?

'Here we are,' says Lou.

From what I can tell from the blindfold she is now at the passenger side door. I can feel her leaning over me and then I hear the pop before my seatbelt pings undone.

'Can I take the blindfold off yet?' I ask.

'OK, then.'

Ripping off the blindfold I suddenly have to cover my eyes as for once the sun is shining. Of course the sun is shining today. This means that it will be raining next week on my wedding day, as we all know that you can't have two nice weekends in a row with British weather.

'Where are we?'

I look up to see we're parked next to a static caravan. A caravan? For my hen do? Really? Mark gets to stay in a hunting lodge and I get a caravan?

I look at Lou for some explanation for this.

'Don't kill me. This is your sister's idea, but they're apparently luxury caravans and there's a spa on site.'

I'm trying not to project my sceptical feelings on to my face. I'm reminding myself that people are here for my enjoyment and I should stop being such a princess.

'Great. Let's get in there then. I could do with a glass of water,' I say.

'Glass of water? I may not be drinking, but there will be none of that.'

I walk into the caravan and I hear a champagne cork pop.

'Surprise,' shouts my sister Becky.

The caravan is a lot roomier than it looked from the outside; it is positively a Tardis. Instead of having the makeshift seats and the annoyingly restrictive fixed tables that I remember of caravanning when I was a child, there is a giant L-shaped leather sofa and a kitchen that is actually big enough to cook in.

'Wow, this place is great.'

I go over and give my sister a hug before taking a glass of champagne and saying my hellos to the rest of the crew that are here.

'This is suddenly very exciting,' I say, sipping on my champagne. 'What are we going to do?'

'We figured we'd chill out in the hot tub for a bit before we get ready for our night out tonight,' says Becky.

'Hot tub?' I ask. Did I really hear that right?

'Out the back,' says Becky, as she opens up the patio doors.

I poke my head outside to see the wooden veranda with a hot tub on one side and patio furniture on the other. Caravanning has suddenly gone up in my estimation.

* * *

The hot tub turns out to be just what I need to relax after the week I've had. The tension caused by worrying whether Nanny Violet was going to spill the beans has well and truly left my body. Now I am in a relaxed state of bliss. I will just have to channel this Zen when we go on our night out, as I don't think somehow it is going to be as calm and tranquil.

'Right, time to play Mr and Mrs,' says Becky, clapping her hands.

Oh God. I hate Mr and Mrs. OK, maybe hate is the wrong word; I hate the thought of me having to play it. I don't want people to know what Mark's favourite sexual position is or which of my friends he fancies.

I sit down on the sofa and I'm amazed at Becky when she pulls out an iPod projector and a laptop and suddenly there on the wall of the caravan is my lovely Mark. *Oh Mark, what have you done?*

A horror unfolds on the screen. There is my father dressed in a tuxedo introducing the Mr and Mrs game.

'Really? You got Mum and Dad involved in this?' I hiss at my sister. I try to rack my brains to think what we did at her hen do and I don't think we humiliated her that much, did we? An image of her dressed as Little Bo Peep in Brighton flashes in front of my eyes; maybe I could be in trouble after all.

The first question is tame enough. How did we meet?

Surely Mark will tell the version of the story we all know and love? Surely he will? I'm going to bloody kill him if he tells the truth. Only Lou knows the actual truth. And that's if she remembers I told her – we'd had a lot of tequila the night I confessed it to her.

'So, Pen, how did you and Mark meet? Or should I say, how will Mark say you two met?' asks my dad.

Becky pauses the video and she and the rest of the girls look at me expectantly.

He'll have to give the approved version. Surely he knows better than to tell the truth?

'We met at the gym. He came up to me in the juice bar and asked me out on a date,' I say as confidently as I can.

'Let's see what Mark says.'

Oh no, there's something in the way Becky said that which makes me think Mark's version isn't going to be the same as mine.

Mark pops up on the screen again. I'm such a lucky girl – he looks amazing.

'We met at the gym,' says video Mark.

'See,' I say, with a triumphant grin. I know my fiancé just fine.

'Wait for it,' says Becky.

I strain my face to keep the grin as Mark keeps talking.

'You want me to tell you how we met at the gym? Oh boy.

So I was walking out of the men's changing rooms and Penny walked out of the girls' changing rooms just ahead of me. At first I was looking at her arse as I thought it was cute, and the next thing I saw that she'd dropped something. I bent down to pick it up and called after her. Only when I picked it up I realised it was a pair of knickers. Penny of course was mortified, but I told her if I'd already seen her knickers then I might as well take her on a date.'

I'm going to kill him.

'That's it, laugh away,' I say to the much-cackling witches.

'How did your knickers get on the floor?' asks Becky.

I take a deep breath. I've lost all my shame at this point anyway.

'They were in my trouser leg. I must have taken my trousers and knickers off at the same time the night before. I guess I picked the trousers off the floor and shoved them straight in my gym bag without noticing, and when I put them on at the gym I hadn't realised.'

'Oh my God, that's too funny,' says Sasha, crying with laughter.

I roll my eyes. Six years we've been telling the juice bar story. *Six years*. How had he not picked up on that?

And now everyone at the wedding will know too. Jane's here in the caravan so she'll tell Phil, and Phil will tell all of Mark's friends, and then everyone will know. Heaven help me, if this is what Mark is saying at the hen do, goodness knows what he is going to say during the wedding speeches.

'Question two,' says my dad. 'What part of your body does Mark find most lickable?'

Shoot me. Really shoot me now. It is probably a good job we aren't on Mark's stag do as I don't think it would be wise for me to be around a lot of guns.

The questions progress from there and send me into a pit of humiliation so deep I think I'll never be able to climb out. I just about manage to survive without spontaneously combusting, which I thought was a possibility as my cheeks are that hot.

As the girls, who are all laughed out, start to peel off to the shower I I'll send Mark a cheeky text about what reprisal he's going to get when I get back from the hen do.

PENNY

Just played Mr and Mrs. I can't believe you told everyone about the gym. I'm going to have to get you back tomorrow night. I'm thinking those handcuffs you got me are going to come in very handy. Excuse the pun. Hope you're having a nice afternoon x x x

I stare at my phone, willing Mark to text back immediately like he did earlier in the day, but my screen looks blank and motionless.

Before I can pine over the lack of text a cocktail appears in my hand thanks to Jane.

'Don't think you're going to be able to text your *munchkin* all night,' says Jane, pointing at my phone.

I can't quite believe that Mark would tell everyone that the most embarrassing nickname I've ever called him is munchkin. I'm secretly relieved that either he's too embarrassed or he hasn't remembered the phase I went through when I called him the muffin muncher. I'm neither confirming nor denying that Mark calls my lady bits my muffin.

'In fact, why don't I just take that off your hands? I'll give it back when you get in tonight.'

It all happens in slow motion and I reach for the phone but Jane really is quick as lightning. I should have known – I've lost enough times to her and Phil when we play tennis doubles. Under duress, I may add. Who actually likes playing tennis doubles? Except Jane and Phil, as they always win.

'But what if there's an emergency?' I plead.

'Well, then I'll sort it out.'

'What if I lose you?'

'Then one of the other girls will help you.'

'What if I lose you all?' I know I'm whining but without a phone I feel like my arms have been chopped off.

'Don't worry, you're going to be handcuffed to one of us all night as we know how you just walk off when you're drunk.'

Dammit. The problem with being on a hen do with your friends is that they know every move you're going to make and they're just one step ahead of you.

'You'd better go and get ready anyway. Your clothes are on your bed,' says Jane.

Those are the words I've been dreading. When I asked about what I needed to bring clothes-wise they said not to worry. So of course all I have done since then is worry.

I slowly get up from my seat; there is no point delaying the inevitable.

'Oh, my goodness,' I say, clapping my hand over my mouth. There on the bed is a full-on toga dress.

'We're all wearing them,' says Lou. 'Look, you can't even tell I'm pregnant.'

I am going to ask whether togas are a safe choice to be wearing to go drinking but I think better of it. Instead I down the cocktail I'm holding; it seems like my only option.

I wake up the next morning to the sound of tiny drums beating in my head. It takes me a minute to work out where I am, but as I roll over, I see Lou on the other side of the bed with green leaves falling out of her hair.

It hurts to think back to last night. I can only just remember leaving the caravan; details after that are pretty hazy. Either we've been to a Greek restaurant or I must have got into a lot of trouble as I have very vivid recollections of smashing plates.

Jane was true to her word though – my mobile phone is next to my head. I pick it up expecting to see a text waiting for me from Mark, but there is no little message symbol.

Maybe Jane gave me back the phone last night and I read it and in my drunken state forgot about it.

I open up my messages from Mark and I'm confronted with all my texts from the night before. It seems like I was having a very one-way conversation.

PENNY
HELLLOOOOOOOOOOO

PENNY
Where's my finance at?

I have to read it a couple of times but I'm guessing that was supposed to say fiancé. That's clearly down to the winning combo of fat thumbs, drunk texting, and the dreaded autocorrect.

PENNY

This time next week we'll be sealing the deal.

I really wish that phones didn't show you what you sent any more. Remember the phones that only allowed you to have ten text messages in your inbox? Oh, those were the days. Now you get two years' worth of conversations in black and white.

PENNY

I'll be Mrs Robinson now!!!! Next week obvs.

PENNY

Had the best night. LOVE YUUUUU

And then I get back to the original text I sent him before I went out. Why hasn't he replied? I know that I didn't contact him when he was on his stag do. I figured that I should leave him alone as he was with the boys, aka he didn't have any signal in his country lodge. But still, it is probably Mark just being nice and not wanting to get in my way of having a good time.

Yes, that's it. He's giving me space to let me get on with the hen do. There is really no other plausible explanation, unless he's lost or broken his phone. Oh, I like that idea so much better. He dropped his phone down the toilet and he doesn't know he has all these messages from me.

That is the only explanation. Not to worry, I'll be home in a few hours. I can tell him all about my weekend then and I'll just skip over the part where I sent him all the stalker-like text messages. After all, if he's lost his phone he'll never know, and what's one more secret in the grand scheme of things?

chapter twenty-one

Lou tells me on the drive home that it's best if she doesn't fill me in on the blanks I had from last night. From the flash-backs I've had, that include me dancing round a pole and shimmying on a podium, I think she might be right.

It seems sad to leave our caravan; I'd grown quite fond of it in the end. My sister Becky is staying in it for the rest of the week with her husband and their two little rug-rats. I hope she can get the smell of tropical punch out before they arrive. They'd get drunk just walking in.

As much fun as it was being away with the girls, I have really missed Mark. Yes, I know, I've been away one night and it's pathetic. But I guess I wouldn't be a very good bride-to-be if I didn't miss him now, would I?

Lou has managed to get us home in a speed that I don't

think is quite legal, and it had me wanting to reach for the blindfold again.

'Thanks for a lovely weekend,' I say, as we pull up in front of my terrace.

'No problem. It was such a fun time.'

'Despite you not drinking?'

'Especially because I wasn't drinking. I have enough stories to blackmail you with forever.'

'You wouldn't?' I say, wincing.

'No, but stand by your laptop. I'll be popping the pictures up on Facebook later.'

Ah, the dreaded Facebook tags. Whatever did we do in the days before Facebook?

'Can't wait. Anyway, thanks again and I'll call you tomorrow.'

I can't wait to get in the house and see Mark again. His phone being out of action has made me feel like part of me was missing.

'Hello,' I call as I walk over the threshold. The house is far too quiet for Mark to be in.

I expect he's gone to see his nan or gone to the gym. He didn't know what time I was going to be back, so I really can't blame him for not being here to be the welcome committee.

To be honest I feel exhausted anyway. I'll just have a nice

long relaxing bath and get into my pyjamas. I'm sure by the time I get out of the bath Mark will be back.

I always know that it is a bad idea to lie on my bed once I've got out of the bath. All those sleepy thoughts going round your head when you're so relaxed. Yet when I got out of the bath I ignored all those thoughts and got into bed anyway. Of course I fell straight to sleep and now that I've woken up I feel groggy and more tired than I did before.

It's dark outside and I scramble over to Mark's side of the bed to see that our alarm clock says that it is just after eight o'clock.

I bound out of bed as that must mean that Mark is home, yet the house is still eerily quiet and pitch black.

Now I'm starting to get worried. I'm sure that there is a perfectly logical explanation and if I can just find my phone and call him I'm sure he'll tell me what it is. When I eventually find my phone still next to the bath I ring Mark and it goes straight to voicemail.

The hairs on the back of my neck go up and I start to run through *Crimewatch*-style reconstructions of what could have happened to Mark and none of them have a happy ending. I wonder if I should phone the police, but even I know that is being far too dramatic. As I wasn't here last night I don't know how long he's been missing.

Instead I'll try to find him myself. Now with it being dark outside I can only guess that he isn't playing golf. I'll start by phoning his mum just to check he hasn't snuck off there for a cheeky roast dinner.

'Hello,' says Mark's mum, Rosemary.

'Hi, Rosemary, it's Penny.'

'Oh hi, Penny, I thought you might be calling soon.'

'You did? Is Mark there? Is he OK?'

'Yes, he's here.'

Thank goodness for that. I breathe the biggest sigh of relief. I'm so happy that I'm not going to have to be at a press conference crying and making some heartfelt appeal for Mark. At least he wasn't abducted last night. Although I'm not entirely sure who would want to abduct a thirty-year-old man.

'Can I speak to him?' I ask.

'I don't think that's such a good idea.'

'What do you mean it's not a good idea? Is he OK?'

'Yes and no. I'm not entirely sure what is going on with you two, but Mark is pretty upset.'

'He is? I've just got home from the hen do. What's wrong?'

'I don't know. He arrived here about an hour ago, after he'd been at Mum's.'

Nanny Violet. She wouldn't have told Mark my secret, would she? She'd seemed so sincere when she said she wasn't going to tell him. I was convinced that she was going to leave it up to me to break the news to him. Not that I was going to but still, it was my secret to tell.

'Did he tell you what had happened?' I ask.

'No, just that he didn't want to talk to you and I wasn't allowed to let you come round.'

'But Rosemary, I have to talk to him. I have to make him understand.'

'Oh Penny, I didn't think you would do anything to hurt Mark.'

'I haven't, or at least I didn't mean to hurt him. I thought I'd fixed everything.'

'Whatever is going on, I don't think Mark sees it that way,' says Rosemary.

'But I've got to talk to him. I'll come round.'

'Penny, he's quite adamant that you're not to come over. I think he just wants some space.'

'Some space? We're getting married on Saturday.'

This is so frustrating. I understand that it must have been a bit of a shock to have found out, but I can't believe that he won't let me tell my side of the story. Especially when we're getting married in a week. *One week!*

'Penny, why don't you just let Mark sleep on it tonight and give him a ring tomorrow? Give him some time to get his thoughts together.'

'But–'

'Penny, just leave it for tonight. I know Mark and he needs his space.'

'OK,' I whisper. I can't believe this is happening.

'Bye, Penny. I'll call you tomorrow.'

I hang up the phone and just stare at it. I can't believe that his mum was telling me how she knows what Mark is like. *I know what Mark is like*. I know everything about how he'd react. I know that he's a hedgehog, as the marriage class taught us. He goes into a ball and doesn't want anyone to come near him when he's angry, and he puts his spikes out. I'm the opposite. I'm a rhino so I like to charge into arguments. Rosemary doesn't need to tell me that Mark would rather not talk about it.

And usually I'd let him stay in his ball, but not when we've got a week to go until we get married.

There is just one person that I need to phone before I go over to Mark's parents' house.

'Hello,' says Violet. I love that you can guarantee that she'll pick up with one ring in the evening as she's always sitting right next to the phone.

'Hi, Violet, it's Penny here.'

'Oh, Penelope.'

I'm still obviously in the doghouse with Penelope being trotted out.

'I've just spoken to Rosemary on the phone and she says that Mark is there and he's furious.'

'Yes, dear, he is. He came to me in such a state. He kept going on about you hiding something from him and bank statements and I had to tell him what I knew. I'm so sorry, Penelope, but he is my grandson.'

Oh no. The bank statements. I'm so sure I hid them all. They were in a shoebox underneath a pair of boots. *In the spare room*. There was me worried that Mark would find my secret shoe collection and I never even gave the bank statements another thought.

'Oh Violet,' I say.

'I'm so sorry, but Penelope, you should have told Mark the truth while you had the chance.'

'I wish I had. I just want to explain to him why I didn't tell him but he won't talk to me.'

'Well, I can't blame him.'

'But didn't he at least seem relieved when you told him what you saw?'

'Of course he wasn't. He was practically inconsolable. Beforehand he'd been confused, but by the time he left he was furious.'

'But didn't it make him feel better knowing that I was getting over it? You know, trying to sort myself out and get help?' I ask.

'What are you talking about, dear? Getting help? I didn't know you were. I don't know, you young people going to counsellors over the littlest of upsets.'

Why doesn't Violet know that I was getting help? Isn't that how she knew what my little secret was?

'Wasn't he pleased that I was going to a gamblers' support group?'

'Gambling? Penelope, I don't have a clue what you're on about.'

There is definitely something weird going on with this conversation and I'm wondering whether Mark was right: that Violet is losing it. Of all the times that I need her to be lucid, this is most definitely it.

'What did you see me doing at the community centre?' I ask in frustration.

'I saw you holding hands in the coffee shop with another man.'

Holding hands with another man. She must have seen someone else. This must be a huge big misunderstanding. I'd never hold anyone's hand but Mark's.

'Hang on, Violet, I think you've got it wrong.'

'No, I haven't. I watched you holding hands with him and then I saw you hug him goodbye.'

'That wasn't me, that . . .'

Oh, hang on. An image of me and Josh pops into my head.

Now it all seems to be crystal clear. She hadn't seen me going to one of my support group meetings; she'd seen me meeting Josh that time when I was feeling weak in willpower. It all makes sense now. That's why she told me the story of Geoffrey and Ted. She confided her story of infidelity to get me to tell mine. But I didn't have one.

'Violet, that wasn't what it looked like.'

'That's what they all say!'

'It's true! I have a gambling addiction and I've been going to a support group and Josh is my mentor.'

There's complete silence from the other end of the phone and I suddenly wonder if Violet is still breathing. This probably wasn't the most sensible conversation to have with a woman in her late eighties.

'I think it would be best if you started from the beginning,' says Violet.

I really feel that I should be explaining this to Mark first rather than his nan, but at the moment that doesn't seem like an option.

I tell Violet the whole sorry story. From wanting to have a princess wedding to me becoming a regular fixture on Fizzle Bingo. I go on to explain about the bank and the Citizens Advice Bureau before filling her in on my support group, Josh, and my Saturdays spent at the museum. By the end of it I am exhausted, both physically and emotionally.

'Well, well, well. You have been a busy girl,' she says.

'Yes, it's been quite a hectic three months.'

'I'd say. I still think that Mark would have understood, you know, if you'd told him from the outset.'

That is not what I want to hear right now.

'He's just so sensible with money. I didn't want him to see me as a disappointment.'

'I think he'll see your lying as more of a disappointment.'

I don't want that to be true, but I guess in my heart of hearts I know it is.

'It's such a mess, Violet. How am I ever going to fix it?'

'Oh Penny, I just don't know. You know what Mark is like.'

Yes, *I do*, I nearly scream. At least Violet recognises that I know my fiancé. And did you hear? She called me Penny! It seems that I have won her over at least with this conversation.

'I just need him to know my side of the story. The *whole* story,' I say.

'I think that's the only way. I'm sure if you explain to Rosemary, she'll let you see him.'

Rosemary? I can't tell Mark's mum the whole story. I'm tired enough from telling Violet. What is it with the women in his family acting like gatekeepers?

'I just feel that the next person I tell should be Mark.'

'Then go and see him, love. I don't think he's going to like what you have to say, but at least it isn't as bad as what he thinks it is.'

Well, that's encouraging, surely? Although I have a sneaking suspicion it is going to take a lot more than just telling Mark my side of the story to get him to forgive me.

'Right, Violet, I'm going over,' I say determinedly.

'Good luck, Penny. And I'm so sorry that I made the situation worse.'

'Violet, I only have myself to blame.'

It's true, it's all my fault. Somehow now the fact that I spent the money seems like such an inconsequential part of it. If I had told Mark the truth in the first place, before I tried to sort out the wedding, then he would have seen how much I've changed as a person. Instead I've built a house made of lies that has come crashing down around me.

I rush out of the house with just my keys and my phone. I don't know how I'm managing to drive normally, but I am. It's like I'm driving on autopilot. Mark's parents only live fifteen minutes away but tonight it seems to take fifteen hours to get there. The thought of what I've done and the magnitude of the repercussions keep swirling around my brain.

I do quite possibly the worst piece of parking on their drive and run up to the doorstep. I feel like I'm in a dramatic scene in a romcom movie and I can suddenly hear the power ballad playing as a theme tune behind me. All I have to do now is beg Mark to come back and he'll sweep me into his arms and we'll live happily ever after. Isn't that how it's supposed to happen?

As the door opens I'm faced with Mark's mum, Rosemary. Her hair is in her usual severe up-do and her lips are pursed. This isn't going to be easy.

'Rosemary, I've got to see Mark,' I say, practically barging her out of the way. I start to run up the stairs and that's when Rosemary tells me that Mark isn't here any more.

'What?' I say, collapsing on the stairs.

'He's gone, Penny. He said he knew you'd come round once you'd spoken to me and he doesn't want to see you.'

'But I've spoken to Violet and she had the wrong end of the stick. I've got to tell Mark what was really going on. I've got to tell Mark the truth.'

'You're making about as much sense as Mark was earlier. Do you want to tell me what's going on?'

I can't face telling the story again. It is far too draining. And besides, I do owe it to Mark to tell him before his entire family.

'I can't, I need to tell Mark.'

I suddenly have this sneaking suspicion that Rosemary is covering for Mark and that he is actually upstairs hiding. I stand up again and go racing into Mark's old bedroom only to find it empty.

There are crease marks on the bed where he'd obviously been lying. I sit down only because it makes me feel closer to Mark.

'I'm sorry, Penny. I was telling the truth – he's gone,' says Rosemary, poking her head round the door.

'Did he say where he was going?'

'No, he told me he'd text me when he got there, wherever there was. I have a feeling that he's going to a hotel rather than someone's house.'

Perfect. There are loads of hotels in the local area that he could have gone to. I'm going to have to face the fact that Mark doesn't want to be found.

I can feel my mobile vibrate in my pocket and my heart suddenly leaps. Maybe Mark has spoken to Violet and now he wants to speak to me. But it's not Mark. I'm disappointed when I see that it is Chris from the band calling.

'Hello,' I say, in the most unmelancholy voice I can muster.

'Hi, Penny. I was just phoning to confirm our set times for Saturday. Do you want us to start off at eight for our first set, and then our second set at ten?'

I don't have the heart to tell Chris that there might not be a wedding. They've already had one cancellation on that date. Maybe that was a bad omen. Maybe booking the band that had been due to play at someone else's wedding has jinxed mine and Mark's big day.

'That sounds perfect,' I say, lying.

'Great. And we've learnt "Mrs Robinson", so we're all set to play that for your last song. Have you picked a song from our playlist for the first dance, or did you want to play a CD of your own choice?'

'We picked "Kiss to Build a Dream On".'

I can feel the tears welling up in my eyes at the thought of Mark and me dancing in the kitchen to the Lou Reed song earlier in the week. We'd been dancing to the different options and seeing which we liked best. Mark had spun me round to that song and I'd felt like a princess. Ironic that Mark made me feel like a princess having spent no money, and yet I was convinced it would take at least twenty thousand pounds.

'Excellent choice. I've spoken to the venue and we've got it all sorted for our set-up and sound checks. So we'll see you on Saturday night. If you give our fee in cash to us then, minus the deposit you posted, that would be great'.

'Brilliant,' I say, without any enthusiasm. We're going to have a band playing for no one at this rate. Or maybe all our friends will want to go to a big party without us; after all, I've already paid for it.

'See you then,' says Chris.

Great. We've got the band confirmed and all I need to do now is make sure the groom is still going to attend. Somehow I don't think confirming Mark's attendance is going to be as easy.

chapter twenty-two

I am proud that I managed to make it through an hour and a half of work before I left. I'd love to tell you that I was highly productive in that hour and a half, considering I've only got two days of work before I'm off for two and a half weeks, but I wasn't. Instead of starting on my massive to-do list I sat staring at my computer screen, the desktop image being of me and Mark looking all happy and loved-up on holiday last year in Greece.

I'd managed to answer two phone calls, including one where I'd agreed to host the annual 'handrail safety awareness day' which, in our department, we usually rock, paper, scissors to avoid. But as I'm a tad preoccupied with my impending wedding and missing groom, I said yes just to get the health and safety officer off the phone. It now means that next month I'm going to have to spend a whole day walking scores of people up and down the stairs making sure they know how to hold the handrail.

With Mark not answering his phone, and the receptionist at his accountancy firm telling me he's off site, I've got no choice but to go to his office in person. The receptionist always says the accountants are off site – it's like their default do not disturb. I don't really want to go to his office, but he's left me with no other option. I'm starting to lose my mind, and who knows what else I'd agree to at work in my current state?

Pulling into the Brown and Sons car park I scan it for Mark's car but it isn't here. I reassure myself that he could still be at work. It might just mean that he is staying somewhere so close he can walk.

I climb the stairs to the second floor where their office is and I take a deep breath before pushing the door open to reception. I've only been to Mark's office once, when I went to deliver the lunch he'd left on the kitchen sideboard. I don't know who was more embarrassed, me or the receptionist, as I handed over Mark's Tupperware tub of smelly leftover curry. I hope it will be a different person today.

As I open the door I see that it is the same receptionist. She looks at me like she's trying to place me and then her eyes widen in recognition and she looks down at my empty hands. I do a jazz-hands wave to symbolise that I'm not carrying any Tupperware. And this is me trying not to cause Mark any embarrassment at work.

'Hi, I'm here to see Mark Robinson,' I say as professionally as I can manage.

'You're his fiancée, aren't you?'

'That's right,' I say.

'You must be so excited about the wedding this week! And the honeymoon, eh? Where are you going again?'

'Mexico.'

'How lovely.'

The receptionist is just smiling at me and I wonder if she's forgotten why I was here.

'So is Mark around?' I ask again.

'Oh, yes, sorry. No. No, he's not here.'

Surely Mark wouldn't have called in sick, would he? Mark hates missing work. I practically have to chain him to the bed if he has flu or else he'd go to work pretending it's just a sniffle.

'Do you know when he's going to be back?' I ask.

The receptionist clicks around with her mouse.

'It looks like he's on site at Kinetic-Co all this week,' she says.

'Oh, OK,' I say, despite the fact there are a number of expletives in my head that I wanted to say instead.

'You'll have to give him a call on his mobile,' says the receptionist.

What a genius. Why didn't I think of that? See, this whole not being able to talk to Mark thing is turning me into a mean person.

'Thanks ever so much,' I say, before turning to leave.

'Good luck with the wedding,' she says.

'Thanks,' I mutter. At this rate I'm going to need it.

Slumping back down into my car I'm wondering just what I'm going to do. I know that Kinetic-Co is a big local company, but can I really just go there and hunt Mark down? I can't think of any other option, so I start the engine and try to remember where it is.

As I stop behind a car going on to the Kinectic-Co site, I'm thinking there might be a slight hitch in my plan. There's a barrier in my way, literally. I'd forgotten that Kinetic-Co is a quasi-military establishment. The car in front has pulled forward and the guard in his little hut is waving to me and I've got nowhere else to go but towards him.

'Have you got an appointment?' he asks, as I wind my window down.

'No,' I say honestly. 'I just have to see my fiancé. You see, we're getting married at the weekend and I need a quick word with him.'

'OK, so your fiancé works here. What's his name?'

'No, no, he doesn't work here,' I say. I can see the guard is looking puzzled. I look in my wing mirror and there is quite a queue forming behind me.

'Right. Well, if he doesn't work here, then how can I help?'

'Because he's here on site all day, all week in fact. He's an accountant.'

'Well, do you know who he's meeting here?'

'No,' I say quietly.

The guard is not looking impressed. 'I'm afraid you're not able to come on site unaccompanied. Can't you just phone your fiancé on his mobile?'

I'm about to start venting steam from my ears, if one more person tells me to ring his sodding mobile. What did people do before mobiles anyway? What if there was an emergency and his phone battery was flat? Perhaps I should have made that my cover story.

'He left his phone at home,' I say, lying. 'Look, can't you just check the guestbook and see where he is?'

'I'm afraid I can't, love. Security and data protection. Without you knowing who I should contact, I can't help you. I'm going to put the barrier up and then you're to loop round the roundabout and come back through that side. You got it? No funny business.'

He's actually wagging his finger at me as if he thinks I'm capable of funny business. If only I knew what funny business

I could try. Even if I do get loose in the car park this site looks huge and I'd never find Mark.

I've just got to come up with another plan. Like waiting until he drives out from behind the barrier, that's what I can do. I can then follow him back to wherever he's staying.

'Thank you,' I say, smiling. Now that I have my new secret plan I drive as instructed round the roundabout and outside again. I then position myself in the lay-by further down the road where I'll have a perfect view of him exiting. I turn the engine off and congratulate myself. Yes, if I look round I have an excellent view of gate F.

Uh-Oh – Gate F. That seems to imply there are multiple gates. I dig around in my bag to find my phone and pull up the internet. I hurriedly type in Kinetic-Co Farnborough directions and I click on a PDF map to download. As the colourfully illustrated map loads I see quite clearly that there are six gates on what appears to be a site the size of a small town. I had no idea that this place was so big.

I'm never going to be able to find Mark at this rate. I've got about as much hope as finding a needle in a haystack.

That's it then. I turn on the engine and resign myself to my fate. With no other options for finding Mark I may as well head back to work before I get into trouble for going AWOL in the middle of the day.

Back at my desk I'm even more depressed. At least for

the hour and a half this morning when I was pretending to work I was deluded into thinking that Mark was fifteen minutes down the road and that I could go and see him any time I want. Now I'm sitting here in the knowledge that he's working on a site that is guarded like Fort Knox.

There's nothing else for it. I'm going to have to actually do my work. I glance over my to-do list, trying to find the task that requires the least amount of brainpower, when I see number 6: find a venue for our graduate event. I clap my hands with delight. Not at the fact that I get to spend a whole two days meeting snotty-nosed, brainiac scientists, but because we usually host the day in a conference room. And where do you find conference rooms? In hotels.

We didn't like the hotel we were in last year so it's been on my to-do list forever to sort out a new venue. It hasn't been high on my list of priorities to phone the venues and find out rates and availability, but now it seems terribly important.

I pick up my list of hotels that I printed off Yell.com weeks ago and I dial the first number and wait patiently as I go through to reception.

'Good morning, Reddington's Hotel, how may I help you?'

'Oh, hello there. I just wondered if you were able to send me some information about your conference facilities. I'm looking to hire a place for a graduate recruitment day. We need one room that we could have lectures in, and then another where we could set up like a fair and have tables and chairs so that our staff could interact with the students.'

'Certainly. We have several rooms that could fit that description. Did you want to make an appointment to come and have a look first or did you want to give me your email address and I can send you over some information?'

'Just some information would be great at this point.'

I rattle off my email address details to the very helpful receptionist who makes me repeat everything back to him, and then he repeats the details back to me.

'Yes, that's right,' I say, desperately trying to move the conversation on. 'Also, I think we have one of our employees staying with you at the moment and I wondered if I could leave a message.'

'Certainly. What was the name?'

'Robinson. Mark Robinson,' I say. Perhaps not what I should be doing on a work call, but I like to think of it as killing two birds with one stone. A bit of multitasking. At least this way I actually might achieve something workwise today, even if I am using the conference as a bit of a ruse.

'I'm sorry, Miss Holmes, but we haven't got him listed as a guest. Would he go under another name?' asks the receptionist.

I think about this for a moment. Would he have gone under another name? What would he have picked? My mind is a whirl of possible names Mark could have chosen and then it hits me: Mark isn't a famous movie star, and as far as I know this is the first time he's run away to a hotel and I doubt that a fake name would have crossed his mind.

'Miss Holmes?' says the man on the phone. I'd almost forgotten about him.

'I'm sorry, no, he wouldn't be under another name. I must have the wrong hotel. But thank you for your help.'

'No problem, and I'll email you the corporate hire pack straight away.'

'Great, thanks.'

I look down at the list – only another thirty to go. I hadn't thought I'd phone all of the hotels on the list, as not all of them would have the conference facilities. But I might have to if I want to find Mark.

By the time I get to number thirty on the list I've almost lost the will to live. This place is also trying to do the hard sell and get me to visit.

'I think I'll just start with the price list,' I say, trying to keep my cool.

'OK then, I'll send it over.'

'Great. Also, while I'm on the phone, I think one of our employees is staying with you. His name is Mark Robinson. I wanted to drop something off for him.'

'Robinson, hmm. Oh yes, here he is. M Robinson.'

I nearly bite through the biro I'm chewing – I've actually found him!

'That's great,' I say, trying to hide the excitement from my voice. 'I'll drop it off later tonight.'

'OK, great, and maybe while you're here you can check out our conference facilities.'

'What an excellent idea,' I say, lying. Why was it that out of thirty hotels in the vicinity Mark had to pick the one with the pushiest sales team?

'Thank you so much for showing me around,' I say to Emma, the events manager at the hotel.

This hotel seems like it could be perfect for our needs, which is lucky as I did bunk off work just a little bit early to check it out. I just wanted to make sure that I caught Mark before he barricaded himself in his room. This way I can camp out in the lobby until he shows up.

'It was my pleasure. Now you've got your full brochure there and an up-to-date price list. Just let me know if there is anything else you need.'

'Thanks, Emma.'

I watch Emma disappear back out towards the conference room and I look around reception for the best place to wait.

'Can I help you?' asks the receptionist.

'Um, yes, I was just waiting for one of your guests. Mr Robinson,' I say, approaching the main desk.

'He's not picked up his room key yet tonight.'

'That's OK, I'll just wait over there,' I say, pointing to a group of upholstered chairs in the corner.

'Perfect. Help yourself to tea and coffee from the machine.'

'Thank you.'

What a nice hotel. I walk over to the coffee machine and get a coffee. It has been a long day and I didn't sleep well last night – a coffee might be just the thing to perk me up. The chairs are perfectly placed near the lifts and opposite the reception desk, and more importantly they're hidden from the main entrance and they can't be seen when you walk in the door, so Mark won't be able to see me and make a hasty exit.

I pick up one of the magazines and flick through it. It's an in-date copy of *Hello!* magazine. I can never resist a magazine profiling the lives of the super-rich and famous, but today it is doing little to relax me. I'm a bundle of nerves sitting here waiting for Mark. I admit that perhaps drinking the coffee was not the best idea as I'm now on the wrong side of jittery.

I think I'm also freaking out the receptionist as I keep looking up at the clock behind her head. It's 5.30 p.m. Mark should be arriving any time now.

The revolving doors start moving and I look up in anticipation and hold my breath. But it's not Mark. It's an old man wearing a mac over his suit and carrying a briefcase in his hand. As he walks over to the reception desk I go back to reading about celebrities I don't recognise at an opening of an art gallery.

I look up from my magazine as suddenly I'm aware that I'm not alone in the chair area. There, standing in front of me, is the businessman who just walked in.

'Hello, there,' says the man. 'I understand you're looking for me.'

I look up at him, tilting my head to the side in Mark's trademark move while I desperately try to work out what's going on. 'Eh?' I say. It's about all I can manage.

The man takes me speaking to him as a signal to sit down and he sits opposite me.

'The receptionist said you were waiting for me. Now I know that Mrs Lexington said that she would be in contact but I didn't think it would be this soon.'

Again I want to just say, eh? 'I'm sorry, I think there might have been some mistake.'

'I don't think so. You're after Mr Robinson, aren't you?'

I nod my head slowly, wondering just what is going on.

'Well, that's me,' he says, grinning from ear to ear.

'I, um, I think there's been a mix-up,' I say, trying to work out who this man is and why he isn't Mark.

The man sits upright and the smile drops off his face. 'Am I not what you were expecting?' he asks.

Not really, I want to say, but before I get a chance he launches into a bit of a rant.

'I mean, Mrs Lexington just said that she'd have no trouble getting someone for me. I hadn't realised that you would be fussy about it and that you'd judge me. I just thought that you came along and that we had dinner. If I'd wanted to be rejected in person I would have gone on Match.com. I'll be telling Mrs Lexington that I'm not too impressed with her service and–'

'There really has been a mistake. I don't know who Mrs Lexington is and I don't know who you think I am, but you're not the Mr Robinson I'm after. I'm looking for Mr Robinson, my fiancé, who's gone AWOL five days before our wedding. And I'm afraid, Mr Robinson, that you're not him.'

'Oh,' he says. We both look at each other with new-found embarrassment as it dawns on me just what type of woman – or, more accurately – madam Mrs Lexington might be, and it dawns on him that I'm not his date/escort/hooker – Mr Robinson can delete as applicable.

Mr Robinson gets out of his chair, straightens his tie and says, 'I do hope you find your fiancé.' He then walks calmly to the lift and waits for it not so calmly; he jabs the up button about ten times in ten seconds.

I walk over to the receptionist. 'That man who just got in the lift, is he the only Mr Robinson staying here?' I ask.

'Afraid so,' says the receptionist. 'Not your guy?'

'Not even close,' I say, sighing.

I thank the receptionist and walk out of the hotel.

I stand for a moment on the curb wondering just where I am going to go. With only five nights left before our wedding, time is running out. I have to find my missing groom and I have to find him soon.

'Mr Mark Robinson, just where are you?' I mutter under my breath in some cosmic hope that the universe will tell me.

chapter twenty-three

This has to be the worst pre-wedding week ever. I'd planned to take Wednesday, Thursday and Friday off work to do spa-like treatments to myself. Getting myself primped and preened to be the most beautiful bride the world has ever seen. Yet in reality I'm going to have to spend the time trying to stalk my husband-to-be until I get a chance to talk to him.

Today at work has gone no better than it did yesterday. In fact today has been one of the worst days of my working life. Not only have I been so preoccupied that I agreed to let a number of key engineers all have Christmas off, which means I won't be having a happy Christmas when my manager finds out, but one of our senior managers has got a secretary pregnant. Which has meant there have been a lot of meetings and sensitive whispering going on as we try to manage the situation.

I think that will see the end to our team-building weekends in Wales. Not that I mind that – I hated them with a passion. All that mud and seeing your colleagues in tracksuit bottoms – it was just wrong. But I would rather the Wales weekends had come to an end naturally than because a manager's wife came tearing into our office and told us all what had actually happened in Wales.

It made me realise that I'm glad Mark wasn't in his office yesterday and that we didn't have a similar scene in front of his colleagues. Everyone has been tiptoeing around the manager and the secretary since the outburst and they've been treated like they've got bubonic plague. I wouldn't have wanted to embarrass Mark like that.

Work-related disasters aside, my team gave me a lovely send-off before the wedding. A few of them are supposed to be coming to the evening do. I didn't have the heart to tell them that there was quite a big likelihood that it wasn't going to happen. Especially when I could see through the bag that there was a gift box in the exact colour you would get from Tiffany's and in a size box that would fit champagne flutes nicely. Yes, I'm that shallow.

As it's Tuesday, I'm going to my support group meeting. I can't help but feel queasy when I push open the door to the community centre. If only I'd never come here to meet Josh for coffee. Out of all the places to pick, why did we come here? Not that I guess it would have changed things. Mark would have found out eventually. Maybe it was better that he found out what a lying toad he was marrying before he said *I do.*

'Hi, Penny,' says Rebecca, as I enter our little room.

'Hi, Rebecca.'

'You must be so excited – only a few more days to go before you're married!'

I can't cope any more. I've spent the last two days smiling and hugging work colleagues who kept popping over to give their congratulations and I can't bring myself to do it with these guys too. Before I know it tears are rolling down my face. And when I say rolling, I'm talking rolling waves like over the top of Niagara Falls.

I've surprisingly managed to hold my tears in over the last couple of days but it's as if the dam has been breached and all of a sudden I'm practically drowning in salty tears.

'Oh, Penny, whatever is the matter? Was it something I said?'

'No, it isn't you,' I say, hiccupping. 'It's the wedding. I don't think it's going to happen.'

'Why ever not?'

'Mark found the bank statements and he knows I've been lying to him.'

There is a collective sharp intake of breath and I look through my foggy eyes and see that the whole of our group is sitting down ready and listening to me. I bet Mary wishes she could open every meeting like this as there are usually a few lingerers at the tea and coffee as she starts. But not today. Today, everybody is poised to hear my woes.

'But haven't you explained to him what you've done?' asks Rebecca. 'You've worked so hard, what with the group and your wedding planning on a budget.'

'Oh yes, Penny. You've done wonderfully. Can't he see that?' says Mary.

'I haven't been able to tell him. When I got back from my hen do he'd gone. He went to his mum's first and now I don't know where he is. He hasn't even let me explain.'

'Well, surely when he knows the truth . . .' says Mary.

I shake my head. 'That isn't all of it. There was a bit of a miscommunication with Mark's nan. She saw me and Josh having coffee and she put two and two together and got five.'

My cheeks flush as Josh is sitting on the other side of the room looking confused. And then he laughs. OK, so I know Josh is slightly like an Adonis, but I'm sure if we were both single then it wouldn't be out of the question that we could get together. Was it really that laughable?

'She thought you and Josh were a couple?' asks Mary.

And now she is laughing too. What is so bloody funny? Yes,

I might have a little bit of a spare tyre around my waist, and OK, my hair isn't in the best condition and I might be a little cross-eyed, but I reckon I could get a Josh. It just makes me cry even harder to think that people find me that unattractive as a person. Don't personalities count any more?

'Penny, I'm gay,' says Josh.

'You're what?'

'Gay,' says Josh slowly.

'But what about Mel?'

'What about him?'

Oh. Mel is a him. I thought – well we all know what I thought. Now on top of feeling sad I feel like an idiot. Could my day get any worse? Don't answer that as yes, it quite possibly could.

'Right. Well, it doesn't matter if you're gay or not. Mark doesn't know that and Mark doesn't know that I'm not having an affair with you either.'

I'm still slightly shocked that Josh is gay, but I guess that just reinforces how little we actually know about each other. It is all so frustrating; if only Mark could see that.

'So what are you going to do?' asks Rebecca.

'I don't know. I went to his work and he's working off site all week and I tried to go there and they wouldn't let me in. I tried to find what hotel he was staying at but that didn't go very well.' The image of the man in the mac floats into my mind before I shake my head and get rid of it. 'I don't know what else to do. It's all such a mess. And when everything had come together as well. I've worked so hard to plan the wedding and now he's not going to see any of it.'

'Don't say that,' says Mary. 'You've still got a few days to go. Maybe he'll want to sort it out once he's calmed down. Have you told his family the truth? Couldn't they talk to him for you?'

'I've told his nan; I couldn't face telling his mum. I've got both of them trying to contact him to tell him he needs to speak to me, but he won't pick up the phone to them either. He seems to be shutting everyone out.'

'But all that hard work,' says Mary, shaking her head. 'There must be something you can do, something you can try.'

I know that everyone says that a problem shared is a problem halved but this time it doesn't feel like it. In fact, it feels like my problems are multiplying like frogspawn.

'I've got an idea,' says Josh.

An hour later I'm sitting in Josh's living room wondering just what the hell I'm doing. I've just been introduced to Mel, the man, and he is busy helping Josh set up.

'This is so exciting,' says Rebecca, squeezing my arm.

'I'm really nervous. Do you think it will work?'

'I don't know your fiancé, but I hope it will.'

'Right, Penny, we're ready for your starring role,' says Josh.

I get up from the sofa and go into Josh's dining room where he has the video camera set up. The idea is that I am going to send Mark a video message. I know it is a risky strategy and there is the very distinct possibility that he won't play it. But if I wrote a letter there would be a chance he would rip it up before reading it and he clearly isn't listening to his answerphone messages, as he hasn't called me back.

Josh came up with the idea and I think it is my best chance of getting Mark to listen to my explanation without him shutting me down. We're just going to have to hope he actually watches it when we have the finished video and have managed to find him to give him a copy.

'Right, Penny, just sit down here,' says Josh.

I do as instructed and I then smooth my hair down. I know a bit of frizz is probably the least of my worries, as I'm sitting here with eyes all puffy and red from all my crying.

'And action,' says Josh, smiling.

Seeing Josh in director mode brings a smile to my face for the first time since the hen do.

'Mark, I know you don't want to hear anything I have to say, but you have to hear my side of the story. I'm going to tell you the truth, which I should have done from the word go, when you proposed. The truth was, I was scared that you would be disappointed in me and I couldn't bear for you to look at me in that way.

'I just thought if I could make it all better then I wouldn't have to hurt you. But that hasn't really worked, has it?

'The truth – if you haven't already worked it out from the bank statements – is that I have a problem with gambling. Online bingo to be exact.'

I close my eyes as I can just tell what Mark is going to be shouting at the screen.

'I know you're going to tell me that I was stupid, and I was. But I can't tell you what came over me. It was like I was in a trance. I just wanted the perfect wedding so that we could have a fairytale day, where everything was magical and everyone would be amazed. When I say it out loud it seems ridiculous. I know now that none of the chair covers, the table confetti or the white doves would have been the key to a happy marriage. I know now trust and honesty are the foundations of that, and I've destroyed them.

'You wondered why you didn't recognise Josh as one of my work colleagues, and that is because he isn't from my work. He's my mentor in the gambling support group. Think of it like an AA sponsor. He's my go-to man when I'm thinking about gambling. And that was what Violet saw. She saw me with Josh and assumed that we were having an affair, but in truth he was helping me to get over my problem.

'I know you're probably thinking that it was your job to help me with my problems, and to some extent you should have been. But Josh has been through what I have. His gambling stories are worse than mine. He understood what I was thinking, and more importantly, he's made me see what is important in my life. Which is you.

'I want to marry you, Mark. That's all I ever wanted to do. I want to go to stage six with you and start our family and I'd love to go to stage ten with you and retire to our country cottage. But I don't really care about the stages, I don't really care what happens as long as I'm with you.

'I know that I made the biggest mistake of my life when I started the whole "don't tell the groom" business, but the funny thing is that it's made me a better person. I now don't take for granted what I have and I know what is actually important. And being a princess for sixteen hours is not.

'I'm not cancelling our wedding, Mark. And it has nothing to do with me wanting to put on my dress or not wanting to cancel the caterers – it's because I know we belong together. As long as there is even the slimmest possibility that you will be at the altar then I'll not cancel it. I don't care that I might be humiliated in front of all our family and friends if you don't turn up. I'm just hoping you can forgive me and that you will be there.'

I can't think of anything else to say. There's so much I want to tell Mark and I desperately want to beg him to come back but I do want him to watch the whole video. And sometimes, Mark is right, less talking is actually more.

'Great work, Penny,' says Josh. 'I've stopped recording. Now I think it's time to film some of the segments.'

I'm relieved that Josh thinks that what I said was good enough to end my plea segment.

'You did so well,' says Rebecca. 'I'm so nervous about my bit.'

'You'll be fine,' I say, rubbing her arm in support.

For a moment I'm suddenly overwhelmed by the other members of the group who have given up their Tuesday evening to help me with my video. Mary's bringing cups of tea in from the kitchen and Nick the businessman has popped to the local chippie to bring us back dinner.

I don't advocate gambling, and I know what I did was wrong, but I can't help feeling just a little bit blessed that in all this horrible mess, I've got to meet this bunch of people who I never would have encountered in my everyday life.

When we started in our little gambling group the most important point that Mary stressed was how confidential our sessions were. We weren't supposed to tell anyone about what went on in the room and other people's addictions were closely guarded secrets, bearing in mind that some of them hadn't been honest with their partners and their families.

And yet they are still helping me. It means the world to me that my fellow addicts are willing to share their secrets, to help me.

My phone starts to vibrate in my pocket and immediately my stomach flips and my heart starts to beat faster as I hope that Mark is on the other end of the line. My stomach sinks when I realise it is just Lou. Every time my phone makes a noise I'm like this. My poor stomach thinks I'm on a constant roller coaster with all the ups and downs.

'Hi, Lou.'

'Hey, Pen. Any news?'

I shake my head before realising that Lou can't see me do that. I'm so tired that I'm barely thinking straight. This heartbreak is not conducive to sleeping.

'None. I have no idea where Mark is. His mum told me that he texted her to say he was staying in a hotel. And after last night I've given up trying to find out where that hotel is.'

'But surely you've got to keep trying?'

'I know it's stupid, but part of me doesn't want to find him. I don't want him to tell me that it's over. This way I can at least hope he'll be at the wedding.'

'Well, is there anything I can do? Do you want me to try and find him?'

'Actually, yes. And I want you to make a delivery. In fact, what are you doing now?'

'I'm ironing.'

'Since when do you iron?'

'Since I became pregnant and suddenly the wrinkles in the duvet bother me.'

'Lou, as your friend, I'm going to rescue you from your crazy ironing. I'll text you my friend Josh's address and you can come and see what we're up to.'

'Josh with the eyes?'

'Uh-huh,' I say, suddenly hoping that no one else can hear our conversation.

'I'll be over as soon as I can.'

'Can you pick up some bridal magazines on the way?' I ask.

'What's going on?'

'You'll see,' I say cryptically.

I feel like I've been having an out-of-body experience for the past twenty-four hours. Filming the video that I hope will persuade Mark to turn up at the altar was one of the most exhausting things I've ever done. The upside of it was that I slept last night for a whole nine hours. Which means today I am almost functioning like a human being.

It's Wednesday today – only three more sleeps until the wedding. I remember booking this day off work months ago and I imagined that I would be floating around in a state of ecstasy, excited about what was to come. I certainly didn't imagine I'd be sitting in my PJs at 7 p.m., having not got dressed all day, and wondering if there was going to be a wedding.

Josh and Lou should be here any time now. We're launching 'operation tell the groom' tomorrow morning.

When all this is over I owe Josh a huge thank you. He sent me a text message this morning saying he'd almost finished the video; he'd been up all night. This wedding planning has taught me a lot of things, and one of them is how generous other people can be.

The doorbell rings and I get up. I know I should care that I haven't washed my hair in days and that I probably should have showered before they came over, but I don't. I suddenly panic and wonder if it is Mark, but then I realise that he has his key and he wouldn't need to ring the bell.

When I open the door it's Lou. She has a takeaway bag in one hand and a large box of chocolate fingers in the other.

'Glad to see you made an effort for me,' says Lou, laughing. 'Hope you're hungry.'

I hadn't really thought about eating but all of sudden I realise that I am ravenous. If there is a wedding on Saturday I am going to be in danger of not fitting into my dress after two takeaways in two days. Not to mention the calories involved in a box of chocolate fingers.

'I'm starving,' I say.

'Me too. And I finally fancy curry again.'

I am just closing the door when I hear someone shout.

'Wait.'

I open the door again and there is Josh.

'Hiya, I've got them!' he shouts as he comes up the path.

I hug Josh hello and bring him into the kitchen.

'Do you want to see it now?' asks Josh.

'Absolutely,' says Lou. 'But we need to eat first.'

'We can eat on our laps,' I say, shrugging.

Lou audibly sucks in a breath. I know, it's a deviation from the norm. I usually draw the line at any meals being eaten in the lounge. Mainly as I drop food like a baby and our faux-suede sofa isn't Scotchguarded. But with my life falling apart that seems like the least of my worries.

We scoop out the portions as quickly as we can as we're all dying to watch the DVD.

What Josh didn't tell me is that he's a video-editing genius. I imagined the video would resemble a video made at school with rough fades and cheesy lighting, but it is quite the opposite.

My heartfelt plea comes first, before the slick editing takes us on a journey of my last three months. Mary, Rebecca, Josh and Nick all share their gambling stories and talk about how the group saved them from their problems.

Next comes the cheesy montage of me attempting to make a bouquet of flowers, which I still fail at miserably, but I narrate over the top how I went to flower-arranging classes to try to save money.

I'm then demonstrating my cutting skills as I explain I've been volunteering at the museum to get a discount on the reception. I'm pretty mean with the pinking shears now.

By the end of the video, in which I'm symbolically burning the bridal magazines Lou brought over and I try to tell Mark how much I've changed on this wedding planning journey, I'm in tears.

I can't believe how good it looks. If I were Mark I'd take me back. But then again, if I were Mark we wouldn't be in this lousy situation!

'That's beautiful,' says Lou.

She is crying buckets, but I can't tell whether that is to do with my video or whether it is her pregnancy hormones. Last night she cried when Nick gave her his last chip.

'I just hope it's enough,' I say.

'Well, I'd marry you after watching that, if it were me. And I don't believe in marriage, and I'm gay. That's how good it is,' says Josh.

I can't help but smile at Josh.

'Thank you so much for all your help. I don't know how I'm ever going to repay you.'

'Don't be silly, it's been fun to pull an all-nighter on my computer doing something productive that wasn't losing me money. Anyway, I'm shattered, so I'm going to head home. I've left you six copies just in case.'

'Six?'

Was that going to be enough?

'Yeah, I know it's a bit of overkill, but just in case.'

'Thanks, Josh, for everything.'

As we're walking out of the door an idea springs to mind.

'I don't suppose you're free on Saturday, are you?'

'Let me guess. You want me to video the wedding?'

'Well, that is if there is a wedding.'

'Do I get a free dinner?'

'You most certainly will.'

'Then I'm in. Good luck,' he says, enveloping me in a big hug.

'Thanks, we're going to need it. And Josh, invite Mel to the evening do.'

'OK, great,' he says, as he walks up the path.

I go back into the lounge and Lou has managed to pull herself together and stop crying.

'So, how are we going to give it to Mark and how are we going to make him watch it?' I ask.

Having a video worthy of winning an Oscar is one thing; making Mark watch it is going to be quite another. Having lived with him for almost five years I've never once been able to force him to watch *Strictly Come Dancing*.

'Well, I phoned Kinetic-Co today,' Lou says, 'I might have told a small lie and I might have found out that their finance department is in block 4, which uses gate B. I'm just going to hang out near the exit until I see Mark's car and then I'll follow him until he stops. I'll have a laptop with me on the off-chance he'll watch it with me, and if not I'll force him to take a DVD.'

'You can't just hang around in the car for hours – you're pregnant.'

'I'll be fine. It's not like it's cold outside. I'll just put the seat back a little, listen to Radio 1. Believe me, it will be far less stressful then being in the office for two hours.'

I'm really not convinced by Lou's plan. It doesn't sound like a winning plan to me. I think about doing it myself, but as Mark hasn't returned my calls I'm guessing I'm the last person that he wants to see right now. All I can do is hope that Lou's plan works, as right now I am running out of time and options.

chapter twenty-four

To say yesterday had dragged would be an understatement. Yesterday was the longest day in the history of mankind.

I got up at the crack of dawn; I showered, shaved and moisturised myself in all the necessary places. I blow-dried my hair into little ringlets, which is Mark's favourite style, and I put on a full face of make-up. All before 7 a.m. All in preparation for when Mark watched the video and came running back to me.

I went to bed at midnight on the penultimate night of my single life alone, still fully dressed.

I was hoping that Mark would have come home. Lou had phoned me to tell me the sorry story. Her plan actually worked and she'd followed his car to a petrol station. She apparently waddled over to him and before he had a chance to fill up the car with petrol she started talking to him about the video. He turned to look at her before telling her that he didn't want to hear anything she had to say and that he didn't want to watch 'a fucking video'. Mark *never* swears. He is quite possibly the maddest I've ever known him to be.

Lou said she did manage to frisbee the DVD into his car before he got in and drove away. She said he wasn't rude to her, but I'm guessing that's because she looks pretty pregnant now. The upside of getting a pregnant woman to fight your battles seems to be that the other person isn't allowed to shout at them. The downside is that by the time Lou had waddled back to her car Mark had sped away and we still don't know where he's staying.

I was desperate for me and Mark to have this all ironed out last night as my mum is due to turn up any minute now. I didn't want to have to explain the case of the missing fiancé to her. I sort of hoped it would all come good and we'd get married, live happily ever after, and no one else would have to know.

The doorbell rings. I know I have to answer it, but it's like I'm wading through treacle to get to it. I've stopped jumping when the doorbell rings now as I know it won't be Mark. At this time in the morning it will only be my mother.

'Hello, darling,' she says.

I go to kiss her hello and all I can do is stare at her hand because it is carrying my wedding dress in a garment bag.

The wedding dress for the wedding that probably isn't going to happen.

'My goodness. You look, um,' she says, barging past me. I know I look a state. I've been sitting on the edge of my bed contemplating what the hell I'm going to do rather than washing off last night's make-up, which is smeared all over my face.

'I've made a list of everything we have to do today. Now where's Mark? I need to hide the dress before he sees it.'

'He's not here.'

'Excellent, I'll go and put it in the spare room wardrobe. When's he coming back?'

I don't have the energy to talk any more so I just shrug my shoulders.

'What's going on?' she asks.

Just the sight of my mum and the concerned look on her face is enough to reduce me to tears.

'Penny, whatever's the matter with you?'

I can't face telling the story for the billionth time, so instead I lead her into the living room and plonk her down on the sofa. Pressing play on the DVD player, I take my dress from her hands and head out of the room.

This DVD thing is marvellous. Maybe I should record all my life stories and woes on to disk and then I won't have to tell the same stories over and over again.

I know I should probably be in the room watching it with her, but I can't bear to hear my pleas to Mark again. It seems so much worse now that I know he's probably watched it and it hasn't moved him enough to come to me.

I unzip the garment bag and I gasp again at how beautiful the dress is. I'm so stupid. Why did I ever think I needed to have a dress worth thousands of pounds? Right now I'd marry Mark in a potato sack. I'll tell you what, a potato sack and Louboutins would look fierce. OK, so potato sack and bare feet would be fine too. I know now, too late, that it doesn't matter.

'Has Mark seen that?'

I look up and see that my mum is standing in the doorway of the spare room.

'Lou gave him a copy but I don't know if he's watched it or not. He thinks I was having an affair with Josh!'

'The guy with the gorgeous eyes from the video?'

I nod. I don't appear to be the only person fixated with his eyes.

'And he wouldn't listen to you when you told him you weren't?'

'I haven't spoken to him.'

'Penny, you're getting married tomorrow. You've got your rehearsal in eight hours' time. What if he doesn't turn up?'

'I don't know.'

Oh my God. The rehearsal! With everything going on I'd

completely forgotten about the rehearsal. Being jilted on your wedding day at the altar would be bad enough, but how am I going to get through the rehearsal? How am I going to explain the missing groom to Reverend Phillips? I don't think I'm going to be able to convince him it is part of my 'don't tell the groom'; he wasn't very impressed with that whole idea.

We've only invited our parents and the bridal party to the church, plus Mark's brother to sort out the photography. Will Mark's family even turn up?

I've been speaking to his mum on the phone every day and she knows only slightly more than me. Apparently Mark has told her that he's OK. I don't really want to analyse what OK means; I don't have the energy.

My mum looks at her watch.

'We've got so much to do today. We've got to sort out your cakes and drop those off at the reception venue. We've also got to get you sorted out. Look at your nails,' she says, in horror. She yanks my hand up with such ferocity that I think she is going to rip my arm out of its socket.

'What's the point, Mum? What's the point if I can't get Mark to come?'

'Penelope, if you thought in your heart of hearts that he wasn't going to show up then you would have cancelled the wedding. What we've got to do is focus on getting this wedding ready and getting Mark to watch the video.'

'How come you're not shouting at me for what I did?'

'Penny, we all make mistakes. Your gran once gambled the housekeeping money on bingo and we all had to eat bread-and-butter pudding for a week.'

Blimey, thank God that wasn't me. I hate bread-and-butter pudding.

'Anyone would be able to see on that video how much it hurt you and changed you for the better. I mean, I'm so impressed with your wedding planning skills on a budget. I'm going to ignore the fact that you should have been able to confide in me, and that you should have told Mark. But darling, I'm proud of you.'

'You are?'

My mum sits down on the bed next to me and puts her arms around my shoulders.

'Yes. You had an addiction and you had a problem and you sorted them both out. You also didn't want to hurt Mark and I think he'll understand your motivations, even if they were misguided.'

I can't believe that my mum just said she's proud of me. She's never said that to me. Not when I graduated with my 2:1 from university and not when I beat off stiff competition to get my perfect HR job. I've never doubted that she was proud of me, but to hear it out loud is the boost to my confidence that I need.

It is also the kick up the bum I need to get me into the shower and to wash off last night's make-up. Within an hour I've deep-conditioned my hair, had a bath, and I'm ready to play the part of blushing bride-to-be. I don't really feel like it, but at least I look the part.

Having my mum around is just brilliant. I wish I'd had her over for the rest of this miserable week. Usually I'd take it as an insult if she came round and got the Hoover out, but today I practically smother her with a gigantic hug. Not only has she cleaned my house, helped me take everything to the reception and driven me to the flower wholesalers, but she has also deposited me at a beauty salon.

I tried to protest but she told me that my eyebrows were nearly as bad as Professor Dumbledore's. I've now had my eyebrows plucked and shaped, my toenails painted, and I'm having my nails done; I'm beginning to feel just a little bit special.

'Are you nervous about getting married in front of all those people?' asks the woman buffing my nails.

I don't want to tell her I am nervous that I won't be getting married in front of all those people. I also don't have the strength to tell her the truth or have the DVD with me to play for her.

'No, it's going to be totally awesome.'

Yes, I do think I'm from *The Hills*. It seems like when I lie I turn into an American reality TV star. Next I'll be saying 'totes' and 'amazeballs' and every other word Mark has banned from the house.

'What's your dress like? Is it all big and princessy?'

'No.' I laugh. 'It's really demure and almost Grecian.'

'I bet it's lovely.'

'It is.' I'm trying not to think that there's a possibility that I'm never going to put that dress on.

'So are you going anywhere nice on your honeymoon?'

'I'm going to Mexico.'

That much is true. My name is on the ticket. I am going to Mexico. It might just mean that I am weeping into my cocktails alone all day, but I don't care. What better thing to do to mope over your wedding that never was than to go on holiday? To a couples hotel surrounded, no doubt, by newlyweds. I really hadn't thought that one through.

'I'd love to go to Mexico. You're so lucky.'

'Yes. Yes, I am.'

I think my mum has slipped something in my tea. I've always had my suspicions that she's on Valium, as she's always so perky and happy. How else do I explain why I'm not in tears at this Spanish inquisition the nail technician is giving me?

'You all right, love?' asks my mum.

Thank goodness she has shown up to rescue me.

'Hi, Mum. Did you manage what you had to do?'

'Mission accomplished. I'll just wait for you over there.'

I don't know where my mum went. She just said she had some business to take care of. I hope that was code for she had secretly tracked down Mark and given him a smack up the arse, but I think that is probably too much to hope for.

'Right, you are all set,' says the nail technician. 'Just be careful you don't do too much or you might chip the polish. Now have an amazing day and don't forget to come and bring us pictures of it!'

'Thank you so much! And of course I'll bring pictures.'

They may be of me eating the cake by myself in consolation, but I'm sure tomorrow, one way or another, there will be pictures.

'Right then, love. Time for the rehearsal?' asks Mum.

I nod. There's no use trying to be late for that. At least one half of the happy couple should show up.

I expect the church to be empty when I walk in, but it is far from it. Lou and Russell are here, Mark's parents are sitting in the front row. Mark's brother Howard and his wife Caroline and their children are sitting behind his parents, and my dad and my sister are chatting over the other side of the aisle.

Nanny Violet is standing next to Reverend Phillips and upon seeing me she gives me an incredibly guilty look.

'Ah, Penelope. I'm so glad you're here. I was getting a bit worried,' says Reverend Phillips. 'Mark not with you?'

My heart sinks. I knew it was a long shot that he was going to be here, but I couldn't quite help hoping that he would show up.

'Don't tell me, Penelope that you're going along with this "don't tell the groom" thing still? I thought I told you that the church couldn't be part of that.'

'I . . .'

I hear the door of the church go and my stomach somersaults at the thought that it is Mark. I turn to see Phil walking in.

'Sorry, sorry I'm late. Traffic was a nightmare.'

Phil walks straight up to me and kisses me on the cheek as he would normally, and he carries on walking to the top of the aisle.

'Where's Mark?' he asks, realising that Mark is nowhere to be seen.

Oh my God. Phil doesn't know. Mark left five nights ago and he hasn't told his best friend. Where the hell is Mark? And what is he playing at?

I'm about to open my mouth and tell the truth. Enough is enough. I know that I'm hoping that Mark turns up tomorrow but I just have to accept that he isn't going to. He would have turned up to the rehearsal if he was planning to marry me. I have to face facts.

'He's–' I say.

'He's got food poisoning,' says Howard, talking right over me. 'We went out for a curry last night and I guess his prawns weren't cooked.'

Howard is talking to Phil but looking straight at me.

'Oh dear, oh dear. Well, this isn't the first time we've had to do a wedding rehearsal without the groom. Usually it's when they've had the stag do a couple of nights before the wedding, but you know, these things happen,' says Reverend Phillips.

'I'll stand in for Mark,' says Mark's dad.

I look at my mum and she's giving me a two-thumbs-up hand gesture. I don't really know what she's done, but I somehow think that Mark's family's behaviour is all down to her.

'Splendid, splendid. Right then, positions, people. Now, father of the bride you come and stand at the end of the aisle with your daughter.'

My dad walks down the aisle as happy as ever. Maybe mum has got him on the Valium too. I should really only accept water from her from now on.

'You look lovely, dear,' he says, as he links arms with me.

'Thanks, Dad.'

'Right, then. The organist will start to play and you will walk up.'

As if by magic the organist that I hadn't even realised was

there starts to play the wedding march. I can feel my whole body tingling in the way that it has in so many of my wedding fantasies. I have to admit, though, that this isn't quite like any wedding fantasy I've ever had. For starters, I was never walking up the aisle towards Mark's dad.

I realise just how wrong it is that Mark's dad is standing in for Mark when I have to say my vows. Let's skip over the bit where I practically choke saying 'for richer for poorer' and jump to the bit where I tell Mark's dad 'all that I am I share with you'. My cheeks go as purple as my hair once was. This is not how it is supposed to be.

'You're now allowed to kiss the bride,' says Reverend Phillips.

I look at Mark's dad in horror, and luckily he looks equally as perturbed.

'Only joking,' says Reverend Phillips. 'I don't actually like the bride and groom to kiss in the church. It isn't part of the ceremony as far as I'm concerned.'

Phew. Not that I'd not want to snog Mark, but I draw the line at his dad.

'Right, then. Penelope, you and Mark will now be married and I'll take you through that door to sign the register. Who are your witnesses?'

'Lou and Phil.'

'Great. Bridesmaid and best man. Keeps it easy for me.

So we all sign the register and then I bring you back here in front of the congregation and I announce you to the church.'

Mark's dad has linked arms with me and we turn and face the others. They politely clap and it's then that it hits me that Mark should be here. I can't believe he's missing out on this. A tear threatens to roll down my cheek, but I don't let it out. I very deliberately applied non-waterproof mascara this morning as a tear-prevention method. It is proving most effective. Sadly the inside of my mouth is taking quite a beating as I have to keep biting my cheek to distract myself from crying with the pain.

We walk back down the aisle and everyone claps and waves and I try to join in the jolly mood, but I can't. I know that Mark's family are playing along fantastically but what is the point if Mark isn't going to show up? Are we just delaying the inevitable?

I turn and thank Reverend Phillips and he says he will pray for Mark's speedy recovery. It makes me feel terrible that one little lie has meant that we've lied to the man upstairs, which surely will result in me going to hell.

Reverend Phillips ushers us out into the fresh air and I start to hug everyone goodbye. Lou gives me a big hug and a squeeze and whispers to call her tonight if I need to. Phil gives me another kiss and as he's leaving I see my mum slip him a DVD. Great. Is there anyone who isn't going to know my secret?

Before I can skulk back over to the safety of the car and have a good cry, which is all I want to do, Mark's mum grabs my arm and pulls me off into the graveyard.

'Have you seen him?' I whisper. I suddenly feel like I'm a spy in a movie, as the last thing I want is for Reverend Phillips to find out Mark's absence was a lie.

'No. I've had texts from him and I keep telling him to talk to you but he doesn't reply to those texts.'

'He hasn't said anything about a video?' I ask.

'No, sorry, Penny. Your mum showed it to us. It was lovely. Well, not your gambling, you silly girl, but the message.'

I smile at Rosemary. I hope that Mark does turn up as I want more than anything to have someone as nice as her as my mother-in-law.

'I just want Mark to see it,' I say.

That was all I wanted when I made the video.

'I think I can help with that,' says Nanny Violet.

I'm sure that woman has stealth mode as I didn't see her approach.

'What are you going to do?' I don't think I really want to know what she has up her sleeve.

'Don't you worry about that. Just you make it to the church on time. He'll be here, don't you worry.'

'Are you sure?'

'As the day is long.'

I've never really understood that as a phrase but Nanny Violet is my last shot.

'Thanks, Violet. I really appreciate it.'

'Penny, it is the least I can do. I fear that I made the whole situation worse.'

I don't want to argue with that. Although if I hadn't gambled in the first place there wouldn't have been a situation, but I'm not going to argue over potayto potahto.

'I really do appreciate it,' I say.

'I know you do, dear. I saw the video.'

Is there anyone who hasn't seen the video? Ironically, probably Mark, the person who the video was *actually* for.

'Don't you worry, Penny. This time tomorrow you'll be Mrs Robinson too,' says Mark's mum.

Not even The Lemonheads going round in my head can make me smile. Instead, it just feels like it is taunting me. I wish I shared the Robinson women's faith that Mark will show up. Right now any hope I had is fading fast.

chapter twenty-five

Here I am, about to climb into the jeep that is going to take me to the church, on what should have been the happiest day of my life. Yet it feels like my most miserable day. I've still not heard from Mark and I have no idea whether he is going to be waiting for me by the altar.

Maybe I should have accepted drinks from my mother after all. Fearful of her drugging me up to the eyeballs, I've been making my own drinks all day. And even the champagne I drank, that would usually have had me giggling and giddy, made me feel sick.

'You look beautiful,' says Ted.

'Thank you.'

In all my fantasies this is the bit where I would twirl round and milk the compliments as, after all, this day is all about me, but I can't. I know I look pretty good. My sister has done an amazing job with my make-up. She's even managed to hide my red eyes that looked so puffy and swollen when I got up it was as if I'd gone ten rounds with Mike Tyson. Lou has pinned my hair up in a side bun with a plain hair clip that she bought in John Lewis and decorated herself with diamantes and pearls.

'You look like a young Sophia Loren,' says Ted.

I smile as best as I can and I wonder just how I am going to get into the jeep in my dress. As if reading my mind, Ted pulls a kick step from the back seat. He places it down in front of me and takes my hand.

I hoist up my dress, which looks really classy, let me tell you, and I climb in. Ted has even covered the seats with tissue paper. I hope that he asked Cathy the curator before he stole it as it looks a lot like the expensive conservation type she uses.

I notice that he has even tied white wedding ribbon to the bonnet and the side mirrors. I remember that I need to make a wish when I see a wedding car and I close my eyes and make it. Now I can't tell you what I wished for or it won't come true, but I bet you might just be able to guess what it was.

'Ready?' says Ted.

'As I'll ever be.'

The jeep starts noisily and I cling on for dear life as it

travels jerkily down the road. What should have been a fifteen-minute drive from our house seems to take a lot longer with the engine nearly conking out every time we stop at traffic lights.

By the time we make it to the church I don't know whether I feel sick with nerves or whether it is the post-adrenalin rush of holding my breath every time Ted pulled out in front of a car at a dodgy junction. Which happened a lot.

Ted, ever the gentlemen, comes and helps me out of the jeep. Lou and my sister walk straight up to coo over the jeep. I keep forgetting that they didn't know about it.

The funny thing is that everything about this wedding is so cool and everything seems to be going like clockwork except, that is, the groom.

'Is he here?' I ask Lou. My voice catches in my throat, almost like I don't want to ask as I don't want to hear the answer.

They don't need to tell me the answer as it is written all over their faces.

'Why don't we go in and wait in the little waiting room? You're a bit early, anyway.'

My father has walked up to us and I grab his wrist to check his watch before I even say hello. It is three o'clock on the button. Maybe Mark is working on the principle that I'll be late and he'll be here any minute.

I look around hopefully and all I see are some of my friends sneaking in late, giving me a thumbs up and a wave as they go into the church.

'Come on,' says Lou.

I let myself be dragged into the church.

'Ah, Penelope,' says Reverend Phillips. 'Now then, Mark and Phil don't appear to be here yet, so if you just come with me into the waiting room. I do hope that he is over his food poisoning.'

I can only imagine I gave Reverend Phillips a look which told him that the food poisoning was a lie. His whole expression changes and he suddenly looks like he is having a eureka moment.

'Right, then. Well, in cases like this, we usually give them a bit of time. You're the last wedding for the day so we can wait a while.'

The waiting room is just off the main church and I can hear the organ playing and I can also hear the whispers of the guests getting louder. People know that I've arrived; surely they know by now something is wrong as Mark isn't at the altar waiting for me.

'Can you see if Jane's in there?' I ask Lou after we've been waiting for about ten minutes. I am clutching at straws, but I hope that Jane might have some enlightening news from the boys' camp.

The door to the waiting room opens and in comes Jane,

followed closely by Lou. Lou rests up against the back of the door and takes a deep breath. It's like she's hiding from the paparazzi.

'What's going on?' asks Jane. 'I've been phoning Phil for the last half an hour and it keeps going straight to answer-phone.'

'I don't think Mark's coming,' I say. 'I was just hoping that you could get hold of Phil so that I knew once and for all, before I go and tell all the guests.'

I hear Lou gasp at that, but it's true. Sooner or later someone is going to have to tell the guests that Mark isn't coming and the wedding they are supposed to be here to see isn't going to happen. For once I have to be realistic.

'I'm sorry, Penny, his phone must be off.'

The look of pity on Jane's face is enough to make my heart break. Will everyone look at me with such sympathy? Can I just sneak out the back door and let someone else tell people that the marriage isn't going ahead?

'Penelope, I think it might be a good idea if I give the guests a little update on what's going on,' says Reverend Phillips, walking into the waiting room. 'It might be wise if people could have a stretch of their legs as we don't know how long they're going to be sitting down for, before we get started.'

'He's not coming,' I whisper.

'Sorry, dear,' says Reverend Phillips. 'You'll have to shout a bit louder.'

'I said Mark's not coming. He's clearly decided that he doesn't want to marry me.'

I turn to Lou and she's in floods of tears.

'I'm sorry, Pen, it's just so sad, and the pregnancy hormones just amplify it.'

Becky puts her arm round Lou to comfort her and she rubs my arm with the other hand.

'Do you want me to do it, Penny love?' asks Dad.

'No. This is something I need to do. It's my mess. I should at least have the guts to tell the truth.'

Reverend Phillips looks at me and then in a moment that touches my heart he takes my hand and leads me out of the room. It's a good job that he's got hold of me or else I'd probably fall flat on my face. My legs have gone limp and it feels like I am wading through treacle.

I can see everyone turn to me just like they have in my fantasies, but far from the gasps of doesn't she look wonderful, they are all gasps of shock. No one is smiling and everyone is looking at me with pitying glances. It seems so awful that everyone knows what I am going to say and yet I still have to say it.

Reverend Phillips leads me to the altar and he lets go of my hand where I should have turned to meet my groom. There is no one there to turn to me and tell me I look beautiful and no one to squeeze my hand in reassurance.

I start to open my mouth but nothing audible comes out. Reverend Phillips points over to the lectern that has a microphone poised and I slowly walk towards it.

I cling on to the lectern until my knuckles go white and then I look up at the congregation. There is an eerie silence that under normal circumstances probably would have made me feel awkward and I would have giggled, but not now.

'I want to say thank you all so much for coming. I know that you all came here to see me and Mark get married, but unfortunately I don't think that's going to happen.'

There is a collective intake of breath and I can see my aunt Dorian and even she looks shocked. At least she of all people should be pleased that now I definitely won't upstage my cousin Dawn's wedding.

'Most of you probably know that I was planning this wedding along the same lines as *Don't Tell the Bride*, only I wasn't telling the groom. Please don't think that this is all part of that and Mark has thrown a tantrum because he doesn't like the suit or the hairstylist I got him.'

I am relieved that a couple of people chortle at my attempt at a joke; it relaxes me slightly. But it also relaxes me enough for a rogue tear to roll down my cheek.

'But the truth is, I lied to Mark. I lost his trust and I guess I hoped that he'd be able to forgive me, but he obviously can't. I'm sorry everyone, you've had a wasted trip.'

I know that is supposed to be the end of my speech but I can't let go of the lectern; it is the only thing keeping me upright. I can't move. The congregation don't know what to do either. They are all looking at each other and then looking at me and it is like no one wants to move.

'Mark's not coming,' I say finally into the microphone. It is the most painful thing I've ever said and now I understand what it means to be heartbroken, as my chest is burning in pain.

I look down at the floor, hoping someone will just take me away.

'I am coming.'

I've really lost it now. I must be imagining things as I thought I heard Mark.

'Wait, Penny.'

I look up and there he is. Standing there as bold as brass. In his wedding suit with his purple cravat tied in the most untidy knot. And his feet are in trainers. But even that doesn't matter; all I care about is that he is here.

He's here. I let go of the lectern and I'm about to rush towards him only everything seems to be spinning around me, and Reverend Phillips appears to have two heads.

'Penny!' shouts Mark.

* * *

I try to open my eyes as I wonder where the hell I am. I'm lying on what feels like the most uncomfortable floor.

'Penny, are you OK?'

I can hear my mum calling me and she is shaking me gently. I can also hear Mark's mum ordering someone to get me some water. I feel my head being lifted up and then laid down on what I can only imagine is a kneeling cushion. To be honest I think the floor was more comfortable.

I try and work out what is going on, but my mind is foggy. I try to remember what was happening. I was at the wedding and at the altar, and Mark was here. I open my eyes and through the blur I look for him.

'Mark?' I mutter.

'Penny, love,' says my mum. 'She's coming round, she's coming round.'

My vision clears and I can suddenly see everyone around me. My mum, Mark's mum, Reverend Phillips and Mark. Mark is here. For a minute I thought I'd imagined his arrival.

'Don't try and sit up, love,' says my mum.

But it is useless. Mark is here and I have to talk to him. I start to reach forward but I am powerless to stop my mum pushing me back to the floor.

'I'll take care of this,' says Mark.

And in a flash he's bent down and picked me up, in true *An Officer and a Gentlemen* style. We go back down the aisle in a way I'd never pictured. Our friends and family look just as stunned as I feel at this turn of events.

Mark takes me into the little waiting room at the back of the church and then lowers me to my feet. I collapse almost straightaway into one of the chairs, my legs still unsteady.

'Mark, you came. There's so much I want to say to you.'

'Take it easy. You just fainted. There'll be plenty of time to talk later.'

I can't believe that he is standing in the room with me. All this week I've been desperate to see him, to tell him the truth. And now he's here I feel like I've got mud in my brain as I just can't seem to think straight.

'I can't believe I fainted.'

'I guess it was a bit of a shock seeing me.'

Mark sits down in the chair next to me.

'I didn't think you were coming.'

I can feel myself crying and I don't know whether they are tears of joy or just tears of confusion. Whatever they are, Mark is wiping them from my face.

'Stop crying, you crazy lady.'

'I can't help it. I thought you weren't going to come.'

'So did I.'

'Then why did you?'

Mark sighs. 'Because Nan told me off.'

'But how did she find you? I tried calling all the hotels and I couldn't find a Mr Robinson.'

'I checked in under Mr Holmes. What?' he says, clearly looking at my puzzled expression. 'I knew you'd try and stalk me as Mr Robinson. But anyway, Nanny Violet left me a voicemail that made it sound like she was in trouble. I thought she'd fallen. Of course, when I got to her house she ambushed me. She told me that she'd got it wrong, but I was still furious about the bank statements, the lies and the whole "don't tell the groom" nonsense.'

I felt hot when I came round, but now I am burning even more with the shame.

'I would have helped you, you know. I would have understood,' says Mark.

'I couldn't see it then. I was so ashamed of what I'd done.'

'Nan told me I had to watch the video too. But I didn't. I didn't want to know.'

So everyone else has seen this bloody video and Mark still hasn't.

'I texted Phil this morning as I didn't know what to do and he came to my hotel room and he actually handcuffed me to the bedpost.'

I raise what I hope is a suggestive eyebrow.

'Not like that. I was walking round the end of the bed and he grabbed my arm and attached me to the bedpost. He put his laptop on and played the video. As soon as I saw you, I couldn't not watch you. You *always* make me watch you, whatever you're doing.'

I can feel tears welling up again, but for completely different reasons. My heart is starting to beat faster.

'Do you think you'll be able to trust me again?' I ask. There is just a little bit of me that is scared he's only come to let me down gently.

He looks straight into my eyes as if he is looking into my soul for the answer. And then he kisses me on the lips, so suddenly and so sweetly that it makes me cry again.

'Once we take those vows there will be no more secrets between us, OK?'

He said 'take our vows'. Does that mean he still wants to marry me?

It is a good job that we have some privacy as I pull him into me and I kiss him in a way that probably isn't appropriate for a church.

'I'll take it that's a yes?' says Mark, pulling away.

'I promise, no more secrets,' I say, doing a cheesy salute.

'Not even shoes that you hide in the spare room?'

'I promise.'

Now I may have my fingers crossed behind my back. I totally agree that we shouldn't have big secrets between us any more, but he really doesn't need to know about all the shoes I buy, now does he?

'I guess we'd better get this show on the road,' says Mark. 'I'm sure everyone's wondering what's going on.'

'I love you, Mark, more than anything in the world.'

'More than Jimmy Choos, I see,' he says, pointing to my shoes.

'More than anything,' I repeat.

He kisses the top of my head and he goes to walk out of the waiting room.

'Wait,' I say, pulling him towards me. 'I just need to fix your cravat.'

I could forgive the trainers – they actually make him look cool, a bit Doctor Who. But the cravat really is a mess and Howard is going to take such wonderful photos, we don't want it haunting us for years to come.

As I am fixing the cravat, Amy sneaks over and seamlessly fixes a purple rose to his buttonhole. She gives me a little wink and I scrunch up my eye, trying to wink back. I probably look like I am having an allergic reaction, but I think she gets the idea.

'See you in a minute,' says Mark, grinning at me before he turns to walk up the aisle.

I watch him hesitate. I follow his gaze and see that he is looking straight at Josh holding the video camera.

Mark starts to walk up to Josh and I am about to go and intervene when he stretches his hand out and Josh shakes it.

God, I love that man. Mark of course, not Josh.

My dad slips his arm around mine. 'You ready, love?'

'Yes. You know what? I've never been more ready in my life.'

The organ starts playing the wedding march and a feeling of light-headedness washes over me. And not because I've recently fainted. This is what I've been waiting for. All those years of planning in my head, all those hours of daydreaming and all the different ways I'd imagined this scene unfolding.

I'll tell you one thing, my daydreams never included the dramatic lead-up to the wedding or my slightly tear-stained face. But it doesn't matter that this isn't the way I envisaged it would happen; it had finally hit me that that isn't important. The fact that I am marrying the man of my dreams is all that matters.

I take a deep breath as I feel my father leading me forward. This is it. I am finally going to become Mrs Robinson. I doubt there has ever been a more contented bride than I am at this very moment.

epilogue

There's my aunt Dorian with a face full of thunder as she watches Mark and me glide around the dance floor in serene happiness to the band playing 'A Kiss to Build a Dream On'. Mark is looking at me like I'm the only woman in the room. And the smiles on all the guests' faces confirm that they're at the best wedding ever.

The song comes to an end and I press Fast-forward. I just love watching the first dance over and over again. I always fast-forward to the next bit as the camerawork goes a little iffy while Josh places the camera on the table and has a dance for a song, or a whole set, with Mel.

I can't complain, though. I'm so glad that I got Josh to video the whole wedding. It captured everything so well. OK, so perhaps not the beginning with Mark running into the church and me fainting, but he captured what really mattered. As much as the reasons behind the 'don't tell the groom' were totally wrong, and I fully admit that, the look of surprise on Mark's face throughout the day was priceless. From the jeep that took us to the reception, to the reception venue itself, Mark was amazed.

It wasn't that he didn't think I could do it; it was just that he was amazed that I, of all people, could pull it off on such a small budget. And it was a really small budget. It came to five thousand four hundred and thirty-four pounds exactly. Not bad, huh?

And do you know what? I wouldn't have changed it for the world. It wouldn't have been better if I'd had a dress with a ten-foot train, or if there had been caviar canapés or a photo booth for the guests to take crazy pictures. The Polaroid camera guestbook gave us quite enough crazy pictures. Especially the ladies who took the pictures of their boobs covered by their hands. I would never have recognised Lou's boobs as they're so big now, but I'd never not recognise her bespoke engagement and wedding rings that were twinkling on her finger.

Speaking of Lou, I stop the fast-forwarding at one of my highlights from the wedding: the moment when Lou told me what my *Don't Tell the Bride* surprise was. Never in a million years would I have guessed it.

'Ladies and gentlemen,' said the lead singer of the band, 'while we take a break, please put your hands together for the maid of honour and best man, DJ Loopy Lou and DJ PP-L.'

My open mouth on the video is embarrassing. I swear you can see my fillings as Josh flicks between me and the scene unfolding on the stage. There, in all their glory, are Phil and Lou dressed up in ridiculous hip-hop inspired outfits. Phil even has his trouser leg half rolled up and has my mum's hat on backwards. And Lou has Phil's cravat tied around her head.

'Yo, yo, yo,' said Lou. 'Let the battle commence.'

The next hour was hysterical. I swear it took a week for my ribs to heal from all the laughing. Lou and Phil battled their way through an hour of songs, each pulling out a song that was either one of my favourites or one of Mark's. It got everybody on the dance floor. And I mean everyone, even Nanny Violet.

Which reminds me. My favourite Nanny Violet memory of the whole wedding is in the second set of the band when Ted asked her to dance and they swayed around in a perfect waltz to 'That's Amore'. I couldn't have choreographed it better myself. OK, so I did invite him to the evening reception. And I did give him a nudge when the song came on. But really it was all down to him. I haven't seen Violet smile that much since she drank half a bottle of Bailey's one Christmas before she realised it had alcohol in it.

'You're not watching that bloody video again, are you?' asks Mark, as he walks into the lounge.

'Maybe. I just love it.'

'So did I, the *first* time I saw it.'

I know I'm not supposed to be keeping secrets from Mark, and I'm doing really well on the whole, except I do sometimes secretly watch this video once or maybe twice a week.

'Well, what am I supposed to do now that I'm not planning the wedding any more?' I ask pouting, trying to do my best Jane impression.

'I can think of something.'

He grabs my hand and pulls me off the sofa and leads me up towards the stairs. Stage six! *Stage six* – just kidding.

If there is one thing that the pre-engagement wedding planning taught me, it was not to be in such a hurry for everything to be perfect. Whatever life throws at Mark and me, I don't care, as I know we'll cope with it *together*.

The End

about the author

Anna Bell writes the weekly column *The Secret Dreamworld of an Aspiring Author* on the website Novelicious, and reviews modern women's fiction for the website the Chicklit Club. She is also a member of the Romantic Novelists' Association's New Writers' Scheme.

Anna gave up a career as a museum curator to become a full-time writer. When not at her laptop she can usually be found walking her Labrador with her husband, and dreaming up new plots.

You can find out more about her on her website:
www.annabellwrites.com
or follow her on twitter
@annabell_writes

acknowledgements

I'd like to thank Jay, who did a marvellous job of editing this book. As always, your attention to detail and suggestions were spot on. Thank you also to Andrew Brown at Design for Writers for designing such a beautiful cover, and for being patient with my silhouette panics.

I'd also like to thank my agent Hannah for taking me on as a client and putting up with my many, many ridiculous questions. I'm so excited about this stage of my publishing journey!

Although the topic of online gambling gets a light treatment in this romcom, it is a really serious issue. I'd like to thank those that helped me with those elements of the story by sharing their very personal experiences. Any mistakes that I've made relating to counselling or advice are all my own.

Writing books is an exhausting process and I couldn't do it without the support of my friends and family. A special thanks to Jane, Christie and Steve for reading the first chapter, which I sent them hesitantly; their positive feedback gave me the confidence to write the rest.

I also owe a huge thanks to those online people that give me endless support, Twitter is one of the best companions that a writer can have (other than a dog). Thank you especially to the ladies of Novelicious: Kirsty, Debs, Kira, Amanda, Cesca, Kirsty P, Jenni J, Jenni C and Cressida for all their help with covers, taglines and blurb, and for listening to my rants.

Thank you also to those people who are continuing to buy my books, and for those that have written reviews and tweeted with me. I love nothing more than hearing that I made people laugh or smile.

And finally, I owe this book to my husband. He may have been working away while I wrote this, but somehow he still managed to be a slave-driver. I am going to enjoy him being around for the next book though, as I did really miss him tidying up after me and feeding me chocolate!